Sparks laughed and chucked her under the chin.

His touch set off so many alarm bells that Emma forgot to watch for the inevitable with Trouble and the lake. The dog shook the water from himself, gathering velocity as the shake intensified. Sparks and Emma ducked behind the cottonwood tree that had been there ever since Emma could remember.

That tree would be gone, as well. No need for a shade tree under bazillions of gallons of water.

She turned to Sparks. "It really is true. It's not just that the town is out of money. It could also be flooded?" Surprise tears stung her eyes. Why did she care? She was leaving as soon as her plans were finalized.

Sparks's shoulder, so close to hers, invited her to snuggle into him, hoping he'd tell her everything would be all right.

Dear Reader,

As a teen, I handwrote pages and pages of romance novels after discovering Harlequin books in my Adirondack Mountains village library. Years later, welcome to my first novel for Harlequin Heartwarming, titled *Waiting for Sparks*.

While staying by a lake with the same too-blue-to-believe water as is in my book with my husband and border collie—the model for Trouble—I thought: What if this place was Heaven for one person and another couldn't wait to leave? Then, the hero, Sparks, introduced himself. And I met Emma and her grandmother Nomi. Soon afterward, I knew secrets and running after what you think you want would make a great story.

I hope you get caught up in this special place and its people just as I did. I'd love to hear from you.

Kathy

HEARTWARMING

Waiting for Sparks

—

Kathy Damp

HARLEQUIN®HEARTWARMING™

Recycling programs
for this product may
not exist in your area.

ISBN-13: 978-0-373-36728-3

Waiting for Sparks

Printed in U.S.A.

Kathy Damp loves to write about characters who discover they are more than they know and who realize that saving the world can take many forms. Walking on fire this past summer caused her to wonder what else she could do that she didn't think was possible. When not writing, she rides bikes and kayaks with her husband throughout the West.

To my Adventure Guy and husband, Fred.
Without your unflagging support,
Emma and Sparks would never have gotten
together. Thanks for always being willing to
stop the car one more time to explore a novel idea.
Here's to ever so many more adventures.

CHAPTER ONE

Someone was screaming.

Naomi Chambers clutched at her son's hand, her salt-and-pepper hair plastered wet against her skull. Where terror ought to have been, her son's face revealed only a cocky boredom. Her grip on him was saving him from the abyss, but her hand was cramping with fatigue. Why didn't he fight? Try to help himself? His hand slipped from hers.

Jerked half-awake, Naomi Chambers opened her eyes.

Plants… She'd been watering the plants in the front room and thinking about the upcoming Memorial Day weekend.

Now, she was… She turned her head to the right, toward the *beep-beep* of a machine. She was at the regional hospital, most likely. Where her husband, Raymond, had died. The results on the screen looked a little puny.

Next to the machine, a plastic bag hung on a pole with a long tube dripping into the back of her hand. The two prongs blowing oxygen into her nose rubbed her nostrils; her left hand traveled to them.

Her darling granddaughter, Emma. *I need to tell you...* Naomi had waited too long.

The same night Emma had arrived as a tiny infant, a shrieking duet of anger and anguish between two women had exploded outside the house, a sound unheard in their town of Heaven.

Then the doorbell.

Every detail remained scoured into her being: Raymond checking his Timex, her insisting he take the gun from the bedside table in case a rancher had gotten tanked at The Wayside Inn and decided to persuade the bank president to reconsider a declined loan with the business end of a shotgun...

Some time later, she lifted heavy eyelids toward the beeping monitors. She dashed away wetness from her cheeks, but not before a few tears dropped into an ear. "Tears don't solve problems," her mother had always said. Looking toward the door, Naomi saw only graininess. She blinked. No change. She blinked again, becoming aware that she couldn't feel her left arm. A singeing terror flared from her chest and out to the tips of the opposite arm.

Trying to breathe deeply, blinking again at the hospital ceiling, she fought the shadow of sleep. Two years had been too long for this stalemate between grandmother and grand-daughter. If only Emma would be sensible and return to Heaven. Naomi hoped the young man she'd hired for the Jamboree fireworks would ignite a hometown spark in her grand-daughter.

She'd met him at a Western Alliance confer-ence of mayors, where he'd spoken on the ad-vantage of pyrotechnics for civic events. From the longing in his eyes as she'd regaled him with the wonders of her Rocky Mountain vil-lage, he'd stay. Fall in love with Emma. Then she'd stay, too.

"Naomi? You decent?" A gravelly voice in-terrupted her plotting. Chet Jensen's weathered face peered into the room. He approached, a frown creasing his expression as he took in the machines. "I told the nurse I was your fiancé so she'd let me in." Gently taking her hand in his, he wriggled his eyebrows. "'Course, that means you'll have to marry me now."

Naomi tried to smile, riding the wobbly waves of semiconsciousness. As the crackle of terror began to subside thanks to Chet's pres-ence, she struggled to think. Had he called Emma? Surely, he had called Emma…

"To save you the bother of trying to spit out all the questions, I'll fill you in," Chet said, settling himself in the chair next to her bed. "It's Thursday night. The EMTs got a call that you'd fallen." He seemed to read her mind. "I don't know who called. Good thing someone did. You've had a stroke. Do you remember the ride here?"

On the heels of the horror of the word *stroke* applied to her for the second time in as many years, Naomi tried to recall how much Raymond's ambulance ride had cost and if that irresponsible Juggy Burnett had driven her in the silly thing.

"N-no." But how could she not remember? Memory like an elephant, everybody said. Then her insides were seared with a remembrance. She had not yet told Emma what the girl needed to know, what Emma must hear only from Naomi. Her eyelids fluttered. "Wh-where's Emma?" Bags of flour pressed her lids down. "I almost missed my chance to tell her that…" Sleep closed in.

EMMA TOOK A deep breath and blew it out. Suitcases by the door.

Check.

Mail set to be held at the post office.

Check.

Passport—her first. Big smile.

Check.

Ticket to England.

Oh, check, check, check.

She was doing it. Actually keeping the promise she'd made to her grandfather to get a new life while he'd been ending his. Emma Chambers's lips trembled as she swallowed the thickness in her throat. A crooked smile formed as she glanced at the rest of the checklist in her hand. Her with a checklist. Normally, she was as scattered as leaves in the wind, but not with this trip. It was too important. The smile faded. For almost all of her thirty years, Emma had vacillated between wishing she was more like her grandmother to avoiding any habits that hinted at her grandmother's top three: order, control and action. Naomi Chambers, Nomi to Emma, lived by checklists. And controlled everyone. Especially Emma. She loved her grandmother. She just wanted an ocean between them for a while.

Emma bit her lip and shifted her purse to her other shoulder, peering out the basement apartment window. *Hurry.*

A horn sounded outside as the blue and yellow van pulled up. The shuttle to the airport, then on to Denver to meet Brad. Then—England. *I'm doing it, Grumpa.*

Picking up her suitcases, she shook her head. "Boyfriend. Brad is your boyfriend." She said it out loud to make the point. So why did her heart skitter away from thinking of him as that? Brad was always telling her, "Baby, I'm here for you." The peripatetic day trader was fun. She needed fun. Yet sometimes—she refused to let her thoughts go here often—Brad seemed, well, about half an inch deep.

Her cell rang in the new traveler's purse. Setting down one suitcase, she dug in the bag slung across her chest and checked the caller ID. She wouldn't put it past her grandmother Naomi to try one last ditch effort to get her to her lair, the tiny Rocky Mountain village of Heaven.

Seeing Chet's name, she grinned and punched the green button. Good old Chet, retired pharmacist and family friend. "Hey, Chet!"

Moving to the window, she waved at the driver and took in the dust-covered flowers that were at eye level at the edge of the sidewalk. She'd felt like those flowers until the details for the trip had been cemented. No more coated with other people's ideas. *England, here I come. We come*, she amended.

"Emma?" Chet Jensen's deep voice floated over the line. He sounded old and tired, unusual for this vigorous bachelor, who was in love with her widowed grandmother. "Listen,

E, honey, your grandma's had a stroke. Will you come, even with the—the way things are between you?"

CHAPTER TWO

Doug "Sparks" Turner grunted, curling his lip. A gutless sedan. It wasn't what he had envisioned for his hair-blowing, stereo-blasting drive up Bigelow Canyon to Heaven, his home for the summer. An hour and a half from the airport, Sparks had had enough of the crappy car and intermittent country music on a tinny-sounding radio.

As he reached over to silence the noise, the right wheels caught the dirt of the curving road's shoulder. Only a narrow strip separated him from a long drop. He yelped and overcorrected, shooting the little blue car into the opposite lane—thankfully temporarily empty of cars, RVs and trucks towing boats.

Another thump on the brake and the car shuddered to a stop on the wrong side of the road. The woman at the car-rental desk had asked if he'd wanted insurance. Maybe he should have considered it. He shifted to Park, lifted his quivering foot off the brake and sat very still, breathing in pine and dust.

"Pull yourself together, Turner," his pyro-technics scheduler had said. "Running in every direction gets you nowhere."

"Steady," Sparks spoke aloud. "They can't pay a dead man." He needed this job more than he needed the vacation. His last two firework-design gigs had finished with fingers pointed at him, murmurs that he'd lost his touch.

On his most recent job all of the fireworks went off at once. A show that was supposed to last twenty minutes had lasted ninety seconds. One big grand finale with no build-up.

He put the car in gear, placed one hand at ten and the other at two on the steering wheel. Carefully returning to the correct lane, he forced his thoughts to remain on the twists and turns of the granite and evergreens, instead of his problems.

"Watch out for the last curve before heading down into Heaven," the female clerk had said, brushing his hand with hers and giving him a smile. "I've heard it's a killer." Worse than the ones he'd already navigated? Ah, a sign herald-ing the summit. Downhill run. Good.

After meeting with Naomi Chambers in town to discuss business, he'd be able to offi-cially start his vacation. Playing hard and long would retire the doubts he'd begun to have. It would push that yearning for something just out of reach back into the place where he wouldn't think about it. *Home.*

Compared to his previous occupation— fighting isolated forest fires—and given his vast experience with pyrotechnic displays all over the world, this particular design for such a small town would be a piece of cake. Small towns were hometowns. He'd borrow this one for the summer. Maybe that would help him out.

He had to be getting close to that turn. He flexed one hand, then the other on the steering wheel. *Good.* He was tired of green trees, tired of the canyon, tired of thinking... He turned the blind corner in third gear, where, instead of the road continuing straight or even at a reasonable curve, a wall of rock appeared along with a ninety-degree angle.

He barely had time to stomp the brake, wrench the wheel all the way to the right and hope he would skirt the outcropping of granite.

SHE SHOULD HAVE seen it coming.

Kissing the edge of the speed limit on her way to Heaven, the phone call with Brad— made as soon as she'd ended the call from Chet—bounced around in her brain. Brad's voice, breezy as always, had stunned Emma.

She smacked the old Omni's steering wheel

with a fist, remembering his words. "No problem, you have to go back home," he'd said.

"It's not home," she'd snapped, apologized and, after his next words, wished she hadn't.

"Given all those phone calls you ignored from Granny, I had a feeling family ties would come home to roost. I snagged Carmen a few nights ago. She can fly standby. You remember her."

Carmen was hard to forget with bleached hair, bleached-white teeth…and a husband.

"Carmen? The married Carmen?" Despite wanting to keep her tone neutral, Emma couldn't stop the sarcasm from catching the word *married*.

Emma heard the woman in the background call to Brad and ask him where he'd put the massage oil. Brad muffled the phone to answer. When he returned, he said, "We had some good times, Emma. Let's leave it at that."

Don't hang up on me. Emma's stomach started to grip like it did when she was going to be sick. Then he was gone.

In a swirl of hurt, she'd decided to confront her grandmother. Emma would firmly tell her only relative she was not falling for this ruse, that it was a shame she'd roped Chet into it and that Emma was turning around right now and heading for the airport.

She'd board that plane for England whether Brad and Carmen were on it or not. She could do this. She had to do this. She'd go with, with… a man moratorium in place. Yes, that was it.

Her brain cleared, and her foot pressed the accelerator firmly. No man for her until—well, until a very different type of guy showed up. One that made her see fireworks—or at least a spark. And who was trustworthy. Dependable. One who, when he said, "I'll be there for you," really was. Yet, from her perspective, it wasn't going to happen any time soon.

Ninety minutes later, pulling off the interstate at Evanston, Wyoming, the venerable Omni rumbled along the two-lane highway toward Bigelow Canyon. Emma kept an eye out for deer, skunks and raccoons with their nonexistent road-safety habits. The speedometer climbed; every mile brought Emma closer to the place she had vowed never to return to.

Grumpa had referred to Heaven as the intersection between Are We There Yet and Nowhere. Tucked in a valley with steep canyon sides, it boasted maybe a thousand people, which swelled into many thousands as tourists flocked there for the summer, and especially for the town's main moneymaker—the Fourth of July Jamboree.

The event lasted from Thursday till Monday. A celebration of a small Western town and America.

It was almost nine o'clock now. And as surely as she took her next breath, by the time she crossed the town limits, her grandmother would be fine, Emma reassured herself. Nomi would be formulating some powerful reason for making Chet her minion on a new project.

Emma remembered she would need both hands on the wheel for the final turn. Only idiots blew down this canyon.

No way would her grandmother actually allow herself to fall ill. Not with her riding herd over the upcoming Jamboree in July. When God created Naomi Chambers, He had given her a double shot of stamina, and on the way out, she had snatched another.

Recognizing a familiar landmark, Emma shifted down for the descent. No one else on the road at this hour. Though Memorial Day weekend, travelers would be up and at it quick tomorrow; the early birds were already in their RVs for the night, parked at the local campgrounds, ready for the kick-off of the town's summer season.

The Omni's headlights swept left and right, with Emma letting the engine hold the car back. Biting her lip, she tapped the brake around another curve, readying for the last one.

She recalled smelling tourists' and semi-trailer brakes burning clear through to the center of town, coming from this canyon. Others, who thought they knew better than to slow down, rode with the tow truck or in an ambulance. The slow signs meant slow.

After she downshifted to first for the final blind corner and hairpin turn, she lowered the window; cool canyon air poured in. Here came the turn. She tapped her brakes. What was that ahead? When her headlights illuminated a blue sedan, she squinted. Off into the dark, up against an outcropping of rock spray-painted every year by graduating high school students, was a car lying on its side, steam pouring out from the hood, which was bent at many angles. Emma hit the brakes.

Pulling carefully to a stop at the side of the road along faint double tracks, she eyed the car, heart rate ramping. Yanking up her parking brake, she prayed it would hold on the steep downgrade, shut off the car and regretted that she couldn't use her cell phone. Everyone in Heaven knew precisely where the lack of signal coverage ended for cell phones, and she wasn't anywhere near it.

Please don't be dead. Chastising her short height once again, she ran toward the car, looking around for something to stand on to see into it. Stepping onto a large flat rock that was close—yet not close enough to be really useful—she flung herself toward the car door, hanging on by her fingertips. *Now what, genius?* She couldn't go back and she couldn't let go, so she stretched up and peered into the sedan. She could see him now, see the blue collar of a shirt, a man's head against the seat. He was blond, he was bloody and he wasn't moving.

Do something. What?

The figure stirred as her fingers cramped from clutching the car's side. Any minute now she was going to have to fling herself backward to avoid falling under the car.

His eyes opened, and despite the blood seeping down from a cut on his forehead, she couldn't help noticing the dark blue eyes. Eyes staring right at her. Eyes with—deep questions? *Don't be dumb, Emma.* He has a question as to what happened, not some complicated existential need.

"You're beautiful—an angel? Am I dead?" he asked, then groaned and put a hand to his head. "My head."

That struck her as funny—both the beautiful comment and that he actually did have questions—and she giggled, albeit a trifle hysterically. "No, you're in Bigelow Canyon. The last turn. We call it The Last Nasty."

"Nasty. Sure. About…how…my luck has been going." He squeezed out the words.

Her aching fingers reminded her that she needed to change positions. Bending her knees slightly, she edged to the rim of the rock on which she teetered, and then shoved off the car. Back she fell, rear end hitting the ground first. She rolled to the side quickly and stood up, legs shaking. Dramatic rescues had not been part of the itinerary for the England trip, nor were they a common occurrence in her life.

The car door squeaked and then swung open with a metallic groan. The bloody, blue-eyed guy gazed at her and took in the surrounding area with a fuzzy frown.

She stared up at him. Even bloodied he was a jaw dropper. Blond hair sticking out all over, strong cheekbones that rose above a carved chin. Those eyes. Those questions.

"I think we're both in trouble," he mumbled, and dragged himself toward the open car door.

CHAPTER THREE

WHAT HAD THE angel girl just asked him? Thunderbolts banged around in Sparks's head. The dampness and sting on his chin told him he'd have a souvenir of the Compact Car Crunch.

"I said, do you think you have a concussion?"

Minutes before, he'd started a slow pitch out of the car. Somehow—perhaps he'd recall later—she'd grabbed his long legs at the same moment he'd pushed off from the frame. It took him a few moments to realize he'd landed on his rescuer. She uttered gasping, grunting sounds from underneath him.

After he'd rolled off her, they'd both regained their breath, and she'd lugged his two suitcases out of the trunk and into her car. He focused on standing upright and making his legs move toward it, only to collapse onto the passenger seat. Oh, was his head throbbing.

She'd steered out onto the road, and they were on their way. *Angel girl*, Sparks thought. Short, dark haired and curvy in beige capris and a light-colored knit shirt, she was the prettiest part of the trip so far. And the prettiest thing to ever save him. Now, what was her name? It wasn't like him to miss getting a name.

In the light of the dashboard, the skin over her knuckles was stretched taut, he noticed. Although in the midst of the rescue she'd kept saying, "What do I do? What do I do?" She'd been great.

He winced at the virtual bombs exploding in his head. "I've had concussions. This isn't one."

No response, yet her eyes widened at his comment.

"I'm kind of used to emergencies." It would take more than a car crash to prevent Sparks Turner from getting a pretty girl to relax. She had a smudge of dirt on the cheek facing him. He raised his hand to wipe it off. She shrunk back. The car swerved.

"Man moratorium!" Her voice squeaked on the last part of *moratorium*.

He must have landed on her harder than he'd thought. "Did you hit your head?"

She ignored his question. "Are you sure you're okay? Maybe I should take you to Regional for that cut on your chin. I'm…I'm headed in that direction." Her voice sounded decidedly nervous.

He blamed himself for scaring her. Of course, taking a strange, bloody guy into your car was a risk. "No, ma'am. I'm a former smoke jumper and I've taken some pretty good bangs to the head before. I appreciate it, but a ride to the Safari Motel is good enough for me."

Silence.

The knock on his head had opened a memory he'd slammed the door on five years ago. The tragedy that had driven him from a once-loved occupation and a part of his life that he was trying to forget.

A few more miles passed by, and the road flattened a bit before another plunge. She gestured to the left. "You can't see much at night, but that's the lake down there. Route 12 is Main Street." So this was Heaven, his borrowed hometown for the summer.

This spurt of conversation seemed to empty her, and she once again fell silent.

Keeping his eyes on the darkness that was the lake, he leaned against the headrest and gave himself over to the pain. "Never expected such a big lake in the Rocky Mountains," he muttered to himself. Talking to himself was a habit he'd had since he was a kid. Some counselor had told him he did it so he wouldn't feel alone. He hadn't wanted to think about that then, and he didn't want to think about it tonight.

She didn't respond.

"Heaven's a different name for a town," he said, this time louder.

The silence spread so long he thought she wasn't going to answer, and then she shook herself slightly as though to rouse herself from troubling thoughts. "The original settlers had such a hard time coming down that canyon—" she flashed him a look "—as you can imagine, that when they came to this point and saw the bizarre blue of the lake, they figured they'd died and gone to heaven. Hence the name."

Everyone had told Sparks he was crazy to take a cut-rate job designing fireworks in the middle of nowhere. When he'd been sitting with his feet dangling over the edge of the wrecked car door, he would have had to agree. Now, seeing the size of the lake and with a summer to play in it, he began to doubt his doubts. He could entertain himself watching the spin cycle in a Laundromat and make five new friends before he'd even folded his polo shirts. He would amuse himself in Heaven and get back into sync with his career. A win-win for him and the town.

In fact…he eyed the petite woman next to him. He'd get a summer girl. Summer girls didn't need to know why he couldn't stick around.

The uncomfortable niggling at the back of his mind, the keening loss that often surged within him, kicked in again. He'd been feeling it off and on for months now. A place to call home. A place to be from. Come back to. Sparks touched the cut on his forehead. It had stopped bleeding.

Shooting a sideways look at his angel girl, he wondered where she was from, where she was going. She'd said a hospital. Local girl with a sick husband? He sighed. He hoped not.

Minutes later, she braked at a four-way stop sign with a Qwik Stop in need of a paint job on one corner. The other three corners were the edges of fields that gave way to Main Street.

"It looks like…home," he blurted as yet another crash sounded in his head.

"Don't bet on it." Her muttering landed so softly he wasn't sure he'd actually heard her. After she stopped on Main Street in front of the Safari Motel and put the car in Park, she turned to look at him—or rather, the cut on his forehead. Then she smiled.

Her smile curved up wide, showing white teeth with a tiny overlap of the right incisor. The move pressed her eyes into a delightful squint. He was glad she'd been coming down the canyon when she had. In the reflected light from the motel's office, he saw coppery highlights glinting in her dark hair. A pretty woman preoccupied with something. After her rescuing him, he wanted to make everything right for her. Keep that smile on her face.

Finally, she spoke. "Looks as if Lynette kept the light on for you. She'll want to know why you look as though you got beat up. She's not much on troublemakers staying at her motel." The smile faded and the tone sharpened. "Or unreliable, undependable charmers." She closed her lips in a thin line.

"You're from here?" His spirits lifted; he'd choose to ignore the edge to her last words. *Summer girl.* For the summer, he could be anything she wanted. For the summer.

A look swept over her face. Revulsion? Regret? He couldn't place it.

"Not really."

He slid slowly out of the car, emitting a few spontaneous grunts as he pulled his suitcases out of the backseat. "Thanks for rescuing me."

Her smile returned, lightening her expression. "You rescued me from rescuing you. We're square."

As he came around the front of the car, he spoke in the direction of her open window. "See you around, then?"

She leaned out the window. "I'll call on my cell about your car. The garage will contact the rental company."

"Hey, no problem. I'll call from my room."

Another transforming smile. "I'll call." She put the Omni in Drive.

"Thank you for saving my life!" he shouted belatedly as she left the parking lot. She didn't look back. He knew because he watched her. She knew where he was, so maybe...

Digging a piece of paper out of his jeans' pocket, Sparks gingerly felt around the scrape on his chin. He leaned over, stretching right and left to unravel the increasing kinks, while checking out his home for forty-six glorious days of vacation. To the right was a line of single-level motel units of cinder block with a metal, aqua-painted eaves running their length as they sloped down away to the lake. Probably built in the 1950s.

He pushed open the glass door of the office and the bell at the top of the door tinkled; the theme song for a late-night talk show sounded in a room behind the desk. He was hours past his guaranteed reservation time. As his hand hovered over the bell on the counter for a second time, a bouffant-haired older woman pushed through the bead curtain.

"Don't be pounding that bell. At my age, it takes more time to get everything moving." Of average height, a loose black pullover tunic and legs encased in black knit pants, she didn't look as though she had an ounce of fat on her. Taking in his damaged face, her eyes narrowed. "You got a reservation? We don't allow riffraff here."

Sparks glanced at the confirmation number on his piece of paper and passed it over to her. She snatched it from his hand.

"You're Lynette?" he said.

Looking up from the paper, she seemed satisfied with his right to be there. "I'm the owner, Lynette." She peered at him over half glasses. "You're that hotshot fireworks designer who's going to put Heaven on the map this year." She swung her head back and forth. Her hair never moved. "Why do you look as though you lost a fight at the Wayside Inn?"

"I had an accident coming down Bigelow Canyon."

"The Last Nasty, no doubt. Going too fast, I imagine. Happens all the time."

His head ached in cadence to the throbbing in his jaw. He hadn't eaten anything for hours, and he was feeling that Heaven fell short of Naomi's rhapsodizing about warm, friendly people. Forcing his split lips into a smile, he said, "Yes, ma'am. Fortunately, a woman from town stopped to help me. I didn't get her name."

She shrugged. "Payment's in full. Up front. Cash preferred."

Naomi had warned him of Lynette's affection for cash. No plastic card was accepted, but as he pulled out his wallet, he noted the rest of the office asserted a predilection for plastic. On the counter, plastic—not silk—daffodils leaned out of a hot pink plastic vase with seashells glued on it. The bead curtain was plastic. Plastic covered the lampshade by the cash register. He shifted his feet, heard a crackle. Plastic runner.

After opening his wallet and removing the cash, he glanced down at the registration card she slid in front of him.

"Fill it out completely—including home address. I'll need your license plate number, too, in case you go sneaking off with my towels." She looked out the side window. "Where's your car?" Her eyes narrowed again.

"It'll be towed in." He focused on the card.

Home address. There it was again. *Home.* By habit, he put down the address of the pyrotechnic corporation with whom he contracted. He was rarely at the condo he rented with a pilot.

She took the completed card Sparks offered her. "Doug?"

"I go by Sparks."

A twinkle at last thawed the frosty, faded eyes.

"Bet there's a story there." Her tone returned to business. "The town's got us a drought going on, so we change the towels and sheets twice a week 'stead of every day."

He nodded. A quick survey out the window showed no on-site restaurant. "No restaurant?"

Turning away from him with the card in her hand, Lynette slid it into a pocket of a numbered canvas wall hanging. "No need for me to monopolize making money. Dew Drop Inn Café's over there. Place for those of us over thirty and tourists who want local color." She gestured behind him; Sparks followed. Across the street sat a cinder block building with wide glass windows and a prominent sign announcing a "Squat and Gobble Special" of eggs, biscuits, cream sausage gravy and hash browns. No lights on and a closed sign on the front door. His stomach rumbled.

Lynette peered at him. "Nothing's open this late… Tomorrow, start of Memorial Day weekend, you can also go to the Dairy Delite at the other edge of town or Angel Wings BBQ here on Main." She leaned her forearms on the counter. With money in hand, her tone of voice became positively chatty. "So you're here to bail out Naomi?"

"You must be thinking of somebody else." He dredged up a smile, wincing at the sting. Everything he owned ached. Longing for bed, he added quickly, "I'm only here to design the Fourth of July Jamboree fireworks. Technicians come from Evanston to set up the actual display. Pretty much, I'm on vacation." Before he opened the door to leave, he remembered. "I'll need directions to her office, though."

"Won't do you any good. Naomi's had another stroke." Lynette's watery gray eyes scanned him. "We're waiting for poor little Emma to save us."

He nodded, and moments later, as he stood in the doorway of room number twenty-seven, Lynette's departing statement lingered. Poor little Emma must be Naomi's hapless assistant. Did this mean working for Naomi would be…difficult?

Holding the handles of his two suitcases, he surveyed the room with no relief found from a gathering sense of gloom or his aching muscles. The two full-size beds in front of him, one with a distinct hollow in the middle and both draped with red and saffron zigzag bedspreads, shouted 1970s, as did the crimson velvet paisleys raised on the gold wallpaper. He spied a rotary desk phone on the nightstand. At least there was a phone.

Walking over faded yellow shag carpet, he picked up the receiver to call the rental company. No dial tone. So that hazel-eyed angel girl had already known the secret. Hence her smile, the smile he wanted to remember and see again.

Reminiscing about the four-star hotels he'd enjoyed in Chicago, DC, Paris and Tokyo, he rotated his shoulders. Hadn't he wanted a break from the globetrotting for a touch of hometown America?

He chose the least concave bed and plopped his suitcases on the other. The bed dropped a couple inches lower. He shrugged. "Best to look on the bright side." Mother Egan, a fond memory from growing up at the orphanage, had had a million such sayings; every now and then one popped out of his mouth.

Sleep was his next order of business. Once he'd slept, his head would stop banging and his bones would settle back into place. After he met this unfortunate Emma, he'd explore his summer hometown.

Forty-six glorious days of vacation.

CHAPTER FOUR

EMMA PEERED INTO her grandmother's hospital room where monitors glowed and beeped. Chet sat next to the narrow bed, his arms folded on the railing, head pillowed on them. *Sweet Chet.* The only person in Heaven who wasn't afraid of her grandmother, other than Emma's childhood friend Zoo. Emma stepped forward.

Nomi looked old. Her face, usually bright with vigor or pique, hung sallow. So many machines connected, like when Grumpa was here. So still. Had she—? Nomi moved her right leg slightly under the sheet and blanket.

Letting out the breath Emma didn't know she'd been holding, she moved over to Chet and touched him on the arm. He jerked, then straightened.

"E?" Worry creased his wrinkles into gullies while his remaining white hair stuck up at every angle. She managed to lift her lips into a semblance of a smile as he gripped her hand. "Thank the good Lord you're finally here." No judgment sharpened his words, merely relief.

If Nomi had said the same thing, it would have been clear that Emma had taken too long and someone else had had to shoulder her share of the burden.

Nodding toward her grandmother, Emma returned Chet's squeeze. "How is she?"

"I'm scared, E." He related the few details he knew: she fell, someone—nobody knew who—called the paramedics, and they brought her to Regional. She was stable. "I'll leave you alone with her and wait outside."

Her grandmother stirred. Picking up Nomi's hand, Emma held it as Nomi lay unresponsive. "Tomorrow. I'll see you tomorrow," she whispered.

Nomi's lids rose slowly. "Trr-ouble," she whispered through dry lips. Emma reached for a plastic glass with a flexible straw. Her grandmother sipped with shallow swallows.

"Yes," Emma whispered back, a tear sneaking out of her eye. "It's trouble, but you'll be fine. You always are."

"Sparks. Sparks." Naomi's head jerked against the pillow.

Had there been a fire the night of the stroke? Emma's eyebrows slammed together.

"Take care of…trouble…" Her grandmother's attempt at speaking alarmed the monitors. Emma stroked Nomi's arm. Her grandmother would survive trouble. A plan of action for every crisis.

At Emma's touch, she quieted and appeared to fall asleep.

After watching her grandmother to make sure her sleep was peaceful, Emma joined Chet in the hall. They walked silently through the hospital out toward the parking lot.

As long as there were memories, Nomi and Grumpa were in them. When a fireman came to school in second grade, some kid had asked her if her smoke jumper daddy had been a hero. She wasn't sure, so she asked her grandmother. Nomi had hesitated, her hands stilling on the fridge door. She'd just returned from her office where she served as mayor and was pulling leftovers out for dinner.

"He did what he felt he had to do," she'd answered, then she'd told Emma to go set the table. Heroes did what they had to do. Emma had decided if you couldn't *have* a father, at least you could have a *hero* father in heaven. The *other* heaven.

Emma rubbed the vertical line between her brows that matched her grandmother's. She knew little of her father, other than he'd left to go smoke jumping and had died.

As a child, she'd been told her mother—whoever she was—had had to go away, asking

Nomi and Grumpa to take care of her. Grumpa had said that, so it must be true.

Emma had learned a little more as an early teen. Evidently, her mother had been too much of a teenager herself to handle a baby. Despite the fierce love of her grandmother and the gentle care of her Grumpa, a certain emptiness in Emma had never filled, the being *left* part. Being left had rendered her unable to call the town home. It set a pattern in motion. Temporary relationships only.

After hugging Chet in the hospital's parking lot, she slid into the Omni and drove to the house where she'd grown up. She pulled the car onto the double-cemented lines of the driveway. Tomorrow she'd find out her grandmother's details—or rather, checking her watch, later today—and head back to Salt Lake.

Straightening up, with her stomach continuing to grumble as it had in the hospital, Emma resolved to explore her grandmother's fridge.

Movement next door at Feral Beryl's drew her glance. Naomi's archenemy had peeked out the kitchen window above the Berlin Wall, a tall wooden fence between the two properties. More than a property divider, it divided the have-not Beryl Winsome from the have-it-all Chambers. Beryl was a singularly unpleasant woman.

Emma pulled out her suitcases and approached the bungalow. Fatigue dripped down her neck like perspiration, and her suitcases, rolling behind her, weighed a ton. Lilac bushes that were as high as her waist as a child now towered over her five foot something. They glowed in the dark, lighting both sides of the flagstones to the house. Although chokecherry bushes almost past blooming partially blocked her view, the porch swing peeked through.

Back in the day, when Grumpa could get Nomi to "stop doing and come out and just be," the three of them would sit in silence on the porch. Grumpa and Emma would be on the swing, Nomi sitting on the floor with her head against Grumpa's knees. Nomi would jump up for something; Grumpa would say in the voice Nomi called his "bank president" tone, "Leave it, Naomi. The child's more important." And Nomi would sit down again.

Her grandmother, never quiet for long, would commence talking about how important it was that Emma make good choices. Clearing his throat, Grumpa would interrupt with another story about the fierce Lady Emma, a young girl extraordinaire who fought dragons and won. When his deep voice finished the story, silence would surround them like an old afghan. Until Nomi would make a surprised sound and exclaim, "Raymond, Emma is beyond bedtime!"

"Come along, Miss Beyond Bedtime," he would say, and carry her off to bed. They would pray, her last sight Grumpa's silhouette in the doorway. "Remember, I love you a bushel and a peck and a hug around the neck, Lady Emma."

Smiling now, Emma walked through the open side gate, around the corner of the house and up the back steps. Sure enough, the door was unlocked, as were most houses in Heaven. She was in before she heard a new sound: a low growl and light panting.

CHAPTER FIVE

THE HEADACHE HAD disappeared by the time Sparks awoke later that morning. While orienting himself to yet another new ceiling, he rubbed his neck reflexively. Traveling often left him muddled about which state, which city, even which country he'd landed in. Then, as he stretched his arms over his head, his muscles rushed to remind him, prompting him to recall as well the woman who'd rescued him.

First, there was the immediate intimacy of the little car and how careful she was to keep to her side. Second, her genuine concern for his head, those watchful side glances from the hazel eyes. Where had she been going with such intensity? He groaned again and rolled out of bed.

After a quick shower and shave, he dressed and left his room for the Dew Drop. He needed to get the scoop on Naomi, Emma and the Jamboree deal, and a local diner always had folks in the know. As he stepped off the curb, he winced. Better keep moving today or those muscles would stiffen up.

The pungent mixture of strong coffee and grease filled his nose not unpleasantly as he opened the diner's glass door and stepped inside. Although Sparks had eaten some great food in great places across the planet, he still preferred American cardiac-zone cooking.

Most of the booths were full, and the counter didn't have an empty swivel stool. The clatter of plates, silverware and voices rang against the red-wallpapered walls and aluminum wainscoting. A Coca-Cola clock from years past hung over the half circle of counter space.

"Coffee?" A middle-aged woman waved a coffeepot at him as she caught his glance. He shook his head no, Coke being his caffeine of choice, and continued to look around. When he spotted three men in work clothes crammed in a red Naugahyde booth, he turned toward them. They broke off their conversation, which seemed to center around farm equipment. "I'm here for the summer—fireworks guy for the Jamboree." He gestured to the space next to the one man sitting alone. "Mind if I join you?"

After staring at him as if he'd spoken in a foreign language, the three men nodded, and the one slid over. The server approached. Sparks opened the menu and ordered a Coke and chicken fried steak with mashed and vegetable medley. At eleven o'clock, it was only a bit early for lunch. He'd really slept in.

"You the guy who crashed that rental in the canyon?" A man with a John Deere cap enquired, thick fingers wrapped around a white stoneware mug.

Sparks nodded sheepishly.

"I'm Willard," said a big bald man who looked as if he was meeting a celebrity. Having a license to blow things up had that effect on some people.

The man extended his hand. Sparks nodded, shaking the proffered paw, then swallowed some of the Coke that had quickly appeared.

"We've never had bigger fireworks than what the fire department put on. The rest are illegal…until you cross into Wyoming," Willard explained, rubbing his head.

"Special license for entertainment purposes. I get them all the time," Sparks said.

"That's Mayor Naomi looking out for us—bringing in something that makes more money, knowing what trouble we're in." This was the guy with the John Deere cap. Even with his muttered voice, Sparks had caught that his name was Duff and he owned the Feed-N-Seed in town.

"Lynette mentioned an Emma," Sparks said,

leaving out the part about Emma saving the town. "Who's she?"

Ray, rail thin and appearing older than the other two, leaned back against the booth, lifted his IFA cap and scratched his scalp. Replacing the cap, he pierced Sparks with a look.

"Closest shot we have to pulling our butts out of the fire. She's Raymond and Naomi's granddaughter."

"I don't know 'bout whether she'd come back," Willard said. "You know how she and Naomi left things…" he trailed off, looking like a basset that had had his ears stepped on.

"Oh? So why are your butts in the fire?" Sparks asked.

"Money," the three men chorused.

"She'll come back." That was Ray. He spoke with finality, but Sparks noted the look he tossed Duff.

Sparks jiggled the ice in his empty glass, watching for the server, both for a refill and his breakfast. "Town doesn't look as if there's a money problem…everything here looks freshly painted, well maintained." Sparks tapped his fingers—as was his habit—on the table. He wanted to hear the Jamboree was right on track, meaning his money was right on track, meaning his vacation was right on track.

Duff piped up around the hot beef sandwich

he was shoveling in his mouth. "We work hard to make the town look good. Too many dried up little Western towns." He swallowed his mouthful. "Trouble is, we've had some winters that ate up funds with snow removal. All that snow still didn't kill the drought." A deep drink of coffee followed.

"My money's on Emma not coming back," Willard stated flatly. "She's not been back since—"

"She'll be back. Emma's local," Ray interrupted.

Listening, but not really, Sparks smiled at the server who set down a full plate, plunking another Coke in front of him, as well. Sparks breathed in the aroma of creamy sausage gravy over crispy fried cube steak, lumpy mashed potatoes and a watery pile of vegetables. He picked up his knife and fork. Ignoring the conversation flowing around him, he sliced a piece of meat, ran it through the gravy and slid it into the pile of mashed potatoes. He sighed, the focus on his aches and pains shifted to this gastronomical delight.

Moments later, as he tuned back into the conversation, the three men were now discussing the Jamboree and the cancelled one-and-only volunteer organizational meeting. Naomi's skills must be better than his to run a Jamboree off one meeting. Then again, most people's skills in that area were better than his, and now even his dependability had been called into question by his boss. This job had to go well.

"Can't Naomi's husband plan the Jamboree?" Sparks asked.

The three men looked at him as though he'd thrown a pitchfork of manure into the conversation instead of a question. Then they chuckled.

"Be hard for him," Ray said. "He's been dead for almost two years."

Duff jumped in. "By the way—" he gestured to Sparks's plate "—you don't want to eat that medley."

"Right." Sparks restrained the overcooked vegetables from contaminating the rest of the meal. He didn't see the problem with who ran the event—it was a small-town Jamboree after all. The problem *he* saw was his summer slipping down the drain if *someone* didn't step up. He put another bite of meat and potato into his mouth. He hoped this Emma would show up, and soon.

Willard seemed determined to drive home his morose observations. "I'm telling you, Emma is gone. I was at the funeral that day." All eyes were on him. "Emma and Naomi might have been in the kitchen but most of the US of A heard them, even if everyone pretends they didn't to Naomi's face." He wiped his mouth with a paper napkin. "It was a knockdown, drag-out fight, likely to raise Raymond from the dead."

"Emma's usually so quiet." Ray didn't sound convinced. "I wasn't able to pay my respects till later. Naomi seemed fine then, like always."

"Quiet around her grandmother, maybe," Duff interjected. "She didn't used to be that way. Older she got, less you heard from her." He swirled his coffee.

Sparks squirmed. Add a hair dryer or two and this could be the Hattie's Dyed and Gone hair place he'd noticed down the street. Emma, trained by Naomi, would be a clone of the fire-breathing Naomi. He tried to imagine a younger Naomi. No nonsense. Barking orders and expecting obedience every step of the way.

"Why don't one of you plan it if Emma doesn't show?" he asked.

Ray choked on his last forkful of pie. Willard looked as though Sparks had suggested he strip naked and run down Main Street, and Duff started laughing until tears ran down his face.

"Nobody but Naomi has done the Jamboree since Moses was in preschool," Willard replied.

Looking down at his plate, Sparks leaned back. "Well, bigger fireworks will bring in more people who will then spend money." Although the budget she had faxed fell miles below his usual, he knew the results would still knock the socks off anyone attending this small-town celebration.

Willard opened his mouth, but after catching the expressions on his friends' faces, he reddened, snapped his lips shut and stared at the table. Sparks frowned. What didn't Willard's friends want him to say? Sparks watched the faces close up, wondering if everyone in town knew everyone's business or if they saved energy and focused on The First Family, the Chamberses.

Not having a family, and with traveling so much, people only knew what Sparks told them; nothing more, nothing less. Some things people didn't need to know. Some secrets needed to stay buried.

Looking at his watch, Duff sighed and slid out of the booth, turning a weary face to the remaining men. "Gotta get back to the store. Missus was holding down the fort for me while I went for coffee break." He checked the watch again and headed to the cash register, bill in hand.

Ray inclined his head toward Sparks. "Room okay?"

With a contented expulsion of breath after finishing his meal, Sparks sipped his third Coke. "Yeah, other than the phone doesn't work and it's decorated like a time warp, everything's good with me."

Willard snorted as he held his stomach while Ray slapped his hand on the table and hee-hawed.

"Phones over at the Safari don't ever work." Ray wiped his eyes, then brought the mug to his lips.

Sparks raised his eyebrows. "The sign out front says phones in every room."

Ray explained that there *were* phones in every room; they just didn't work. When Lynette had bought the place back in the early seventies, they didn't work. She'd just left them there so she wouldn't have to redo the neon sign.

Ray punched Willard on the shoulder. "Move. I gotta get."

The two men hitched out of the booth.

"Gotta love vacation," Sparks said, no longer annoyed at the lack of phone service at the Safari. It was a great summer story.

Halfway to the cash register with his tab, Ray turned back toward Sparks, an enigmatic expression on his face. "You think you're here for vacation?" He snorted.

A tall, thin man with a big smile and short white hair sprouting up on the top of his head pushed open the door and strode into the Dew Drop, scanning the diners.

He approached the booth. "Son, you Sparks?" he said, extending his hand. "I'm Chet. Naomi wants a meetin' with you."

Despite the older man's warm voice and kind gaze, Sparks shivered. It was like a summons to visit the queen.

CHAPTER SIX

AFTER A SHOWER, and pulling on shorts and a T-shirt, Emma headed for the ancient Bunn coffeemaker on the turquoise kitchen counter.

The "trouble" her grandmother had talked about last night as well as the heavy breathing when Emma had opened the door turned out to be a black-and-white border collie. *Trouble* was printed on the side of his dish. His favorite place seemed to be under the kitchen table.

One more problem to solve before she left town—who would take care of the dog? And why did her grandmother even have a dog? She'd easily ignored all of Emma's pleas for a pet. Trouble seemed keenly interested in her every move, which was probably why her grandmother liked the mutt.

Out of habit, she glanced over at Beryl's window, the way she had while growing up. When a curtain twitched, as it had last night, she wondered if Beryl had witnessed the ambulance picking up her grandmother and what evil thoughts of glee the bellicose woman had

had. No one, including Emma, knew why the two were such enemies.

Not for the first time Emma thought of the blond guy she'd picked up in the canyon and hoped that he was feeling okay. From what he'd chattered about, he'd sounded wistful, looking for a hometown for the summer. The neighborly-grudges aspect of small-town life would not be on his bucket list. If he was lucky, he might go all summer and not meet Beryl.

Emma opened the back door. Trouble dashed to attend to his duties and seemed to be checking for any sign of intruders since he'd last patrolled the yard. She watched him, tail flagging over his back, joy in every movement. Had she ever felt that free? No need to analyze that. No, she hadn't. She'd always been "poor Emma" to the townsfolk, although she could never figure out why. The Chamberses had money, position.

Holding the door for the dog as he raced back in, Emma shut it and headed to the kitchen. She sat at the round table and stared into space. What would the doctor say about her grandmother? Trouble hitched closer until his nose lay on her lap. An almost snort escaped Emma's lips. Her grandmother must have needed something to replace Emma's presence, although sometimes Emma could still feel the leash.

The dog's nose bumped her knee, and his amber eyes bore into hers. A walk. They both needed fresh air. At the front door, she snapped on the leash and it unloaded the equivalent of a four-shot espresso into an already caffeinated canine. "Okay, okay, a walk along the beach. You sniff, I'll think. But only a short one. I need to get to the hospital."

The doctor would say something that Emma would have to deal with and rapidly. The quick-thinking gene, so lavished upon her grandparents, had skipped her. If she took as long to solve Naomi's health issues as she did her other problems, England would have given up the monarchy by the time she arrived.

Maybe she needed to check out home health aides? Would her grandmother allow a professional caregiver in the house? Would she even need one?

Trouble strained at the leash in the opposite direction from the beach, ears up and engaged.

Emma caught the sound of applause the same moment the dog began to drag her down Seraphim. They were almost at the intersection of Cherubim and Seraphim.

In a normal small town, a street like this one might carry the same name as the school that was located at the southern end. Or it might even be named the quintessential Maple or

Pine Street. But no, that wasn't the case here. Decades ago, the town fathers—before Nomi'd gained a stranglehold on the mayor's job—had decided it would boost tourism to rename the streets to match the celestial nature of the town's name. Tourists found it charming. It had just made spelling in fourth grade more difficult.

On the football field, a bunch of students were facing someone tall and blond and *beautiful*, who was waving his hands and pointing to various pieces of—*artillery*? Mr. Blue Eyes! The guy who had rescued her from rescuing him. A rush of gladness swelled her chest. He was okay—at least he seemed okay—flashing a megawatt smile and gesturing as he explained something.

She was happy he had recovered. His nonchalance about a possible head injury had made her nervous, but she couldn't have done much to make him go to Regional. He now was moving as though all his joints worked. The blue eyes above the cut on his chin came to mind. So very blue and with deep questions inside.

Trouble made his way along the outskirts of the group, startling a rear end here and there. She found it a pleasure watching Mr. Blue Eyes. Maybe she'd just stand there for a bit.

She'd sidled to the back of the group when the idea of a man moratorium jogged her memory.

Oh. Right.

Better to head home and then to the hospital.

"Hi, Miss Chambers! When did you get back in town? How's your grandmother? Who's going to plan the Jamboree?" A cute brunette with a belly shirt and low-riding jeans grinned up at her as she petted Trouble.

When *had* she arrived? It seemed like both forever and a breath ago. Emma answered the girl vaguely and greeted others as a ripple of laughter ran through the crowd.

"What's going on?" she asked one of the kids.

"Fireworks stuff. The dude doin' them on the Fourth is giving us a demo 'cause it's Friday and the start of Memorial Day weekend." The kid bobbed his head.

Each time she thought she had mastered a shift in Heaven's universe, another shudder hit it. What was going on here? Her grandmother had never deviated from the Black Binder of Jamboree Procedures in Emma's lifetime or anyone else's.

Historically, Nomi had the Jamboree organized the day before the Memorial Day weekend started. The parade would be Monday. She wondered who'd taken over the helm, and pitied them.

A murmur went through the crowd that it was almost "time," however, Emma, righteously holding to her no-man policy, had lost interest. She was more concerned with seeing her grandmother and moving on with her new life. Tugging on Trouble's leash, she towed the dog away from the crowd. She would cut across the football field, reach the house in record time and climb in the Omni for the trip to the hospital, and then the ninety-minute drive to Salt Lake. She hoped it wouldn't take too long to get things sorted at Regional. She'd have to arrange for care for her grandmother, the house and, oh, yeah, the dog and...

Should she collect a few personal items for Nomi before she left the house? Good thing her grandmother's place was only a couple of blocks away. Although everything was only a couple of blocks away in Heaven—good for the feet and the Omni, which had been making death rattle noises coming up the canyon. She had planned to run the thing into the ground and worry about a vehicle when she and Brad—when *she*—returned. Dramamine. She'd have to get some Dramamine for the flight. Thinking of the trip helped her keep her goal in mind. *A new life.*

It wasn't as if she was abandoning her grandmother, she thought, picking up speed as she crossed the expanse of the football field. Her cavalier compartmentalizing washed up some guilt. Was she selfish for running off? She halted those thoughts. Why scold herself for *selfish*—why not see it as the travesty it would be to put herself on hold while Nomi took priority again? The fireworks guy with his amazing eyes and the bump on the head could have this hometown. She wanted Europe.

Naomi had always purposely gotten in the way whenever something wasn't her idea. Like when Grumpa and Emma had planned this European trip to celebrate her high school graduation. That was the year town volunteers had put in the boardwalk by the lake, and Nomi had insisted Grumpa would have to assist. Or the time after college graduation... Well, that had been due to Emma's distracted involvement with Professor Sleazeball, but, she amended hastily, there had still been a myriad of other times when Emma's life was restructured to suit her grandmother.

If that way-beyond-beautiful fireworks designer was to know Naomi, he'd change his view of this small town.

She had a stroke, *Emma.* That was hardly in the same category as Nomi conscripting her to plant flowers on Main Street in junior high. Emma set her jaw.

A stone had worked its way into her arch, kicked in by her quick pace. Limping, she continued to trudge along. She was infinitely tired of dealing with how she felt about her grandmother. From behind her, she heard a yell and a thunk from the first firework shell being launched.

Her curiosity piqued, she turned and collided with a broad expanse of white shirt. Her head snapped back and her feet left the ground. Trouble yipped. The chalk of the end zone rushed to fill her nose. Emma lay still, mentally counting the screams in each appendage. Good. Nothing broken. Then, while she was trying to decide how best to eject the dirt and such from her nose, large hands cupped her waist and, with a whoosh that tickled her insides, she landed gently on her feet. Still dazed, she thought it awfully convenient that Heaven's volunteer firemen had such great timing. She shifted onto her back to smile and say thanks when she saw that fireworks designer looking at her like she had looked at him in the canyon. *Questions.*

"You!" With the single word, the scrapes on her forehead and chin widened and began to sting.

"I did yell. I knew it was you." His grin looked satisfied. "I remember your backside—

er, the back of you from last night." He gestured at the field. "You were just about to walk right through my rocket landing zone."

Snorts and giggles greeted that comment and looking further, Emma saw the crowd of teens watching the show.

"Your *landing* zone? Of all the irresponsible—" Now she noticed the orange cones with the yellow caution tape fluttering in the warm breeze, the ends tugged free from their moorings. Great. It wasn't even his fault.

Thinking about her grandmother, she'd wandered into no man's land.

Trouble pulled on the leash. He wanted attention from the crowd. She wanted to say much more, but the dirt in her nose was making it hard to breathe. She wanted it out. With this audience, how was she going to do that?

Sparks faced the crowd and yelled for a tissue and after a pause, a young man parted the crowd and handed her a wrinkled packet of tissues. "Allergies," he whispered.

She grabbed a tissue, muttered her thanks and blew her nose hard. A quick check of her watch told her she'd now have to speed those ninety minutes to reach her grandmother.

She sensed him before he touched her shoulders. His large hands were warm and reassuring. He was such a...such a...*problem*.

"Let me make it up to you," he said. He tugged her toward him so that she could see him, a crooked smile in a sun-reddened face, and a shock of too-perfect hair falling over his wide, tanned forehead. "I'm really sorry. Uh…how 'bout going for food?" Blue eyes stared into hers. More questions lingered in their depths. *What?*

Emma straightened. She needed distance from this man whose gaze gathered her close. Too close. "Man moratorium! Irresponsible— Undependable— I—I have an urgent appointment!" Her voice, intended to be strong and off-putting, wobbled and squeaked.

His eyes widened. "Appointment? Oh, I… uh…" He instantly released her and fled across the field, scattering students in his wake, who looked disappointed that the show was over.

Never in her wildest expectations had she anticipated how good a defense this man moratorium would be. It was a little sad, actually.

CHAPTER SEVEN

NAOMI STARED AGHAST at her granddaughter as she blew into the hospital room—*late, mind you*—to join her, Chet and the neurologist. The child had bits of yellowed grass in her hair along with streaks of dirt on her face, hands and T-shirt. A couple of the facial and knee scrapes were oozing blood. What on earth had Emma been doing?

Soon, Chet, Emma and the doctor, who looked young enough to be one of Emma's students, were watching her eat as if she was some freak exhibit at the state fair. What she would give for a Dew Drop kitchen-sink omelet, hash browns with cheese and a strong cup of coffee, heavy on the cream.

Since the tubes in her nose didn't help the eating process any with what passed for food here, she pushed at the tray. Emma pulled the rolling table away from the bed.

"Are you in pain, Nomi?" Emma's brows furrowed, perplexed most likely at Naomi's swift change of expression.

No, dear, she wanted to say, *that had been a* smile *on my face at seeing you here in town, where you belong.* Drat it. Would the girl never pick up on one of her cues? She sighed.

The girl probably didn't understand she was talking about either the dog or Sparks last night.

Though seeing Emma here now set some of Naomi's world to rights. Getting on with the Jamboree would stabilize everything. Now, what she needed most was for that charming young man to arrive, so Naomi could let them know how it was going to be for the summer. Then she could work on getting out of this terrible place and supervise the rest of the event details from home. Home.

Chet put an arm around her shoulders. "Relax, Naomi. You have to depend on others this year."

How did he read her mind, and more important, had he also lost his? Who did he think could pull off the town's biggest moneymaking opportunity, especially this year when the event was do or die? She turned her head so she could see her granddaughter full-on. Only Emma could be trusted with organizing the Jamboree, and then, only with Naomi's assistance.

Emma understood tradition, or at least had, until the two of them had had a misunderstanding at Raymond's funeral. Emma had made too much of it.

"I've seen worse strokes," the neurologist was saying to Emma, as though discussing cuts of meat. He lounged against the bathroom doorway, one hand resting on the monitor, the other loosely in his pants' pocket. Naomi thought his bedside manner needed work. After several more minutes of being treated as though she was invisible, Naomi struggled to get words out, ignoring Chet's pressure on her shoulders. "You can t-t-talk to me, d-doctor. I—I'm not dead."

The doctor's face reddened and he shifted over to face Naomi. "The stroke has affected you a great deal, Mrs. Chambers. Due to the trauma to your left side, you'll need six to eight weeks in a rehabilitation center to regain the use of your hand and increase stability. Therapy's essential." He slipped the stethoscope from around his neck and checked his watch.

Naomi wanted to snort, but her mouth wouldn't cooperate. She'd never neglected a thing in her life. Except—the sting of the secret burned—neglecting that one thing Emma needed to know.

"She'll recover completely, though, won't she?" Chet asked.

She wanted to cheer; someone was finally

asking a decent question. The next one should be, "When can she be discharged?"

Emma was chewing on her little finger like she always did when thinking deeply. Naomi had never broken her of the habit.

The doctor glanced at the time again.

Straightening, Emma tugged at the hems of her scruffy shorts. She looked at Naomi, and then at the physician. "She'll get there," she answered, determination clear in her voice.

Naomi cocked her head. She'd been racking her brain to think of a way to get Emma to come home and give up the silly trip Raymond was always encouraging her to take. Had something good come out of this horrendous event?

The doctor nodded. "She'll be ready to go, most likely, in a day or two." He typed in notes on his tablet. "I'm writing orders for eight weeks' on-site physical and occupational therapy at an extended-care facility. Garden Terrace is good."

An old folks' home? Naomi about lifted straight off the sheets. If any of them thought she was going to an old folks' home, they had beets for brains.

Where was Sparks?

What had happened to Emma's face?

Someone had better start doing some talking, and fast.

WITH HIS STOMACH reminding him how close lunch was, Sparks dashed up the wide steps of the hospital two at a time, sweating in heat more typical of Las Vegas than Colorado. He wanted Naomi to confirm one thing: yes, his contract was a go.

He'd been having too good a time so far, he chastised himself. He would have to stay focused. His job was everything to him.

Still, it'd been easy to get caught up in the charming flavor of the town. Besides knowing he would enjoy Monday's parade, there were the barbecue invites from Duff, Willard and Ray and their families, and fun at the lake with new friend Ben, owner of Washed Ashore Marina.

On the heels of that enjoyable thought came the image of Emma. Yes, from the kids at the football field he knew that he'd flattened "poor little Emma," who was Naomi's sidekick and had been a favorite teacher at Heaven High. That bit of a woman who'd saved his life and looked as though she had too many heavy concerns weighing on her mind... She was the miracle the town was waiting for? His gallant tackle had delighted the crowd. Her, not so much.

He winced, remembering the laser stare and the knifelike words—*irresponsible, undependable*—as they'd left her rosy lips. They were taking turns saving each other, he thought, and wished he'd said that when she was telling him, among other things, that she wasn't a tackling dummy.

Forcing himself to slow to a trot, he strode through the hospital room door that he'd been directed to. There lay Naomi Chambers, mayor of the town, glaring at him; Chet; the doctor and— His breath caught. Dirty, bloody and gaping at him wide eyed was his summer girl. Hopefully.

The doctor nodded to Sparks on his way out. Chet stepped over and clapped him on the shoulder. "Thanks for coming, son."

Son. Something deep inside stirred, melted a bit.

"L-late," said Naomi, closing her eyes as though his tardiness was too much for her to bear. "Emma, go f-find out when someone is coming to t-take this tray."

"I'll take it, Nomi." Emma moved to pick up the tray, but Naomi waved her off.

"You d-don't g-get paid to do that. They d-do."

Emma's face froze and she abruptly left the room.

Wow. Growing up under Naomi's thumb

suddenly made him traveling the world alone not seem so bad.

Naomi waved again; this time a royal sweep of her hand drew him to the chair beside her bed.

"Mrs. Chambers…" No matter how far he'd travelled or who he met, the manners he'd been taught by Mother Egan would always remain with him. He leaned in. "I don't want to bother you. I just want to make sure everything is still a go for the fireworks."

Now, up close and personal, he drew in a breath.

Light from the window showed every line, all the gray folds in her face and neck. Word at the Rexall soda fountain was that Naomi Chambers was "too stubborn to die." Judging from her pasty complexion, death had nearly succeeded.

Naomi drew the covers up to her shoulders with her right hand, while Sparks waited for her to continue.

But the silence grew.

Chet stood by the window, peering outside.

Am I in trouble? Sparks rubbed his neck. *I can't be in trouble.* He sneaked a peek at Naomi. *Why do I feel as if I'm in trouble?* The silence persisted.

"How are you feeling?" Sparks ventured.

She twitched slightly. "As w-well as... c-can be expected with—" she swallowed and closed her eyes, then reopened them "—s-somebody w-waking me up every fifteen m-minutes to see if I'm still alive." If she hadn't spoken, he might have done the same.

At breakfast, the guys had mentioned that folks were taking bets on whether Naomi would go to rehab if ordered. Had Emma been speeding to see her grandmother when she'd stopped to help him? His respect for her flourished. She'd taken the time to help him, a stranger, while needing to be with family.

"T-to be honest, young man, finances are tight, but you'll be paid."

A whoosh of relief left him. "My fireworks always draw a good crowd, so that'll raise quite a lot of money for the town."

Summer was *on*. He only needed one good pyrotechnic event to get back in the game.

As he heard Emma greeting some nurses in the hallway, Naomi wiggled closer, gesturing with a beckoning finger. Sparks hunched forward.

"You'll be p-paid, but I want you to h-help Emma—coplan with her. But don't b-breathe a word...until I say so."

Sparks's face flushed with heat and embarrassment; his mouth dried so fast he could feel its hinges creak. Help plan the Jamboree?

There were two immediate problems with that edict. First, he didn't know a thing about planning a Jamboree. Fireworks, yes. But that was it. Second, if he worked closely with the townsfolk and they really got to know him, they would eventually find out he was the type to let them down.

He frowned. Hadn't the guys at the Dew Drop said Emma was leaving?

EMMA SWUNG OPEN the door, her back teeth grinding in the old familiar way, ready to tell her grandmother that the nurses said someone would be right in to take the silly tray, when Sparks leaped up and barreled out of the room. She watched him go.

What had caused his face to blush so deeply?

Even though there were more pressing issues, such as Nomi's rehab and Emma's own escape, she showed her grandmother the Organic District cinnamon-bomb bread from the tote bag she'd left by the bed. "I forgot. I brought this for you." Then she looked at the empty chair. "What did you say to him?"

Nomi's eyes gleamed. "We…were talking about the Jamboree…telling h-h-him…fun."

This wasn't the way to stay on track with her

goal. This was her grandmother trying to control the situation just like always. "Not for me."

Emma summoned her courage. Here goes. She took in a big breath. Think new green suitcases, think British Airways.

"Emma..." Nomi's lips, lopsided now, twisted as she spoke. "You...liked it. Miss F-f-fire...crac...ker...you r-remember?"

Emma did remember and was glad Sparks wasn't around to hear the tale. What had made him tear off like that?

What had she just been thinking about? Oh, yeah, the Miss Firecracker pageant. Indeed, she did remember. Short the required number of contestants for the kiddie pageant, Naomi had coerced Emma and her best friend Zoo to participate.

As they did every year, a group of townspeople protested this exploitation of women. Required to wear a red, white or blue T-shirt and blue shorts, each five- to seven-year-old contestant sang a patriotic song or twirled a baton to the same sort of tune. No bathing suits, no interviews about world peace.

Emma and Zoo, unfortunately, did not sing on key and were not particularly coordinated. Zoo agonized through "Yankee Doodle Dandy," and Emma gave herself a black eye from her baton. Neither of them won, and

Emma had thrown the baton in the lake. She now changed the subject. "Think how fast you will progress with twice-a-day therapy."

A vehement shake of Naomi's head.

"Nomi—"

Naomi stretched her lips with effort. "Me..." She stopped and drew in a deep breath. "P-planning would be a little much..."

A little? Denial is a warm bedfellow on a cold night of reality.

Naomi nodded. "Someone else...plan it."

Emma's spirits soared. Here was a breakthrough. If Nomi was going to be reasonable about this, why not the rehab?

"Someone will turn up," Emma enthused. A girl had to move on. *Right on to England, Lady Emma.* "The Jamboree has always been and always will be around, so there's no need to worry. Now, let's get you ready for transport to the facility, Nomi. I'll have the nurse bring the transfer forms."

Her grandmother rose up on her good elbow like Napoleon on his deathbed. "Emma," her imperial tone commanded. With eyes boring into Emma's, the left one slightly unfocused, she said, "*You* must p-plan the J-jamboree."

CHAPTER EIGHT

SHE KNEW SHE sounded juvenile, but *it wasn't fair*. Dashing away the wetness on her cheeks, Emma half ran, half walked out of the hospital.

Every time she reached for something, her grandmother would snatch it out of her hand: sleepovers rejected for civic service, particular friends deemed unsuitable. The list ran on and on.

Emma crossed the parking lot, the asphalt so heated it felt squishy under her sneakered feet. A tall woman dodged out of Emma's way and then grabbed her by the arms.

"Zoo!" Emma exclaimed.

"Hey, Emms." Zoo hugged her. "I've been spending a lot of time with the bulls at Jem Silver's ranch. Sorry I didn't text as soon as I heard you were in town. I've been swamped."

Zoo would be a voice of reason in this mess. They'd been friends forever, as different as two people could be. Zoo, thin, with black hair and pale blue eyes, attracted boys like flies on manure, as Emma was fond of saying. Zoo spoke her mind and got away with it. Zoo had sweated away on ranches and farms since she was old enough to ride her bike from town.

This work ethic of Zoo's had earned her Nomi's seal of approval. Zoo was everything her grandmother wanted, and Emma never heard the end of it. Fortunately, Zoo was also fun and kind.

Emma steered her friend toward the Omni. "Do you know what she did to me this time?"

Zoo grinned. "Haven't heard that in a while. What's the tyrant up to now?" She had, on more than one occasion, stood up to Naomi, inspiring awe in Emma.

Emma rationalized that it was easier to butt heads with Naomi when you weren't related. Chet did it all the time, and he lived. Then again, it could be Zoo and Chet were vertebrates, unlike herself.

"She told—no, ordered—me to plan the Jamboree. Never mentioned my trip to Europe once." New situation, old anger, she acknowledged, but it seemed fresh each time it happened.

A flood of words gushed forth as Emma unlocked the door to her car. Heat poured out. "My only family member, and she pulls rank like when she got me a teaching job at the high school without asking me—and I went along with it. Like when Nomi overrode Grumpa on…on just about everything." She moved around the outside of the car, opening doors and windows. "Darn it, I hate feeling like I have no backbone."

"Lighten up, Emma. Tell your grandmother you won't do it. But don't hate her for asking—um, assuming."

Emma hid a grudging smile. "How can I love someone so much and still want to put massive distance between us?"

"You don't want Nomi out of your life, just out of the *way* of your life."

"You ruined a perfectly good temper tantrum, you know?"

Her friend smiled. "My day, I guess." She laughed as she said, "Just told Jem Silver his sperm count's too low to breed. That ruined his day, too." She laughed some more at Emma's open mouth. "For his *bull* to breed."

Emma imagined the scene with the handsome rancher and a giggle slipped out. She slid into the sizzling seat. "Yow. Hot. Okay. I'll go back to town, drum up a replacement—before I hit Nomi with my decision." She turned the key and squinted up at her friend, standing next to the car. "Thanks, Zoo."

"Any time, you reactionary, you. Hey, what's this I hear about the summer stud tackling you in front of the entire student body? That where your face got messed up?"

As Emma entered town, loneliness wormed its way around her heart. Sparks's offer of food to make up for driving her into the dirt came to mind. If she hadn't imposed a man moratorium, she'd go out with him.

He'd be fun. She wanted fun. She wanted— oh, blast—she wanted to stuff her face at the Dairy Delite. Emma punched the brakes and careened into the hamburger stand's parking lot. The squeal drew the looks of those lined up by the order window, including a blond man towering above the others.

With his head thrown back, Sparks was laughing at something someone in the group had said. By the time she cooled her face enough to get out of the car and walk to the window, the others had drifted away, leaving Sparks to watch her approach.

"Hi," he said.

Zoo's teasing zipped through her head, and she blushed. Their complexions matched, red for red. On the heels of that was Zoo's suggestion she find a replacement to plan the Jamboree.

Emma needed someone who got along well with everyone, although why that would be a requirement since her grandmother didn't, Emma wasn't sure, but it seemed a good thing. And the best person would be one who didn't know how...how her grandmother could be. That left no one who lived in Heaven and the surrounding area. "Hi, yourself," she replied.

Those fabulous blues scanned her face, and then his gaze flickered away.

"You ran away from my grandmother." Really, she didn't blame him.

The redness of his face deepened as he glanced down at his foot and scraped some gravel.

She continued in a brisk tone, "Can you believe my grandmother ordered me to plan the Jamboree? I'm about to go to England." She'd leave out the part about being dumped by Brad. About how "baby, I'll always be there for you" was merely a fairy tale.

Today she was especially looking for someone to lift her spirits.

"Imagine that," he muttered, and stared at the ground, watching an ant struggle with a crumb of bun. "She say anything else?"

"No." Somebody ought to tell Mr. Gorgeous about SPF 45. If he kept burning his face like that, he'd be getting bumps frozen off with liquid nitrogen by age forty.

"Nothing else?" He seemed somewhat disappointed; no, bitterly disappointed.

Obviously, she didn't know him well—but still, she expected excitement, interest. Instead, he seemed as stimulated by her pronouncement as an eighth grader assigned to plot a time line for the Revolutionary War.

Starla Fleming slid the window open with a bang. Sparks startled.

"Are you gonna order something, Emma? If you're not, I'm gonna sit in the back and watch my soaps," Starla rasped, then peered at Emma's scraped face.

Emma ordered an orange cream shake after a wary look at the scab Starla was scratching on her arm. The woman disappeared from the window, the roar of the shake machine following.

Emma turned back to Sparks. "My grandmother thinks she can con me into organizing the Jamboree. I have my own life." Who could she find to take her place? Someone ignorant of her grandmother's schemes, that was who. She scrolled through a mental list… Empty.

Her red-faced companion chewed his bottom lip and swept the toe of his sneaker back and forth. Finally, he looked up at her. "She trusts you, Emma. It's a big year."

Emma's disgust came blurting out in an ugly

noise. *That* was feminine, she thought, duly embarrassed. She cleared her throat. "Big year, my foot. The Jamboree hasn't changed in my lifetime. She's charmed you like I hear you're charming the rest of the town. You don't know what it's like. All you have to do is design the fireworks, pass your instructions over to your techs and skip on to the next adventure." *Stop it, Emma.* Transferring her anger at her grandmother to this innocent visitor was not cool.

"Hey, Spaaarks!" kids yelled from a passing car. "Dude!"

The man was a magnet. Everyone liked him. The hair on her arms prickled, then she gave him a broad, welcoming smile, like a hungry spider that had spotted a fly.

And he's new in town.

The window being flung open startled them both this time. Starla's arm emerged. After a quick look for the scab, Emma slid her money through the window and grabbed the shake. The window slid shut. A moment later, the blast of a TV sounded.

"I've had things not turn out. I know what it feels like," Sparks said, his brilliant blues on her boring hazels.

She jutted out her chin, momentarily forgetting her mission in the rush of resentment. "Sure you have." But her tone was not friendly.

She'd be the first to admit she was acting the drama queen. *Pull yourself together, girl.*

Should she ask him straight out to run the Jamboree or make more small talk? Hadn't he wanted to make it up to her for slamming her into the end zone in front of the under-eighteen population of Heaven?

"My dream was to have parents. It never happened." He said the words matter-of-factly, as if he'd commented on the heat, which was substantial and was pitting her underarms out in a most unbecoming way.

The ant in the crack by her feet suddenly seemed immense compared to how small she felt. "I'm sorry. I didn't know," she managed to choke out.

Sparks must have sat on the front steps like she had on birthdays. She used to imagine her mother was a lost princess held by a wicked king.

"Maybe you ought to go see your grandmother and get it straightened out," he said.

This reminded Emma of her brilliant idea. She sucked up another mouthful of shake while she scrutinized his burned face. "You might want to wear a heftier sunscreen."

"My face isn't always this red." He mopped his brow.

But Emma was barely listening. "Didn't you

say you wanted to make it up to me, you know, for tackling me?"

The color of his faced plunged to a deeper shade. "With food. I said, food."

Perhaps, Emma thought, looking more closely—easy to do with Sparks—he was blushing. What had she said that would make him blush? *Oh, never mind the man's skin tone*, she chided. *Get to the point.*

She leaned toward him, eyes wide in entreaty. She hoped it looked like entreaty and not that her contacts had dried out. "What if you planned the Jamboree? You're getting to know a lot of people here. They like you."

"Me?" His voice shot up. Somewhat cute, really. "I…already have a job. You really should talk to your grandmother."

Emma released an exasperated sound. "You only have to design your fireworks. You don't even have to blow them up. So you'll have all sorts of free time. Nomi's created this gigantic black binder with all the procedures already mapped out." She snapped her fingers. "Piece of cake."

Sparks's Adam's apple bobbed. "Emma, talk to your grandmother."

She stepped back. Sparks looked as if he wanted to crawl under the ant.

A familiar emotion crept up Emma's neck.

"What is it you don't want to tell me?" she asked. "I can see it in your face." She hadn't taught junior high for nothing. Very good liars aside, she'd learned to spot *omissions*.

He gulped. "I'm no good at keeping secrets, but she made me, Emma, I swear."

So that was the reason for his flushed face and repeated urges for her to talk to her grandmother. For "she" could only mean one person. One person who didn't need a first *or* a last name. One person who thought she was the master puppeteer. Emma's back teeth fused. She gritted out, "What did my grandmother make you promise not to tell me?"

CHAPTER NINE

EMMA LEANED INTO the heavy glass door of the IGA, still minus a replacement after a night of thinking. One day left to clear up everything and still make her flight.

Her grandmother was an adult, as Brad had said repeatedly. Nobody could blame Emma. She'd done everything.

Everyone was afraid of her grandmother. And it didn't matter that it would probably be a kick to work with resident summer-fun guy Sparks Turner. Chet had been no help. Zoo had run through the same options Emma had conjured up.

Then Emma had felt guilty about wanting others to solve her problem, then gotten mad about feeling guilty, then guilty about being mad about it. Then she'd eaten way too many slices of butter-soaked cinnamon toast to forget the whole matter.

The pungent odor of extrasharp cheddar cheese twitched her nose. Mr. Telford and his wife had sold the grocery store to their son

Vince. He'd graduated a few years behind Emma. Vince broke off his whistling to greet her from behind the meat counter. Resting his big forearms in front of him, he grinned. "Emma, what can I get you? Got some nice chops. How's your grandmother?"

"My grandmother is going to be fine. She's a Chambers." Her eyes roamed the deli case. *Mmm.* Twice-baked potatoes. A little comfort food might help tonight while she changed a lifetime pattern and came up with a good idea fast.

One crummy day to get it right.

Vince's gaze shifted up and beyond her shoulder. "Sparks! Looking for lunch?"

Emma whirled to find Sparks looking at her, his expression changing the second she locked eyes with him. Those questions when she caught him watching her... Was he thinking, "What is her *problem*? What is the big *deal* here?"

As she hurriedly began to inspect every single item in the deli case as though it was the most fascinating deli case on the planet, a new idea struck.

"Hey, Vince, I'm looking for someone to run the Jamboree. Wanna apply?"

Vince laughed as if she'd told the funniest joke he'd ever heard. "Em, this weekend has been a great start to the summer so far. My barbecue went out the door in slabs." He tied the string around the potato wrapped in white butcher paper and pushed it toward her. "Hope the Jamboree will be enough."

Emma grasped the package and tucked it in her basket. "Enough for what?"

As he bent across the deli case to respond, a bullhorn voice, elevated to carry into the next county, vibrated through the store. "Vincent, how do you expect to stay in business if you don't have what people need?"

Vince patted Emma's hand and stepped aside to wait on Sparks, whose eyes had widened at the stentorian bellow.

"It's only Beryl," Vince reassured him.

Feral Beryl wore a chip on her shoulder the size of Heaven Lake, daring anyone to breathe on it, much less knock it off.

While Emma was growing up next door to the woman, balls that went over The Berlin Wall never came back, at first. Grumpa would have to go and get them. Then one day Beryl started returning the balls over the fence and that was that. To be fair, Emma thought, Beryl had had her share of hard times.

After leaving the deli counter, Emma dropped a loaf of sourdough from a local organic bakery into her basket alongside the tomatoes, lettuce and bacon.

Beryl and her alcoholic husband had screamed at each other for years until the night he'd gone for beer and didn't come home. Old Mae Cunningham swore that evening's events had sealed the deep line between Beryl's eyebrows and gradually added more than a hundred pounds to the woman. Now Feral Beryl lumbered around in a caftan and sandals. Once she retired, she spent most of her time working in her backyard and criticizing town events.

A warm hand landed on Emma's shoulder and caught her attention. Sparks. In the produce aisle. Standing very near to her.

"Look," he said, his hand remaining on her shoulder until Emma shot a pointed glance toward it. "You don't want to plan this Jamboree."

"I don't." Finally they agreed on something.

He spotted the items in her basket. "BLTs! How 'bout I buy some more bacon and we make 'em together?" At Emma's silence, he shrugged. "Sorry."

Although…maybe the sandwich making would give her an opportunity to convince Sparks to take on the five-day Fourth of July event.

"I don't want to plan it, either, to be honest.

I'm on vacation. A man of the world, committed to no one. So let's find someone else." His grin indicated his pleasure at solving both of their problems.

Emma sighed and moved toward the checkout. Great. Only she'd already solved both of their problems.

As she opened her mouth to reply that she was busy—*man moratorium, you know*—the phone in her pocket buzzed and played the opening chords of "I Will Survive." She moved a couple of steps away and answered the call. "Hello?"

It was the nurse she'd spoken to at Garden Terrace, the temporary facility for the next step of her grandmother's recovery. The doctor had cleared her grandmother for rehab, but Naomi was having none of it. "There's no medical reason to keep her at the hospital…and I think they need the bed…" The nurse's voice trailed off. She thanked the woman, said she'd be in touch and ended the call.

Emma decided on and then added shortbread cookies and chunky chocolate fudge ice cream to her basket as she tried to think of something helpful. A breath later, she felt, rather than saw Sparks beside her, his warmth reaching out to her.

What was she going to do? Her mind flashed

to a picture of her grandmother grinning and holding up a map of England, taunting her.

She changed directions and headed toward the checkout, and heard Beryl again, informing Vince of more of her opinions. "If I was running the Jamboree, there'd be changes, I can tell you."

Evidently, Beryl's changes would start with changing the organizer's title from Jamboree coordinator to supreme empress of the universe. Her grandmother would hitchhike from Garden Terrace as soon as she heard crazy news like that. Not that it would ever happen. Nomi would never allow it.

Emma stepped up to the checkout, Sparks at her side. He had the sense, she was relieved to find, to not say a word. Something. She had to come up with something to get her grandmother to rehab. If she didn't get better—Tears smarted in Emma's eyes.

"I'd get rid of that Cadillac Naomi rides in during the parade. It smacks of elitism. And if you ask me…"

Nobody had asked Beryl. Nobody ever did. Naomi had first rode in a Cadillac in the early 70s as mayor when an Evanston car dealership offered it; Grumpa had ridden with her as fire chief. Eliminating that tradition from the Jamboree had as much chance of happening as Beryl did of running the show this year or any year.

Emma's feet stopped moving. If Nomi knew Beryl was thinking of changing the Jamboree… Of running the event? This…this might work. Her grandmother would never agree to go to Garden Terrace unless—unless her grandmother got something she wanted in return. This time the tears were for Emma herself.

She hit Redial and was connected to the nurse. "I'll get her there," Emma promised. It took only minutes to make the arrangements. A pang in her heart struck deep. But the longer her grandmother was not in rehab, the less she'd recover. Could Emma depend on the lengths Nomi might go to keep Beryl out of the Jamboree?

Emma closed her eyes, feeling faint. Had it come down to this? The shores of England began to cloud with fog. An image from the movie *My Fair Lady*, which she and Grumpa loved, faded quickly.

With the basket slung over her arm, Emma forced her legs to engage and continue walking to the register.

"Are you—" Sparks began.

Emma flung up a hand as if to ward off his kindness. "Please."

"Can I help?"

"No." To get lost in those eyes would ruin everything for her. The man moratorium had to get her through.

Another intense gaze, and then he nodded as though confirming something to himself. Sparks turned and strode out of the store.

AFTER LETTING TROUBLE OUT, filling the Omni with gas and grabbing a yogurt at the house, Emma headed for the Organic District before driving to the hospital.

Emma had no doubt that her grandmother would take the bait, once she dangled Beryl's potential involvement in the Jamboree in front of her. The chasm between Nomi and her neighbor had erupted long before Emma had had memories, and nothing could induce her grandmother to let Beryl replace her.

A special loaf of bread would, however, hopefully reward the hospital staff for taking care of her difficult relative. They would need a treat, for her grandmother was, so far, still refusing to go to Garden Terrace.

A few miles out of town, a large carved sign heralded what was referred to as the OD. Organic farmers, ranchers, artisans and crafters rented small wooden stalls and sold their wares to residents and tourists passing on the county road. Organic gardens stretched behind the buildings.

Emma pulled the car off the county road and onto the dusty gravel drive, heading for the Quonset hut that was Jennifer Bread. A small house stood next to the hut, connected to it by a breezeway. Emma had not met this relative newcomer to the area, as the bread baker had appeared after Emma's flight from Heaven.

As she reached for the bakery door, glancing through the small-paned window, she spotted a familiar male. He was standing with his arm around a fragile-looking woman, who was even shorter than Emma. Sparks and most likely Jennifer of Jennifer Bread? Quicker than Trouble could gobble a treat, she recognized the taste of old bitterness in her mouth.

So he wanted to make it up to her, did he? Yet he'd apparently found other, more entertaining things to do with his time. That she'd brushed off his consistent friendliness and attempts at reconciliation food, she ignored.

She was furious with herself for softening even for a moment in the IGA, with Sparks next to her, touching her without touching her.

Her new life was turning out to be just like the old one, she thought, catching Sparks's startled expression. He dropped his arm from

Jennifer, who turned and smiled at Emma. Emma waved feebly.

She stormed off, almost sprinting to her car.

I've lost my boyfriend, my dream trip and my freedom.

And she'd given up her job.

Summer heartthrob Sparks, who had made her think that maybe the man moratorium wasn't needed, was no doubt telling Jennifer, "Baby, I'll always be there for you."

Well, there was one thing she could do that nobody could take away: maintain the man moratorium until she shook the dust of Heaven from her feet.

At the hospital, Naomi pursed her lips in her familiar way. A decision always hung in the balance with those lips positioned so. It didn't matter whether it was permission needed to go to a friend's house or to buy a new truck for the town.

"You stay? If I agree to g-go to that place."

Emma blinked three times, hard, as the nurse came in, pushing the pole with the vital-signs machine attached. The woman cut the tension with her chatter while she checked Naomi's levels and rolled the thermometer ball over her forehead.

"Yes."

"Heart rate's a little elevated." The nurse swished out of the room.

So's mine. Emma stood up and walked to the window. Outside, a maintenance man troweled mulch around some newly planted flowers. Turning back, she regarded her grandmother. "Or I could go ahead with my trip to merry ol' England and Beryl can run the Jamboree. She's always wanted to, you know."

"B-beryl, you say. C-can't...have that." Her grandmother lifted her head from the pillow, regarding Emma from under still-furrowed brows. "Of course, you have t-trip insurance, not like it's a sacrifice."

A new despair clutched at Emma. If she had been her grandmother, certainly she would have purchased trip insurance. But she was not her grandmother. And while her grandmother saw this as a slight blip in Emma's silly scheme, for Emma, the lack of insurance was a small catastrophe. But then, Nomi never did acknowledge Emma's goals as important if they deviated from her own thinking.

Emma managed a quick nod. Ironic—told to "stay," just like Trouble. She'd been put in her place again.

Emma clasped her grandmother's hands. "You have to get better, please."

Naomi squeezed back with her right hand.

"W-we'll do…Jamboree like every other year…just w-work harder." Slowly, she signed her name on the transfer papers to Garden Terrace. Then she sighed, and plucked at the edge of the blanket, the straight line between the eyebrows, like Emma's, sharply carved. She muttered, "Don't… Francine… Navajo Taco… Binder."

"You've already told me three times, Nomi. Don't let Francine do anything with food. Stick to the Black Binder." Once again Emma was playing the village idiot.

Nomi was silent once again. No word of thanks. No comforting reassurances about planning the next few days. As far as her grandmother was concerned, the world had been restored to its normal axis. Emma pulled her hand away from her grandmother's, as close to hating her grandmother as she had ever been.

She said her goodbyes and closed the hospital room door behind her.

Emma's steps dragged as she walked away from the hospital amid the fragrance of the lilacs nearby. At least now her grandmother would get the help she needed. A relief, for sure.

But now Emma had nothing to look forward to but days of dealing with everything from traffic jams on Main Street to the proper placement of trash barrels. Even the prospect of Sparks sharing—hopefully—those duties with her didn't raise her mood.

Clenching her fists, Emma lifted her head, a new vision forming. So she had sacrificed for her grandmother's health, without gratitude, she might add. She would do this Jamboree. It hadn't changed since she'd been born.

The same events, booths and entertainment spread over five glorious July days, from Thursday through Monday.

But if she reminded everyone of their jobs now, she wouldn't have to actually be here for the Jamboree. Sparks could run that.

Surely her grandmother hadn't said *we* regarding the running of the actual Jamboree? Surely Emma had misheard. She desperately *hoped* she'd misheard.

Yes! She'd call the travel agent to ask if she rescheduled soon enough, could she salvage her trip. Then she'd fly through the same, established routine for the Jamboree's setup. And she'd go to England—alone—and never ever return to Heaven.

CHAPTER TEN

NAOMI BREATHED IN until her lungs were full. She smiled. That cotton in her brain had cleared. A good thing, since she'd needed her wits about her with Emma's visit.

Her beautiful granddaughter was not, after all, going to leave her. The only way to save Heaven was through the Jamboree, and the only one she trusted to run the Jamboree was Emma. So when Emma had broached the idea of Beryl planning the event in Naomi's stead because Emma was determined to make her plane, Naomi suffered a momentary panic.

Emma gone and Beryl Winsome with power? *Her* power?

Then, in the middle of that day terror, she'd seen Emma blinking rapidly and had almost laughed, her fear dissipating like clouds before a stiff wind.

The girl never could lie worth a lick.

Try to trick ol' Naomi by promising to stick around if she went to rehab, but if she refused, Emma would defer to Beryl being in charge

of the Fourth of July Jamboree. Considering—
here the old hurt rubbed—how Emma's father
had turned out, it was a blessing the girl didn't
lie like a rug.

Since the night that child had been left for
her and Raymond to raise, Naomi had faithfully disguised her son's deficiencies with her
own strengths.

"Naomi? You decent?" Chet didn't wait for
an answer, entering the room in a familiar golf
shirt, merely a different color. "I saw Emma
in the hall. Did you tell her finally?"

A twinge of remorse stabbed, but didn't kill
the self-satisfaction she felt. "No, I didn't t-tell
her *that*." She relayed the good news about
Emma staying.

"How did you con her into it? What about
her trip to honor Raymond's memory?" The
pang deepened with the disapproval on Chet's
face. "One of these days, Naomi, you'll reap
a rotten harvest sowed from all this manipu-
lation."

Naomi shifted to a more comfortable position on the rough sheets. She would tell Emma.
She would. Now not only would the Jamboree
go as it always had, they would make enough
to put the town back in the black, and Sparks
would provide a needed jolt for Emma. The
Cunningham sisters had filled her in on the

tackling incident and Sparks's apparent interest in her granddaughter.

"It's not going to be any easier the longer you wait to tell her, woman."

Forcing another deep breath, Naomi closed her eyes. Chet was right. In elementary school, Emma was too young. In junior high, the girl cried at the squint of an eye. By high school, the battle over Emma's college and career goals had carried them through freshman year in college. In grad school, there had been the sleazy professor...and then the incident at Raymond's funeral. Emma didn't need to hear ancient family history...right now. After the Jamboree would be soon enough.

BY LUNCHTIME THE next day, Emma felt her first sign of returning cheerfulness. She'd walked the dog along the lake, taken in Promise Island in the middle and remembered her and Zoo's adventures out there in kayaks and rafts. A quick sneak through her grandmother's room at home and soon the laundry was done, although she knew she hadn't done it Nomi's way. Now what?

Tomorrow's one and only volunteer meeting couldn't come soon enough. One meeting and she was gone. Well, gone as soon as she convinced Sparks that he only had to stand around and smile until after the Jamboree. It practically ran itself. Taking a look at the Black Binder sitting on the round kitchen table where it had been since she got it out of the living room bookcase, she could recite the pages from memory.

Everything was in there. List upon list, spreadsheets, warnings, exclamation marks and red pen underscoring items. She'd seen it all before while growing up. She could probably do it in her sleep. Tomorrow she'd run through the lists; people would do what they'd always done. The biggest hurdle now was bringing Sparks into compliance.

Walking to the Dew Drop, she flopped into the booth that had been hers and Zoo's since high school.

Ally, a former student of hers now in college, appeared by the table, smiling, pen twisting back and forth in her hand.

"Hi, Miss Chambers, hot enough for you?"

Ally, on her way up and out. Emma hoped she would make it. "Unbelievable. Home for the summer already?"

The girl nodded. "I'm lucky Alice takes me back every summer. I really appreciate this job." She used the back of her hand to rub her forehead, then her gaze slipped to her pad. "What sounds good?"

Besides running away? While she stared blankly at the menu, Emma remembered Ally had heard her speech in junior high history. The follow-your-bliss speech. "Don't settle for what's ordinary," Emma had told them. "You're not ordinary. Why live an ordinary life?" Now she—the speechmaker—was living neither the challenging what-if nor the bracing why-not, but the insipid whatever. Pushing the menu away, she responded, "Iced tea for starters. Then I need some time to consider my options."

Ally nodded and turned away, glancing up with a blush to greet Sparks, who slid in across from Emma.

"I've been looking for you." His crooked smile lit his tanned face.

Emma kept her eyes on the nearby menu until she realized she'd read *salad plate with crackers* several times.

"I convinced Nomi to go to rehab," she said.

Sparks nodded, thanking Ally for the Coke she set on the table. He sipped. "She finally see reason?"

"Not exactly. I manipulated her into it."

Trepidation, or maybe disappointment, slid over Spark's face. "Funny. I wouldn't think you'd be that kind."

He was right. How could Sparks know her

so well so soon yet Emma didn't know herself? She sighed, hated herself for sighing, and crunched some ice in the iced tea Ally had placed in front of her.

To give herself some time before she answered him, Emma read the menu again. Too hot for soup; a whole dinner was too heavy. Her eyes strayed to the dessert choices. In view of the man moratorium, comfort food might have to do.

No dessert before dinner. The memory of Naomi's voice filled her ears. She twisted in her seat and waved Ally over. "Blueberry pie à la mode. And French fries."

"Got it," Ally said.

"I'll have the same." Sparks grinned across at Emma. "Sounds great."

Emotional eating. It would do her no good past the pleasure of it sliding down her throat.

"Ah," he continued. "See? I can buy you food and we can start over. It's summer after all."

Careful, her inner voice warned. But what if she did just have fun? With him, she argued back. Could she avoid the heartache that she'd experienced with Brad, the married professor in grad school and the rest of the guys on the Let's Dump Emma list because they had shown an interest and she was needy enough to want somebody to love her.

Man moratorium or not? So difficult to decide.

A warm hand covered one of her own. Sparks's blue eyes bored into hers. Again with the questions. "You okay?" As before, the expression slipped away and changed to him looking as if today was his birthday and she was his present.

In the days she'd been back in town, there wasn't a woman under the age of one hundred who wasn't talking about Sparks Turner. He was cute, he was helpful, he looked hot without a shirt and he even liked Feral Beryl despite his first exposure to her. He was helping her reclaim her front yard. Of *course* he was all that, Emma thought sourly, listening to him tell her about his day on the lake. The nice-guy routine worked for Sparks, like Brad's seductive attention had worked for him.

Even the guys liked Sparks. His canyon wreck was fast developing into a local legend instead of a stupid stunt. She'd heard he was fearless on the lake. He'd joined the volunteer fire department, for Pete's sake. Such a saint. Bitterness seeped into her throat, souring the tea.

"I think I need more than pie and fries. Let me order and then I'm all yours," he said.

A smile was her reply. She figured she could still honor the man moratorium without being snarky about it.

"A turkey club with extra bacon," Sparks said, glancing up at Ally, who'd reappeared with her order pad, grinning like mad at him. He leaned back with a happy sigh, lean muscled arms up along the back of the booth as he described yesterday's wild single-track bike ride down Hopkins' Canyon, the ride on the lake monster boat, the kicking marina by the beach. All things Heaven.

All things Heaven.

"I can't wait until the Jamboree," he said, sucking down the Coke.

The Chamber of Commerce should film him for commercials.

Emma's shoulders were jammed up to her ears in responsibility and resentment, and he raved like the tourist of the year. Wait until he hit the volunteer meeting. She simply wanted to finish the task bestowed on her and get out of town. With the two of them here in the booth, she should make this a planning session. Should.

Weariness tightened its way up her neck. How long did she get to pout over the deal she'd offered her grandmother that had gone unappreciated? Time to move on. With her new goal, she'd still reach her happy place. She rubbed her neck, tilting her head against her hand.

"I met a guy in Athens who was a masseur." Sparks's eyes darted from Emma's face to her neck. "Built like an ox. He says some people carry all their stress in their necks."

Rather than respond, Emma didn't answer, tipping her head forward to stretch the back of her neck. Tears from the concern on his face threatened to leak from her eyes.

"He taught me a few techniques. Here, let me show you." He was out of his seat before she could protest, strong fingers on her neck, pushing away all the hurt. *Mmm.* She should pull away, turn, should drop him dead with a look. This was out-and-out a violation of the man moratorium. The tension oozed from her knotted muscles. *Mmm.* More shoulds. Really, she hated shoulds.

As the blood began to flow again through her loosened muscles, she became aware of the interested gaze of several Dew Drop patrons. One last small "mmm" escaped her when Ally set down the food. The girl hid a smile and sped off.

Sparks flopped back into his side of the booth. "How was that for you?" he murmured, digging into the fries with gusto.

Not daring to look around, she spooned into her warm pie and ice cream. Her neck had been romanced—in the Dew Drop. What would people think?

Sparks turned his attention toward his dessert, now that he'd consumed half the fries. "I love Alice's pie."

He seemed oblivious to what his small act of kindness had meant to her. She swallowed the mouthful of pie and ice cream, gulped tea and ate a fry. Brad's touches had never felt like that, she thought reflectively, savoring the warm, greasy food. Still, she had to demur. "You can't go around doing that—" Doing what? Sneak a little humanity on her? "You... Oh, never mind. Thanks. Yes, I do feel better."

Sparks dragged a fry through the melted ice cream on top of his warmed pie. She followed suit, minus the French fry. The sweet-sour taste of blueberry squished with ice cream was a favorite of hers. Eating dessert without dinner was *good*.

They continued in silence before Emma recalled the Black Binder and her goal. Mr. Heaven. A flush of victory warmed her face now, and she ignored her plate. He loved Heaven. This would be a piece of cake—or pie. "Okay, as much as neither of us wants to do this, we need to get started. On the way here from the hospital, I called Tilly to set up the volunteer meeting for tomorrow morning."

Sparks looked disappointed. "I have a para-sailing lesson tomorrow morning."

Emma scowled at him.

"I can reschedule," he said after a pause. "You're doing the Jamboree exactly the same as Naomi would have?"

"Yeah. It's all in the Black Binder." She pushed around the remaining pie. The ice cream had melted into a flat puddle. Kind of like her life. "Apart from my grandmother hiring you for fireworks and contracting with Rockin' Sounds as a music headliner, it's the same as it's always been. We'll have the one and only volunteer meeting and, bam, it's all set in motion. Then—" she eyed him over the three fries she'd inserted into her mouth and spoke through them "—all you have to do during the Jamboree is walk around and smile."

"What will you be doing?" His tone was almost disinterested as his turkey-bacon club arrived with more fries. Abandoning the dessert, he picked up a triangle of sandwich and got to work.

"I'll be gone. I can reschedule my trip if I do it right away."

Sparks's face became scarlet as he coughed and spluttered, muttering about a wayward

French fry. "Emma," he said slowly. "You can't…leave. Don't you want to shake things up a little? Make some changes?"

"No. I just want to get it done and get out of here."

She needed Sparks's hands on her neck again to relax her. A picture of the English countryside floated through her mind. She wondered what the weather was like there today, what type of little sandwiches they were serving for high tea in some charming tearoom, whether she would have chosen clotted cream or lemon curd for her scone. Both, she decided. She would have both.

"And go where?"

"Away. Toward—something."

He shredded his straw's wrapper, staring at it. "Are you telling me you haven't heard that the town needs a more successful Jamboree this year? That the budget is bone-dry?" His fingers stilled as his blue eyes held her gaze.

CHAPTER ELEVEN

WHEN THE ALARM shrilled Monday, Emma's eyes flew open. Today would have been departure day for her. Sleep had teased and danced away from her for most of the night, returning only as the morning brightened. No plane, no England, no countryside, no boyfriend. And worse than all of that, there was no early escape to recoup her losses. She had no plan C. Maybe she should just give up. *Should.*

Heaven's budget was in the red.

There were too many roads that needed repair, utilities that had to be updated. Honestly, she'd stopped listening to Sparks soon after the "out of money" part. Maybe Heaven would just have to wait to fix a few streets. Really, how much could Emma and one easily distracted codirector do to ramp up a small-town holiday event?

And here her grandmother had let her think it would be business as usual, knowing it couldn't be. Swinging her legs over the side of the bed, she stepped around the dog and headed for the shower. While standing under the water, she recalled previous Jamborees. What could they do to make more money from the Fourth of July celebration without sinking thousands into the attempt?

Turning off the water, she stepped out of the shower, wrapped herself in a faded blue towel she remembered from when she was younger and dashed to her room. She surveyed the beige clothes in the smaller suitcase, now a laundry receptacle of sorts. A sorry comedown for adventure luggage. Pushing it away with her foot, she opened the larger suitcase and selected a turquoise tank top. Her trip would have been new attitude, new clothes and a new future. One out of three accomplished.

Ideas. They needed ideas. While standing in the kitchen and drinking iced tea rather than something more breakfasty due to her stomach being in knots, she thought ahead to the meeting. She would have to stand up and say it was different this year. Then what? Her crowd-control skills were connected only to junior highers when she had a lesson plan. Now there was no plan. Not even the Black Binder would do.

An ominous cloud of need hung over Heaven.

What happened when a town ran out of

money? Did they shut Bigelow Canyon and hang a sign that read, Sorry, Closed for Lack of Funds?

Moments later, she stomped down the last of the front steps, the binder cradled in her left arm. Sparks had better show up for this meeting and not be parasailing over the lake or...

"Oh. Hello." She blinked against the glowing light that backlit Sparks Turner, rendering him an angelic apparition. He stood at the bottom of the steps, smile big and bright. He looked good. His signature sage-citrus combination flowed from him to her. She managed a weak smile. *Real* good. The voice in her head shouted, *Man moratorium!*

"Good morning." He stepped forward and took the binder from her. "Have you recovered from the bad news? What's the plan now?"

As if she knew. Frustration that her *co-planner* had asked the million-dollar question as if she was the sole creator of miracles stiffened her neck. She narrowly escaped spearing him with a look reminiscent of her grandmother's Incoming. *Maintain, Emma. Don't shoot the messenger.*

He linked her arm with his and they proceeded onto the sidewalk. Sniffing, Sparks threw back his head. "I love that smell."

Grudgingly, she knew what he meant and

allowed herself to draw in a cleansing breath. The air, like the summers when she was growing up, hung spicy and sweet with the scent of carnations and roses. Immediately after the fragrance filled her nose came the gritty fact that they were in big trouble.

Resisting the urge to turn into his shoulder and bawl out her insecurities about what were they going to do, she picked up her pace, waving at Bev Cluny, a physical education teacher at HCS. The short blond woman lived a couple of houses down from Naomi. Bev was out early, sweeping her front steps in a HCS T-shirt over Lycra shorts. Emma had never seen her in anything else.

"Hey, Emma." Bev stopped sweeping and moved toward her fence.

Emma groaned inwardly. You did not have a short conversation with Bev. She sneaked a glance at her watch. There went her stroll to the church that served as the community center. She'd been convinced that if she could just have a few quiet moments with her co-planner, some great notion would rain down on her head. On her own last night she'd come up with nothing.

"How's your grandmother? Heard from the Parkers that her color's good. Glad you're planning the Jamboree this year." Bev's ponytail bobbed as she leaned on the broom.

Gesturing to Sparks, who had smiled and waved as well, Emma said, "It's not just me planning. Sparks Turner, the fireworks designer? We're doing it together." She backed away from the fence.

"Hold on there, Emma." Bev shifted the broom to her other hand. "Since, especially this year…" Her normally strident voice had faded. "Well, Naomi can be—reluctant—when it comes to new thoughts."

No kidding. The nod came as a reflex and seemed to vanquish Bev's cautious expression. Dropping the broom and gesticulating wildly, Bev exclaimed with the same enthusiasm she did outlining a basketball pick and roll, "Wouldn't it be great if we had Heavenly Hosts? You know, have the Jamboree volunteers wear gold halos and little strap-on wings?"

A chuckle burst from Sparks. "Sounds fun." He shot a sideways look at Emma. "Something different for this year. We could sell them as souvenirs."

Emma waited for Bev to laugh and tell them she was joking. When she realized the other woman was serious, Emma made some noncommittal remark and escaped, Sparks catching up with his long legs.

"That's a great idea." His smile lingered as he turned to wave to Bev, who returned to vigorously sweeping her front sidewalk.

"With the town broke, where would we get the money to buy the wings and halos in the first place?" She shook her head. Was she the only one who saw the crisis for what it was: *unsolvable*?

They passed Mr. Higgins in his porch recliner reading the paper.

"Morning, Mr. Higgins!" She lifted the back of her hair to cool her neck and waved. The man was probably looking for a few minutes respite before Mrs. Higgins found something for him to do.

They had reached Main Street. Emma checked her watch and paused. They had no time to spare, really, and no ideas yet. As they passed the Book Nook, she glanced at the display in the large plate-glass window. Faith had a business theme presently. *Who Moved My Cheese?* Nobody would dare move Naomi Chambers's cheese. *How to Swim with the Sharks.* Her grandmother was an expert in the water. What would Emma's title be? *Heaven Can Wait?*

"Emma! Sparks!"

Emma shifted her gaze from the window. Sparks poked at her elbow. "Juggy Burnett," he said.

As if she didn't know who Juggy Burnett was. A short man with a perspiring face was fast approaching them. Two years behind her in school, and according to her grandmother, the town's current, less-than competent public-works superintendent.

"Hi, Juggy. How's it going?" Sparks greeted the man like a long-lost friend.

"You look warm," Emma remarked, hoping Juggy wasn't going to go off on the latest evidence of alien sightings. In addition to his hobby, he was one of the town's most fervent volunteers and a friendly soul. Emma had always liked him.

Juggy wiped his forehead with the back of his blue uniform sleeve. "Listen, gotta talk to you 'bout the Jamboree." Moving in close, Juggy continued, "I've got an idea so great, we'll make a million this year!" He beamed expectantly at her. "Especially this year."

Wow. If one more person said, "especially this year" to her, she'd lose it.

"That's great, Juggy, but we're in a bit of a rush. The volunteer meeting starts in a minute, so…" Emma checked her watch. She appreciated Juggy's interest in her problem, but needed to have a moment or two or twenty to compose herself before getting the proceedings underway.

"Whatcha thinking about, Jug?" Sparks sounded as if he had all the time in the world.

To encourage Juggy to be brief, she sidestepped away from him and took another glance at her watch.

"Flying Elvis. A bunch of 'em." Pressing his lips together, Juggy danced in place. "Over the lake, dude."

"Flying Elvis?" Emma repeated. Right. Elvis impersonators dressed in white sparkly jumpsuits à la the King. They parachuted from airplanes into festivals, fairs and Vegas parking lots.

Think about practical things, she reminded herself, avoiding Spark's laughing eyes. *Breathe*.

"We're all in this together this year, huh." Sparks patted the man's shoulder.

Emma contributed a polite, affirmative nod and walked on, imagining the sea of expectant faces she'd be seeing shortly. Very shortly.

From the Book Nook, all she and Sparks had to do was hang a right on Main, pass the Sweet Buy and Buy Fudge Emporium and turn the corner at the west end of Cherubim. A short walk, really.

With an increasing clutch of dread, she faced the front doors of the church that doubled as the community center and stopped. Her legs refused to take her any farther. This year was so different and all she knew was the old way. Despite her roiling stomach, she wished she had eaten breakfast.

"Emma, before we go in, let's talk." Sparks's smile slid toward the corner of his mouth.

"No time," she said, forcing her feet up the steps.

She would start with how thankful they all were that Naomi was still with them. *Remember, you* are *grateful*, she cautioned herself. Shifting the binder to her other arm, she surveyed the noisy hall. Looked like the regular crowd. Business owners, widows, teachers, farmers, ranchers. Some people she knew by sight, if not by name. Some people she didn't recognize who looked as if they came from the Organic District. People who'd been doing the same volunteer job year after year.

She had the Black Binder, a beyond-gorgeous partner out of reach because of the man moratorium and two off-the-wall ideas. Sure, she had a dependable list of workers, but what could they do this year to increase the town's return? It was all up to her, and she had no answer. As a teacher, she was used to always having the right answer. Her moments of pure invention were few and far between. The closer she got to the podium at the front, the more she sensed the mood was subdued, even...tense? Her intuition always annoyed her grandmother. *Not everything has a deep meaning, Emma. Some things just are.*

But Emma was sensing something.

A raucous burst of arguing rose above the conversations in the air; she swung her attention to the far wall. Against the background of a colorful mural showing early town fathers shaking hands in front of the lake, Starla and Francine were going at it about the Navajo tacos and how Francine had set off a rash of food poisoning with improperly heated meat.

"Sure you're up to this?" Father Jack's florid face reflected the uneasiness she'd noticed on her way up to the podium. He pastored the Catholic church in town. Beefy in his black shirt and clerical collar, he was best friends with Pastor Ned, the leader of Heaven Community Church.

"Going to be quite a year, especially this year," echoed Pastor Ned, his wife hovering at his elbow, immaculately attired in beige linen.

Realizing she couldn't carry out her threat of clocking the pastor for using the phrase *especially this year*, Emma told herself sternly to just take a look around. After all, many of these people ran businesses. Obviously, they had business ideas. Strategies. Scenarios. That was it. Look for collaboration. It wouldn't have to be just her. Relief flooded her. After her speech about Naomi, she'd throw the meeting open to ideas. *Especially this year.*

The room quieted for the first order of business, the blessing on the Jamboree and its preparations. As Pastor Ned asked for wisdom and protection for this Jamboree season, Emma cast a look at the crowd. No multicolored caftan. Where was Feral Beryl with her annual bellow about praying at a public meeting? "Where's Beryl?" she whispered to Ned after the group chorused, "Amen." He, too, was scanning the crowd for the unmissable Beryl. "It's not a Jamboree without her disrupting the volunteer meeting."

The pastor shook his head. "I haven't seen her this morning. Maybe she's sick." Pulling out his phone, he tapped in a note. "I'll stop by her house afterward and make sure she's okay."

This was how some people liked to think of Heaven. While Beryl would never darken the door of a church, both Father Jack, no doubt, and Pastor Ned kept an eye on her, made sure someone shoveled her walk in winter, offered her rides to Evanston for errands and the like. Never a thank-you from the woman, mind you.

Volunteers milled about with cups of coffee or soft drinks, and snacks donated by the Quick Stop.

Stepping to the podium, Emma tapped the microphone, sending a bone-stiffening squeal through the gym. As she took a deep breath, she saw Feral Beryl slip in, a bulky shadow in a gray-and-black caftan. Instantly, Sparks was by the woman's side, nodding and greeting her. Swallowing the T. rex blocking her throat, Emma all but shouted, "Good morning!" To her ears, the reverberating voice sounded young, childish.

Year after year, Nomi strode to the mike, grasped it with authority and barked out orders. People did what she said. It was that simple. Emma begged the ground to open up and swallow her. When that failed to occur, she opened the Black Binder to the first tab: Volunteer Meeting. No tab for Especially This Year.

"Well," she began, "if we could, I'd like to get signups as usual. It'll be quick and we all can get back to our Saturday." She pointed to three banquet tables positioned along one wall. "Coordinators, you can pick up your corresponding list. Contact the same people you used last year. We all know the drill." Surely someone would step up and offer better ideas now. They all knew they needed to make more money this year.

She moved back and made herself take a deep breath. Breathing was good. It indicated she hadn't died. Yet as she slipped her clammy hands down her sides to dry them, she noticed no movement of people toward the tables. People turned from one to another in small groups, a wave of whispering rising like fog from the lake. A knowing rose in Emma.

Something worse was in the air. In lieu of her grandmother saving the day, they were looking at her. Juggy, looking disappointed, leaned over to whisper in Pitch's ear. Pitch was Starla's husband.

Whispers again.

"There's no point," she heard a grizzled old man hiss to his equally grizzled friend. "T'ain't no point when they're goin' to flood the town."

Emma's knees gave out, but before she could hit the floor, microphone still clutched in her sweaty hand, Sparks's arms had slid around her and set her upright.

He murmured into her hair, "I just heard about it when I went to get a doughnut. It's unbelievable, but it's true."

CHAPTER TWELVE

FENDING OFF QUESTIONS for which he had no answers, Sparks excused himself after the meeting and headed at a trot toward the lake and Emma. Drop followed drop of sweat down his back. He neared the park and spied Emma sitting on the dogs-allowed side of the beach, while Trouble played by the shore.

Sparks didn't relish telling her the rest of the bad news that had spilled out after she had fled the church.

The town needed three hundred and seventy-five thousand dollars by the end of July, combined budget and surplus. And no one, least of all him, had any idea how to get to that total.

For the first time since he'd acquired the role of co-planner, the responsibility of the Jamboree weighed on him like he guessed it had on Emma. Her sharp edges now made sense. So what could he say to make her feel better? Whatever it was, he wanted to say it. He paused at this thought, then shook his head and began to walk more quickly. Until now, his style with women had been fun, noncommittal. Surface. Safe.

Reaching the tree, he sat down beside Emma. She drew up her knees and wrapped her arms around them. Comfort. She needed comfort. What to tell her?

Trouble glanced upward. For a moment, it seemed the dog was hesitating between sticking with his waves or tearing after his new best friend. Chasing a human won out; the black-and-white dog hurtled up the hill, flipping water from his coat.

Emma exclaimed and leaped to her feet as Trouble sprinted toward them and began to shake. "Here comes Trouble." She ducked behind the tree.

A nervous laugh spurted from Sparks. *Nice going.* He joined her behind the tree. "Sorry about that. It was just, well, sort of funny."

She slanted a wry look at him as if she agreed, but didn't want to admit it. Placing her palms against the bark, she directed her first words toward the street beyond the park. "Can you imagine millions of gallons of water flooding this place? Bulldozers knocking down Lynette's motel and the Dairy Delite? Or would the water board officials simply flood the town just as it is, once they removed the people and animals?" Wide, panicked eyes stared at him hard. "Especially this year, they said. Those crazy ideas. Why didn't I hear about the real money problem? I'll tell you why. I was too busy feeling sorry for myself and thinking folks were offering those zany ideas because they saw me as a poor second to my grandmother."

Make her feel better? It would take a miracle. "Um. Would it help to cry?" he offered.

Her lip curled even as her throat worked convulsively. "Cry? Tears don't help." The phrase sounded as if it had been memorized.

Not knowing what else to do, and feeling the burden of further unpleasant news weighing heavily on his conscience, Sparks took her hand.

Emma twitched as though she would jerk it away, but then gripped his fingers. He led her around the tree to sit facing the lake. At least the scenery would be pleasant.

Once they'd settled on the ground, their backs to the rough bark, he cleared his throat and wished simultaneously that he was both a million miles away and sitting close enough for her to use his shirt hem to dry the tears he figured would come, despite what she had said. "There's more I have to tell you."

As THE NEW revelation circled around in her head, mainly around the amount of three hundred and seventy-five thousand dollars, Emma remained silent once Sparks had relayed the financial picture.

"Wow," she finally said, drawing in a deep breath. Turning toward Sparks, she caught his expression and laughed. She didn't need to have known him for years to know the man had no clue what to do next and was apprehensive about her reaction to his news. "You were brave to tell me that after my meltdown at the meeting."

He shrugged. "You were brave enough to lead the meeting you didn't want to lead. Thought it was the least I could do."

I could fall for you, fireworks man. Another time, another place. It was nice, in the midst of this upheaval, to sit with him. Would it be so bad to relax the moratorium? Beachgoers passed them nearby on the path to the lake. Trouble lay on his side, flank gently rising and falling.

She reined herself in, the money issue spinning wildly in her brain. "Flying Elvises, though. Really?"

"Juggy says thousands of Elvis fans pay to see any of the different teams parachute." Sparks's easy smile appeared. "What about the angel wings?" he added. "Could that be off the wall enough for lots of people to buy them?"

"No idea." Hearing the screams from the

lake, Emma smiled. Tourists didn't know the lake only warmed up past bone-chilling in August, and that was a maybe.

"Why are you smiling?" Sparks rearranged his position so he was lying on his side, arm supporting his head. Watching her.

"Oh, nothing. Just a Heavenite inside joke."

"You know," he said, but he looked uncertain again, "you were leaving Heaven. As soon as the planning was over. But just now, you sounded as though you cared, as though you belonged here."

Talking to him was easy. He made her feel as if what she had to say was important. "I don't know anymore. I told myself I was done with the whispers that followed me around town growing up. Then at the meeting, I heard them again, when—" She swallowed the emotion clogging her throat and began to shred a leaf on the grass. "When what I thought would get the plans rolling, didn't."

A frown crossed his tanned face. "You didn't know. You couldn't have done anything different. And what whispers?"

A flush mounted her cheeks. Would he think she was foolish to still be trapped by the past? Somehow she thought he would understand. Perhaps it was the look she'd first noticed the night they'd met. That maybe he wasn't done with his past yet, either.

"I was—maybe four years old." The words picked up speed and she was racing through the memory. "My grandmother and I were at her office, doing stuff for the town." She shook her hair away from her face and straightened her legs. "I asked her, 'Who's the other Emma, Nomi?'"

"She'd replied, 'What other Emma?'"

"'The poor little Emma some people whisper about, but I hear them.'"

"At first my grandmother didn't answer. Then she sounded pretty mad, though somehow I knew it wasn't at me this time. 'There is no poor little Emma, only ignorant people who don't have enough to do.'"

Sparks tossed a twig at Trouble, who rearranged himself and snored on.

"What was she talking about? What were the people talking about?"

My parents, she nearly said, but pulled back the words. Comfortable or no, she'd just met Sparks, and they'd only crossed into friendly. *Let's leave it at that.*

"So you came for a vacation and to blow some things up. This isn't what you planned on, either." She stood up, peeled the back of her T-shirt away from her skin. "Since we're talking about my grandmother, there are a few things I'd like to say to her about leaving out this small, yet highly relevant piece of information about us needing three hundred and seventy-five thousand dollars to save the town." Maybe this time she'd be angry enough to get the words out of her mouth, instead of keeping so much inside.

"She's not well, Emma."

Her friendly feelings toward him wobbled, then stabilized. "I'm sure you mean well, Sparks. It's just—you don't know my grandmother. Thanks for helping me at the church earlier. We'll have to come up with… something."

It took only one try to grab Trouble's leash and tow him with her toward the street. However, the closer she came to her old home, the more she'd convinced herself that driving all the way to Garden Terrace wouldn't net her hearing her grandmother say she was sorry and that she'd change.

No, Chet would be there with Nomi. He'd told Emma that she flat-out refused to have anyone else see her at "that place." Emma would wish her well from town. Maybe some distance would clarify their relationship.

Oh, Nomi. Her heart felt tired.

She'd keep away for a few days anyway.

The image of the lake and those tourists swimming popped into her head. While Emma was growing up, Grumpa would take her out in a speedboat. She had loved it when he'd pushed the throttle forward and spun the boat around so they bounced on top of their own wake. The boat would skim off the first wave and for a moment, before the *thud* of meeting the water, it had hung suspended. What she felt now was the coming down, with nothing there to catch her.

CHAPTER THIRTEEN

"IT'S BEEN NEARLY a week. Emma's not coming, Naomi. You've finally alienated that girl for good." Chet's voice was stern, while his stroking of her arm warmed her. "You're reaping what you sowed all these years. You better come clean with her or you'll lose her forever."

Naomi said nothing. Last night, after she'd awoken, gasping from the nightmare, she'd rung for the nurse and a sedative. It wasn't like her to need one, nor was it like the nightmares to increase in their frequency and ferocity.

She, who didn't put stock in dreams, was beginning to wonder if she should ponder *why now*. In the restless time before the pill kicked in, she remembered more of that girl who'd brought Emma to them that night. The words flung back and forth between them rang as clear as if she'd only just heard them.

Naomi had come down the hallway, seen Raymond and the young brunette in the doorway. The dark-haired girl had been wearing one of those trendy shag haircuts, low-slung bell-bottoms with a bit of a stomach roll hanging over the waistband and a sheer peasant blouse that left little to the imagination. She'd held a crying bundle of blankets as if it was the last thing she wanted to do.

"Naomi, we have a situation here." It had been Raymond's bank-president voice. He could quell just about any sort of request with that voice, although he'd never been able to say no to their son.

"How do we know it's even Kent's?" Naomi had demanded, but when Raymond took the bundle and turned back the corner of the blanket, they knew. A face akin to Kent's as a baby stared back at them.

"You don't abandon children," Naomi remembered saying, and the girl had begun backing away.

Then the woman all too familiar to Naomi had hissed from behind the girl, "You're not God. How dare you judge us."

Tonight, as the sleeping pill took effect and Chet left, Naomi's breath caught as it had that night, exhaustion seeping through her. It wasn't a big jump to think of her own death, here in this rehabilitation place where people were at lunch and then not at dinner. She'd been abrupt with Emma nearly a week ago, the pressure on the Jamboree forcing out words that could have been softer and kinder. Again, Naomi felt the icy fingers of terror that she'd almost left the planet without telling Emma truths too painful to think on, much less speak of. In this season of Naomi's life, however, there was no getting away from the telling. Time was not her friend.

"I'll tell her to come see me," Naomi said through dry lips and throat. She would also tell her about the flooding problem. Probably should have made a clean breast of everything at the beginning.

EMMA AND SPARKS walked along Main Street eating ice cream cones. She couldn't remember the last time she'd had one and enjoyed it this much. Too busy counting calories to conform to Brad's idea of womanhood. She'd at first demurred at the treat until Sparks had said, "You're not one of those women who freak out over every calorie, are you? You're perfect the way you are."

When he handed her the cone and their fingers touched, Emma was certain she'd been zapped with some sort of jolt. She'd hastily removed the cone from his strong fingers. Those fingers on her neck were never to be forgotten. His grin let her know the shock had gone both ways.

"Man moratorium," she muttered, stepping

fast in front of him. Unfortunately, their easy camaraderie made it more difficult to remember that Sparks was "a man of the world and committed to no one." While she was temporarily not interested in dating until she arrived in England, and even then, who knew?

"I can never tell what you're saying when you mutter." Sparks easily caught up with her.

"Never mind." The ice cream no longer pleased her tongue. The Jamboree loomed again, big and problematic. "I can't get past that everyone expects me to pull a grand, town-saving Jamboree out of my hat just because I'm Naomi's granddaughter."

They had reached the park. "It's *because* you're Naomi's granddaughter that they believe you can do it." Sparks eyes were troubled; he tugged her down next to him on the grass under a tree. If this was someone's normal life, Emma thought, this would be a date. Instead, it was another business meeting within a particularly bad series of events. What were they to do now?

"I do know, I guess." She gripped Sparks's knee, causing him to jump. The scoop on his cone fell off onto the grass. "Thinking we can simply work harder and make more money is silly. That won't cut it."

"Ten-second rule," he said, and made a dive

for the ice cream, but Emma's foot slapped it first.

"You won't starve." It oozed around her shoe. She gingerly removed her foot and grimaced at Sparks. "Sorry." Her apology was genuine and lasted a full three seconds before she reverted to crisis mode. "Don't you see?" She pounded his knee again.

"Waste of good ice cream." The megawatt smile. He looked down at the melting mess, then at her. "And yes, I do see. It doesn't take a genius to figure out to get more from the Jamboree you have to put more into it. More than angel wings anyway." He paused and sent a wicked glance in her direction. "Although the Flying Elvises might be quite the draw."

Might be, that was the problem.

Any new plans this year would obviously be untried. Recipe for disaster. She scanned the lake. Several sailboats and a Hobie Cat flowed back and forth on the breeze. Such a serene sight.

Even up on the hill where she and Sparks were, the wind brushing her skin, though warm, was pleasant. If only the churning in her stomach could catch some of the peace. "I have no inspiration, Sparks. I am not a people manager. I can't even organize my sock drawer."

As he chuckled, he cupped his hand over her knee, sending a shiver down her backbone. He had no concept of what his kindness meant to her. In another second, she would throw her man moratorium out the window and beg for him to find a white horse and carry her away. *Keep your eyes on the Hobie Cat. Hobie Cat.* Hobie Cat. The couple on the Hobie Cat leaned in for a kiss. *Great.*

Maybe with Sparks, she argued, it just felt *nice* to have someone to talk over a problem with, and especially, meltdown wonderful to have that person display a crooked smile, smell like sage and citrus and have the most gentle, effective hands on the planet. Could he, maybe, be trusted?

She didn't want another temporary guy. She wanted a forever one. She quickly removed her hand from Sparks's knee. Better to concentrate on saving Heaven.

They would have to come up with something wilder for the Jamboree.

"What about you?" she asked, striving to focus the conversation on the Jamboree and forget his effect on her. "You know anyone important who could sing or make an appearance?"

"There's always Juggy's idea," Sparks blurted, with a sideways look at his empty knee.

Emma groaned. "I can't see the appeal of middle-aged men in white jumpsuits and fake sideburns leaping out of a plane over the lake." She cocked her head at him. "It must be the old smoke jumper in you dreaming of planes and the thrill of leaping out of them."

It was his turn to stare at the lake. He'd moved away from her, even though he hadn't budged an inch. This was a new side to Sparks—evasive. *Hmm.*

Does the man who says he can't keep secrets actually have one? Her warm and fuzzy mood cooled. *New ideas; think new ideas for the Jamboree.* Maybe…

"Yeah," he at last said.

"My father left home to become a smoke jumper," Emma ventured to tell him after a few more moments when the only conversation was what drifted up from the beach. "Or so I've been told. I guess he wanted an exciting life, and it wasn't here in Heaven." *Kind of like me.* "Did you like the excitement?"

A frown broke the smoothness of Sparks's tanned forehead. "I—I don't like to talk about that much. It was a long time ago."

"Kent Chambers was my dad's name. Did you ever work with someone named Kent?"

Ray Smith appeared in front of them, his

old rat terrier on a leash, sniffing around the tree. "Sparks, Emma. Good to see you both."

Emma glanced up, impatient. Although she liked Ray and his quiet ways, this wasn't the time for chitchat. She'd never heard much about her dad, other than he'd left town before she was born. Supposedly, Nomi and Grumpa had tried to find him, and then somehow, news had trickled back that he'd died in a fire in Montana. Years ago. She'd been in elementary school. After that, he'd passed on into a shadowy enigma.

To talk to someone about what his job had been like would at least let her "see" him for a bit.

"Just wanted to say thanks for all the work you're doing on the Jamboree." A smile crawled over the older man's five-o'clock shadow. "I'm happy doing what I've always done with the 'ole litter gitter." He'd been around for at least thirty Jamborees, picking up litter with a long, polished stick with a nail drilled into it.

The lost look on Sparks's face faded; he laughed. "You oughta patent that thing."

After Ray had left, Emma said, "At least there's one volunteer who thinks we're doing something right."

Sparks blinked at the ground as though he'd been far away. "What? Oh, Ray. He's a great guy." Then, abruptly, he said, "No. Never worked with a Kent." Raising his eyes to hers, he asked, "Has your grandmother been curious about the Jamboree's coming along?"

"Chet says she's doing well, but it's slow. I'm not sure."

"Chet says? You still haven't seen her?"

Emma snorted. "No, and I may never speak to her again." Against her better judgment, knowing how guys hated female emotional spillage, she unloaded about all the times her grandmother had ever withheld information. After she finished, the two of them sat in silence for a long while.

Emma finally spoke up. "Since she dismissed me a few days ago, I decided I'm not going back."

"Dismissed you?"

Ignoring his question, she went on, "I need a break from her… It's difficult." She didn't say, *impossible*, but the word was on her lips. She ran her fingers through her hair. "She thinks she can control me and the Jamboree just like every other year. Only this year it won't work." Why shouldn't her grandmother believe she was invincible? Just because the rest of the town had allowed her grandmother to put them through their paces while crushing opposition like Juggy Burnett's blacktop paver.

Noticing a gleam in Sparks's eye as he studied her cone, she shoved it at him.

"Oh, here."

He worked on it some before he spoke. "Maybe Chet will help her see that she can't do the Jamboree justice in her current condition." White teeth crushed a side of the cone. He chewed first, and then spoke. "You know, we'll have to get the volunteers together again." He reached for her hand and pulled her up. If only she wasn't leaving after the Jamboree and he was staying. His hand in hers—it felt, well, like *home*. "We'll have to put some more thought into this. Three hundred and seventy-five thousand…"

As Emma stood, she thought about what he'd said about Nomi.

Maybe she would turn the answering machine back on. Maybe her grandmother would call her and say she was sorry. Maybe…

She shifted her attention back to Sparks. "I suppose you're right, except we don't have a great plan to tell folks about." She swung abruptly toward him. "Hey, you didn't answer my question. About getting in touch with a celebrity. Somebody you've met. Someone big you can call and beg to come and perform at our town-saving Jamboree."

At her words, the last bite of soggy cone

passed over Sparks's lips. He began to cough, loudly cleared his throat and waved her question away. If she didn't know he hated keeping secrets, she'd have thought that choking bit was a tad overdone.

CHAPTER FOURTEEN

THAT HAD BEEN too close.

As they left the park, Sparks kept a hand on Emma's elbow, steering her toward the corner of Angel Way and Main. The Jamboree problem faded into background noise. All he could process was that he was touching Emma and she hadn't moved away. Emma needed him to help her save Heaven, and he wanted to be the one to help her. But her smoke jumper questions had caused him to nearly jump out of his skin. While he had never known her father, he did remember Montana five years ago. If he'd told her everything about *that* fire, the conversation would have taken a decidedly downward turn.

The softness of her elbow teased his callused fingers as they walked. If she knew what type of person he really was, what he had done, or rather, left undone, he'd lose her, and he was surprising himself with just how much he wanted to be with her.

Had she let down her guard with him back

there? Her laugh was something he wouldn't mind hearing for the rest of his life. He checked himself. *If* he wasn't a man of the world, committed to none.

Her comment about him knowing and contacting celebrities had come out of left field. Thankful for a bruised throat from choking on the ice cream cone, he'd managed to create a scene where her question was forgotten. At least for now.

In fact, he did know a big celebrity, or, rather, knew someone who had been a big celebrity. And she was nearer than Emma could ever dream. A few years ago, superstar Trinity, due to go on stage at an outdoor venue in New Jersey, had dashed past him, panic and fear on her pale face. After having a quick look to see who else could render assistance and finding no one, he'd charged into the restroom. Her gratitude had begun a real friendship between them. But asking her to headline the Jamboree? There was a small problem with that.

Entering the cool-hot, cool-hot pattern of crowning trees on Angel Way, Emma's steps dragged, her arms crossed over her stomach as if it hurt. He already missed her skin under his fingers. Perhaps he had been mistaken about Emma being distracted from the troubles of the Jamboree. No trace of her smile now, and she wasn't saying much. She could talk bravely at times, he thought, but the droop of her shoulders and that tempting mouth shouted out to him more than her few comments about getting a grip on their situation.

He'd been told all his life he was a charmer. Now, if he could only charm away her Jamboree worries.

Women had also told Sparks that he noticed everything and understood nothing; however, the gut-wrenching expression on Emma's face struck him. The same feeling sneaked up on him at odd moments, too, like the night he came out of the canyon and saw Heaven for the first time. It was like…being suckered by something invisible. You could never get in a good defensive punch.

"We can do this, Emma. It'll be all right," he said. He raced through his repertoire of things to make her laugh. Right now, it was safer to make her laugh.

"Thanks, but this is a lot bigger than a pat on the shoulder can fix."

The I-don't-need-anybody mask had replaced the lost look, although her eyes blinked rapidly for a second. She made a remark about the weather, the dropping level of the lake, and again fell silent.

He attempted to resurrect the conversation.

"Yeah, it's hot. If this keeps up, these wildfires are going to get worse," he said as they neared Naomi's house.

At the recent volunteer fire department meeting, the potluck dinner provided by the Queen Bees, Chet had discussed the rising fire danger. "Chet says they've been out more than usual for this time of year." What he didn't tell her was that if the dryness continued, a remote—and he hoped it was remote—possibility existed that state or county authorities might ban the lighting of incendiary devices. Although he knew he was setting himself up for an Emma explosion for withholding information—given Naomi's treatment of her—he rationalized he didn't want to scare her. It might not even happen. Ha! Well, welcome to his life.

He was rambling now, unsure what to say exactly. "Ben mentioned he's had to move the gas line out farther this year for the dock. I have a parasailing lesson this afternoon. Being up in the air and looking down on that blue is incredible. Wanna come?"

She shook her head. Naomi's responsible granddaughter. "I've got to think."

In a last-ditch attempt to lighten her expression, he said pensively, "Too bad we can't bottle the blue of Heaven Lake and sell it."

She snorted. "It's been done."

"You're kidding."

"Nope. Years ago." She finally looked up at him, flecked hazel eyes changing from gray to green as the sun dappled the street. "Tourists kept asking why the water was so blue and saying they wanted to take some home. So some obliging Heavenite bought a bunch of blue bottles, filled them with lake water and sold it at a roadside stand. Before too long, however, tourists started doing a U-turn and demanding their money back. After all, the water from the lake is just like any other."

"Is it me or does this town seem to have more than its share of…"

"Quirky people?" Emma squinted up at him, a smile at last breaking the stern lines of her face.

He'd done it; even by accident, he'd still done it. When she smiled, her nose crinkled and those gorgeous eyes sparkled. He liked how the gold flecks in her eyes made the hazel shimmer. On the heels of this admiration, he reminded himself that he came to a town, he blew up the sky and he left. It was what he did. Right after the comfort of that thought slammed the sucker punch, that sense of loss that wiped out his breath for a moment; it was the third time today. He wouldn't be going *home*. He'd just be going somewhere else.

While he wanted to come clean about who he was, keeping Emma near was becoming a need. But she'd been pretty clear as to her feelings about the untrustworthiness of men. What would his confession do to *that*?

"That works." Far better to keep the conversation off her sadness that he couldn't fix…and his…longing that didn't matter.

"It's in the water," she said, darting him a look.

Now humor twinkled in those eyes. He wanted to lean toward them, gently kiss the face that held them, kiss her slowly from the forehead to the eyebrow to the cheek to her lips. And stay there.

"People in the neighboring towns say there's something in the water or because we're so isolated with the canyon. Some say Heaven's not the end of the world, but you can see it from here."

"I wonder if anyone ever thought that about Mayberry."

She snorted. "Mayberry. Talk about fantasy."

"Sounds good to me right about now."

A deep sigh issued from her lips. "Me, too."

Turning on to Seraphim, the lake breeze slipped between the houses, cooling their heated faces. Sparks felt his life mantra slipping away as they walked past drought-faded lawns and porches that people actually sat on and talked to their neighbors who went by.

He'd been wrestling with the Sparks Rules of Engagement with Women since he'd met her. The Rules, which had held him in good stead throughout the world, required he keep it light. *Be genuine, but be sure everyone understands it won't be long term.*

With Emma, something about her told him a summer fling would shatter her. It sounded strange, but more than anything, he wanted Emma to cry on his shoulder so he could provide comfort. She would feel better and so would he. Emotions ignored for too long usually erupted badly. He threw an arm around her shoulder, holding his breath. Would she duck away like she had before? "I was at the Dew Drop the other day—"

"Why does that not surprise me?"

She hadn't moved away. Maybe she'd even moved a little closer. If she wasn't careful, he was going to kiss that teasing mouth. He concentrated on his story.

"Watch it, you," he joked. "So there I was at the Dew Drop and some tourist took off in a hurry after listening to Mae and Violet go on about Pitch's sighting of the Heaven Lake monster when he was sixteen, and how it changed his voice to perfect pitch. Explains why he's so important to the choir."

A burst of laughter shot from Emma. He grinned. Score another one for Sparks. She was too serious. Like how she examined a menu as if it contained varying degrees of caloric danger. There were signs of her changing for the better, though, with her ordering dessert and no dinner the other day. "Naomi must have been a tiger on rules. Mother Egan had had rules, but few on food, figuring if you ate dessert first enough, you'd eventually want real food. Mother Egan was supernice to me at the orphanage where I grew up. She had a saying for just about every situation."

Other parenting stuff she'd done leaped into his thoughts. He'd be a great dad. He was sure of it. A side peek at Emma's profile revealed the small nose and almost pointed chin, her auburn hair brushing the matching freckles on her cheek as she walked. A warning light flashed in his brain; he looked away. This summer afternoon walk with a beautiful, hurting woman had lulled him into la-la land.

He was a man of the world, committed to none.

So what if Emma was off the charts and he wanted to be with her? There was a reason he kept moving from place to place, and no town was friendly enough, no woman smart and attractive enough to change that. He'd kept it hidden, and if Emma found out, she wouldn't want him.

Emma waved at a lady getting out of her car.

As they turned onto the short walkway up to Naomi's house, he returned to the topic of her grandmother. "Maybe Mrs. Chambers can't see that change is necessary."

"Can't or won't?" She opened the door. "Brace yourself."

He stood aside. But Trouble pushed past Emma and went right up to Sparks, who tickled his ears.

"Chet says she's changing," she said, moving through the house.

"How so?" Fanning his shirt collar to get some relief from their journey and the power surge from Emma's nearness, he followed the light lavender scent of her hair as it goaded him forward.

She shook her head, opened the fridge and stared into its depths. "You'd have to ask Chet. It's too much to ponder on a hot night. It's been fifteen minutes. You must be hungry. Want iced tea? I don't have any soda." Pushing a package of the cinnamon bread, the butter dish and a plate and knife toward him, she sat down at the table. For once, the appeal of yet another snack faltered in competition with the delightful face across from him.

If he did try to kiss her, he rationalized dangerously, he'd have to make sure she wouldn't mistake it for the start of something more than a summer fling. The knight in shining armor within him was having a knock-down, drag-out fight with the caveman.

AFTER MAKING THE phone calls to set up the unprecedented second volunteer meeting, Emma sat across the kitchen table from a silent Sparks, who was staring fixedly at the bread in front of her. Normally hungry every moment, and yet he had made no move to open the bread, extract a slice and butter it.

During the walk here, she'd almost, almost given in to his nearness. Being tucked under the shelter of his arm had gone miles toward comforting her. And yet. And yet. It had solved nothing regarding the Jamboree and only created new problems. She knew he was here for a vacation and would leave. He knew she planned to flee the town as soon as possible. Where was a relationship in the midst of all that leaving?

Far better to channel their emotions into brainpower to deal with the Jamboree. They needed something big. And something that would actually work.

Trouble roused himself from the floor; a second later, the doorbell rang. He headed for the door with Emma behind him, checking her watch. 8:00 p.m. Through the glass, she could see Chet. He gestured at the door.

"Hey, E, you gonna let me in?"

Between him and Sparks, she had no lack of male attention today. She would admit it, if only to herself, that she'd slipped into a daydream of her and Sparks walking up to their own house, complete with white picket fence. *What part of* man moratorium *don't you understand, Lady Emma?*

She mustered a smile and opened the screen door. If Chet was courting her attention to have her call or go see her grandmother, he was wasting his time.

"Bad news," Chet said simply. "Fireworks put on hold due to drought."

"Oh," Emma replied.

Trouble led them back to the kitchen, where Sparks was now consuming a slice of bread. He looked…somehow *right* at the kitchen table. Sparks rose and shook Chet's hand. The older man pulled out a kitchen chair and sat, reaching toward the bag of bread, and repeated his bad news. No one seemed inclined to discuss it. You could only take so much bad news and react.

"Eating again," Chet commented to Sparks, but then he, too, claimed a slice for himself and buttered it. For a few minutes, they sat in silence with their snack and iced tea. Chet leaned back in the chair, chuckling as he slipped the dog a piece of crust. "Trouble knows a sucker when he sees one."

"Like my grandmother." The words slipped out.

Assessing her with a gentle, searching gaze, Chet said slowly, "You get wound any tighter, your shoulders are going to be permanently glued to your ears. Your grandmother is not the enemy, E."

She avoided his eyes, repressing the sigh because it sounded pathetic and was happening much too often.

Joining Chet and Sparks at the table, she took a couple of big swallows and stared at her glass. With the meeting tomorrow, the three of them better come up with some out-of-this-world great ideas tonight. Her shoulders were crushing her. Maybe Sparks would read her mind and massage them. As she listened to Sparks and Chet talk about the upcoming drills for the volunteer fire department, she rebuked herself.

Quit looking for someone to solve your problems.

Instead of hoping people would read her mind, what if she *told* people—*steady, Emma*—what she wanted...or needed? Hoping hadn't worked: hoping to find love, hoping her grandmother would act differently, treat her as an equal. She opened her lips to ask Sparks to rub her neck.

Sparks heaved out of his chair. Emma watched his familiar movements and caught herself wondering what it would be like to have him around all the time. If she'd met him in England—or anyplace but here—maybe they could have had something. *Hey*, she corrected herself. *No aberrations.* Here there were too many people spectating. Remembering her screwups. Cramping who she was, or what she thought she could be.

As he once more cataloged the fridge's contents, she spoke. "You're still hungry? No more cinnamon bread, as unbelievable as that sounds. Also no sandwich meat, just peanut butter and jelly. I haven't been to the supermarket."

He nodded and pulled out a loaf of wheat bread and the fixings for a PB and J. Sparks's appetite for food was as big as his appetite for sport, adventure and—women. In a sense, she kind of liked that attitude, admired it even, but it did make her hesitate about being with him.

"It's just your grandmother is so concerned about Heaven and its future, she can't see past the trouble," Chet said. At the sound of his name, the dog opened his eyes. "Your grandmother is the heart and soul of Heaven." Chet nudged the dog with his foot, then looked directly at Emma. "She's slowly realizing she's missed opportunities to make different choices. That's new for someone like her."

Spoken like a man in love. Nobody but Chet would refer to her grandmother in such a warm and fuzzy manner. She patted the kitchen table. "Focus, gentlemen. We've got to go into that meeting tomorrow and get the ideas flowing."

"By the way, Beryl signed up to work with me on the first-aid booth," Chet said.

In midchew on her second slice of bread with peanut butter, Emma choked. Sparks leaped up and pounded her on the back. She sipped some tea; he remained, rubbing her shoulders. *Aah*. Maybe they had a connection after all. Maybe she didn't have to always ask if someone was looking out for her. Despite the admonishment against mental flights of fancy, she let herself imagine that she and Sparks had some special telepathy. "For a moment I thought you said Beryl volunteered to help with your booth."

"That's what I heard," said Sparks, looking from her to Chet, his hands tender on her neck. With a final squeeze and a nearly visible swoon from Emma, Sparks returned to his chair, scratching the front of his shirt. "Beryl's a nice enough lady." A yawn escaped him. "Sorry."

Staring at him as if he'd spoken in a foreign language, Emma made a clearing noise in her throat. "Uh-huh, and how well do you know Beryl?"

He shrugged, eyelids heavy with another jaw-cracking yawn. "I've helped her out in her yard a few times. She was nice. Brought me out lunch."

"That's all it would take for you," Emma teased him. "But not nice enough to invite you in?"

"She said she was embarrassed her house was a mess."

Emma spoke to Chet. "Why *is* she so mean? I asked you days ago, but we got distracted."

Heaving a deep sigh, Chet frowned. "Why don't you ask your grandmother?"

Still trying to get her to contact her grandmother. Nice try. No way.

Rising to his feet stiffly, Chet yawned, too. "Volunteer fire training tomorrow at five. Good thing we decided to have it early, so we can all make this new meeting." He glanced at Sparks. "We'll run through some first-aid drills for heat exhaustion, grease fires, the like, for the Jamboree." Sparks nodded. Chet waved to them and left the kitchen, the screen door squeaking signaled his exit.

Turning to Sparks, Emma groaned. "One rat deserts the ship. So now back to our problem, please. What do we tell them at the meeting tomorrow?"

Sparks stood and was shaking his head. "Emma, everybody understands the situation." He stretched. "And whether they admit it or not, they'll have to step up with some really great ideas of their own."

He had tremendous shoulders, sculpted almost. *Focus, focus, focus.* "Like you've come up with great ideas?"

He flushed. "I'm beat. Too much sun today." He stopped in the doorway. "Sorry about emptying your fridge. I'll bring some stuff over tomorrow."

Here it was already the third day of June, and they were only now trying to redefine the Jamboree with no guarantee of success. And tomorrow morning, at the way-too-early hour of 6:00 a.m. in order to accommodate folks before they had to open for business—and that was, if anyone even bothered to show up—she

had to re-expose her failure at all of this. Not
to mention her support team had just bailed.

A few acid words bounced to her tongue,
but the sight of Sparks standing in the doorway melted them quickly away. He looked
as though he belonged there. The warring in
her brain kicked in again. He made her laugh,
made her angry. She'd miss him after all this
was over. She couldn't wait to get away. She
didn't want to be the Jamboree chief and get
on his case again, but...

"Good night, Sparks," she said instead. On
impulse, she darted up from her chair and
kissed him, her lips missing his mouth and
landing on his cheek. Had he moved? "You
can raid my fridge anytime." This was only a
momentary abeyance of the man moratorium,
she told herself, not a serious breach.

His eyes darkened so rapidly, she took a
step back. He removed his hands from the
doorjamb and put them on her shoulders. The
room grew warmer and Emma swallowed past
a lump in her throat.

He looked deep into her eyes, almost into
her mind where she was screaming, *Kiss
me, kiss me.* All those romance novels about
drowning in someone's eyes had some basis
in fact. Heaven Lake could not compete with

the depth of his blue irises against his tanned face, now bending toward her.

A half step brought him so close that Emma's heart rate zipped up, past any aerobics class she'd ever taken. Summer beamed brighter. Brad's nearness had never rendered her knees so weak. Closing her eyes, she lifted her face.

CHAPTER FIFTEEN

"THE FOREHEAD, ZOO. The *forehead*. Mr. Summer Guy kissed me on the forehead, as if I was his maiden aunt or something. If I hadn't sworn off men, I'd be...*really mad*." Emma sipped the sugar-free caramel brevé Zoo had thrust in her hand as they met on Main Street, heading toward the meeting. They were the only ones on the street at this early hour on Wednesday, although the Dew Drop had a couple of trucks parked out front.

Emma sipped, then yelped as the latte burned the roof of her mouth. "Ow." Touching her tongue to the burned spot, she glared after Zoo. "Slow down. You know my legs aren't as long as yours."

Zoo laughed and waited for her to catch up. "I thought you needed a latte and someone to vent to before the meeting." This morning Zoo was wearing zipped off tan cargo pants and a fitted T-shirt from Colorado State, her alma mater. She looked fabulous, hair pulled back in a still-wet French braid.

Emma glanced down at her wrinkled shorts and gray top. One Birkenstock was still damp from the dog's water she'd spilled on it. Her own frizzed-out hair… Well, she wouldn't go there.

"I need no such thing." The problem with a lifelong friend was that they knew when you were lying.

So what if Sparks had kissed her on the forehead? It wasn't as if they had anything in the works. She was out of here as soon as the event closed, and sooner if she could convince him to play Lord of the Jamboree. If he wanted to, he could leave right after the fireworks.

So why her big emotional meltdown over a less-than-romantic romantic moment, which headed a long list of similar moments titled How to Drive Away a Man?

She decided it was too early in the day to analyze her love life, especially the drama of it, and of course, a latte provided some reasonable comfort.

She tried again, this time more gingerly. "We're facing the town in—" she checked her watch "—twenty minutes to tell them I can't solve their problem. They'll immediately think that Naomi could and would have. Once again, I fall short."

Zoo nodded. "No pun intended, I'm sure."

"So what do I do?" Emma ignored the comment about her height. "Try to fake my way through coordinating the Jamboree and leave town when it flops? I hate pressure."

And then, as she and Zoo walked into the community center, the answer fluttered through Emma's mind, simply, as though it had been there all along. Far fewer people were in attendance than they had at the first meeting. Everyone looked as bleary as she felt. As well as early, it was an unheard-of second meeting. Incredibly, Feral Beryl was there, swathed in a ubiquitous caftan, standing in the middle of the group, talking to Alice from the Dew Drop. She caught Emma's eye and lifted her lips—a smile, Emma supposed. When Sparks sauntered in the door a few minutes after six, the older woman's eyes lit up and she moved over to stand next to him. That man could charm the coat off an Eskimo. Now Emma was sounding like Mother Egan.

Emma cleared her throat and began by stating neither the Black Binder nor her grandmother could fix things *especially this year*.

"Naomi's not going to like this." Willard's bald head wagged back and forth.

Duff, hands shoved deep in his jeans' pockets, elbowed the big man. Tilly and Bull

Bardwell, who were standing next to Duff, exchanged glances.

"Don't you understand? We can't run it the same way my grandmother has." Emma's terse response surprised her, then settled comfortably around her ears. "There has to be more."

All eyes fixed on her. Sparks, by the doughnut table, gave her a thumbs-up. "I can't fix this."

Sparks, now parked between Lynette and a high school girl, gaped, a glazed doughnut caught halfway to his mouth. *And help, Mr. Kiss on the Forehead, is what I wanted last night.* Right after the kiss, naturally. Out of the corner of her eye, she saw Chet jerk his head away from examining his hikers and up at her. The Cunningham sisters leaned their heads together, whispering furiously.

She yearned to blame them for wanting someone else to do the saving for them, but couldn't. Wasn't that what she'd wanted from Brad, from all the other relationships? Make her decisions, tell her what to do, who to be? She had to be Emma, and Emma didn't know what to do.

"Naomi did what she could," Sparks interjected from the food table.

About time the *co-planner* contributed something. *Sheesh.*

"She contracted Rockin' Sounds and my fireworks. She knew she needed to make changes—just not how much." He swigged Coke from a glass bottle—only available at Engel's Mercantile, and a favorite tourist souvenir.

She spoke quickly on the tail end of his words. "I can't fix it. I'm withdrawing as your designated savior."

She hadn't really said that, had she?

SPARKS DROPPED THE maple bar to the plate and set it on the table. What he'd heard could not be what she'd said. But as a cacophony descended, he knew it had been.

A few quick strides brought him to the outside of the circle engulfing Emma. Folks were barraging her with questions and comments.

"What are you talking about?"

"It's not like the softball team you quit in sixth grade, Emma. This is important."

"Emma, I support you. It can't be up to one person. It's ludicrous."

"I knew Naomi made a mistake. You weren't ready for the responsibility."

As one, they all turned on him.

"Hey, Sparks, you're the man now," another voice spoke. In his bewilderment, Sparks couldn't identify anyone's voice, although he knew them all. "What are you going to do?"

A crushing weight pressed on Sparks's chest as the auditorium darkened. His breathing grew ragged. He forced himself to blow out a deep breath.

"Sparks, you okay, man?" A clearer voice, although still one he couldn't identify. Some stranger's. But weren't they all strangers? Besides a contract—which he wasn't sure he was going to get paid for, what obligation did he have to this town? This was supposed to be a vacation, time for him to get his head together, not lose it completely.

Pushing through the throng, he slid his hand under Emma's elbow and maneuvered her out of the crowd, Chet closing in behind them and raising his hand for some silence, which everyone ignored. For a quiet girl, Emma had created quite a stir.

They moved out to the front steps. He still had Emma's elbow, but he was too upset to really enjoy it. What was she thinking? Her hazel eyes were calm and observing.

"What's going on?" he asked. A look at her expression told him little. She had her withdrawn mask on. "Why are you quitting?"

"I didn't say I was quitting," she snapped. "I said, 'withdrawing as savior.' There's a difference." Her arms hugged her chest, and he mimicked the move.

"What difference, a few words? You didn't say anything to me. I should have known before the rest of the town."

Her lips thinned and she took a step away. "Now you know how I feel. I did try. I tried to tell you and Chet last night. You both had better things to do than listen to me."

Last night he'd been sunburned and tired. His world had been rattled with the forehead kiss and when it had hit him that Emma could never be a summer girl. He'd realized with a hurricane force that if he kissed her on the lips—and yet kept his secret a secret—he wouldn't be able to look at himself in the mirror.

Today, he'd meant to get to the meeting early and tell her his revelation, help her with ideas, but the Cunningham sisters, who'd needed assistance getting to the church, had delayed him. "You can't back out now, Emma. What about the Jamboree?" Panic was rising, it wasn't something he was used to or familiar with. Staging shows that dazzled thousands, production problems that paralyzed technicians, none of those evoked a similar horror to the one currently liquefying his bones.

"You mean, what will happen to you since

it's all on you now?" Her eyes stayed on him. "I don't know, Sparks."

Another new expression on her face; this one he knew. Determination. No backing down.

"Don't quit," he begged shamelessly. "I'll help you. I know I've been a little light in that area lately." He was good at broad strokes; details had never been his strong suit.

"A little?" she scoffed.

So she'd noticed. He flushed. "Okay. But you can't expect me to carry the entire thing. I'm only here for the summer. On vacation."

"Now, there's total capitulation."

"Total what?" He was in the dark when she started using big words.

"Never mind." She squared her shoulders and looked over his, toward the building. "I need to go back in there."

Sparks's brain squirmed. "Uh, humor me a minute. You only just told the town you were quitting. Now you're saying you're going back in. I don't get it. What about me?"

No sparkles in those hazel eyes, strictly chips of gold ice. "It isn't really about you, Sparks, but let me explain."

He felt like a kid when he'd ignored one too many chores. Again.

"I am not bailing on the Jamboree. But I am withdrawing as the designated savior of

Heaven. My grandmother has operated as that for years. It's not me. It's not her, either. She just hasn't seen that yet." As she pushed past him, he fell into step with her. "Is that clear?"

Sure. Clear as the mud at the bottom of the lake. The only blazing clarity he knew was the relief he felt that he wasn't in charge alone, and this time he wasn't going to slack on Emma.

CHAPTER SIXTEEN

"AFTER EMMA'S ANNOUNCEMENT yesterday and the reaction subsided, the food vendors huddled and then said they'd donate a larger portion of the profit from their booths to the Jamboree, instead of like other years. Then the food merchants in town stepped up and agreed to donate supplies to help the food vendors. Very cool." Sparks beat a tattoo on the table with his fingertips, while Tilly's big, beefy husband, Bull, examined the Dew Drop's menu. The two men had met outside on the street a little past noon, Bull's green county truck angle parked in front.

Bull grunted, not taking his eyes off the menu. "Better to suck up some profit than lose their entire livelihood with the town flooded."

Sparks nodded, switching tunes with his drumming. He couldn't get Trinity out of his mind. Emma would be dazzled by the addition of the superstar. He kept tapping.

Caught between a promise and a future, he was. Years ago Trinity had sworn him to secrecy and then confided her plan to ditch the success, the lifestyle, all of it to find some peace and anonymity. A couple of weeks later, the world had woken up and she was "gone."

Sparks was as much in the dark as everyone else about where she went. Then, soon after he'd arrived in Heaven, he'd discovered where she'd gone. But her tremulous smile upon his recognizing her had told him the secret between them was still in force.

He would have to think of something else to help Emma.

Bull closed the menu. "Dunno why I even read it. I always get the same thing. Tilly says I should live dangerously and order something else once in a while."

Sparks looked out the plate-glass window from their booth. A truck and fifth-wheel trailer rolled past, young faces hanging out of the back cab window. He watched the truck as far as he could, leaning over to keep it in sight a little longer. A family making memories.

Jerking his mind back to the issue, he pondered. Bigger fireworks? Nope. More money outlay. When the server approached their table, he glanced up, seeing yet another of Emma's former students.

"You going to order dessert first again?" she asked, no smile cracking her solemn expression.

So much for him being the mysterious random stranger who came, blew things up and left. He nodded, sheepish, and confirmed that, yes, he was getting strawberry-rhubarb pie à la mode and then would eat… He decided to try the patty melt and fries.

Bull ordered and stretched his long arms along the back of the booth. "They got you pegged, don't they?"

"Scary. Next thing you know, I'll be here watching the grass grow on my lawn from the front porch." Once, that type of life would have loomed as the pinnacle of boredom. Now, with the tugging at his heart, he wasn't so sure. Not that it mattered, however. The conclusion of the Jamboree and his next assignment would take care of that.

His hands stilled at last. Before he moved on and even if they had no future together, he wanted Emma to know he wasn't a screwup and could pull his weight.

Bull reached down and took a long gulp of his water. "Not a bad thing to sit on the porch and watch your lawn. Get yourself a wife like Tilly to sit with ya." His eyes moistened.

If only. In the short time he'd been here, Sparks had learned Bull cried whenever he talked about his wife. She was his sun, his moon, his favorite of favorites. The bump in

Sparks's gut rubbed again. He hoped food was showing up soon.

Since he'd come to Heaven, he'd had more of those what-ifs than he liked. He'd locked the door long ago on having any family, any sense of belonging, but too many people in Heaven seemed to have the master key to it.

A short time later, the young woman delivered their plates and the men dug in.

Maybe it would be good to have someone all the time in one place, instead of temporary someones around the world. "I'm hoping the fireworks get reinstated or I've got no show," Sparks said, lassoing his thoughts with effort.

Bull's red eyebrows pulled together as he chewed. "It's not the first year we've wanted to make changes. Tilly and I've been saying that for years. Getting Naomi Chambers to change her mind is like getting a chicken to swim."

A companionable silence ensued as the men ate. *Call Trinity.* No. He'd be like everyone else who wanted something from her. Sparks pushed the thought away and swallowed more Coke. Not when each time he saw her out at the OD, her eyes begged him to keep her secret. Despite the Jamboree beginning in three weeks, he couldn't bring himself to blow her cover. So lost in thought was he that he forgot he was sharing lunch with Bull until the man interrupted his train of thought.

"Tilly's ex!" Bull's fork clattered to his half-eaten plate. "That no-good—" He stopped himself, narrowed his eyes and looked at Sparks, who regarded him with upraised eyebrows.

"Tilly's ex owns a midway." His face hardened. "I've never met him, but I have a few things I'd like to say to him." Flexing a ham-like fist, he nodded at Sparks. "Or maybe let the Fives do the talking."

What would it be like, to have someone so completely on his side they'd leap into a fray for him. If things had gone differently, he could try to be that for Emma, but things hadn't gone differently. He would be leaving soon.

Excitement began to build for the idea of a midway. "Time is running out," he ventured.

With his jaw still clenched, Bull looked out the window into the bright sunlight, his Adam's apple bobbing. When he turned back to Sparks, he took a deep breath and let it out slow. "His midway is good. Geared for small to medium towns."

"Why would he do Tilly any favors?" Sparks had worked with a few carnies on his way up in the fireworks business. Some were so slimy you couldn't breathe around them without catching something, but others treated each other like family. He hoped Tilly's ex was like the latter.

Bull shoved a forkful of food into his mouth, chewing furiously and talking at the same time. Sparks heard only muffled explanations of back child support, court rulings and the ex disappearing, but Juggy being able to find him.

Their server zoomed by, tray in one hand, and picked up his plate. Sparks waited. Belching softly into his hand, Bull leaned back and wiped his mouth with a napkin. "I'll talk to my Tilly. Ever since she came here, Heaven's helped her get her feet under her, even when she was—well, kinda rough around the edges." He glared at Sparks as if he would dispute him.

Sparks nodded. After he and Bull paid for their lunch and went their separate ways, the question of his possible, amazing contribution nagged. *Could he ask Trinity?*

AFTER NODDING TO the misses Cunningham and saying once again that no, she was sorry, but she didn't know where Sparks was at that very minute, Emma crossed the street and pushed open the door to the IGA. The two old dears had been the third pair of people who thought that she and Sparks were now attached.

She took in a breath and embraced the cool air. Since Vince used a swamp cooler, it was more humid inside, but still a lower temperature than out on the blistering street. A later-in-the-day leap in the lake sounded appealing. Trouble would love it. Maybe Sparks would be at the marina and come over. Since she'd decided that the man moratorium didn't mean she had to be nasty to Sparks, things had fallen into a comfortable groove. Well, she amended to herself as she headed to the back meat counter, as normal as could be with every crooked smile of his sending her off on a romantic daydream. She needed to work on that, and desperately hoped he couldn't tell. Right now she needed to act on an idea that had awakened her from sleep and solidified through Trouble's morning rounds of the town.

Making her way to the back of the store, she saw Vince feeding a slab of bacon through a slicer. "Hey, Vince. Got an idea for the Jamboree. What's your top-selling item here at the store?"

He looked up. "Hi, Emma. Where's Sparks?" He wiped his hands on his apron and leaned on the top of the counter. "No contest. Our barbecue ribs."

Emma ignored the question. "You willing to put your meat and sauce against all comers?"

Vince threw back his head and laughed.

Fifteen minutes later, Vince was on board as

coordinator for the First Annual BBQ Contest at the Jamboree.

"You got yourself a grand idea there, Emma," Vince said as they parted. "I know guys who would drive two days straight to win bragging rights over me in barbecue." He leaned a little farther over the counter. "Not that it's gonna happen."

As she zipped home, a quiver of excitement ran through her, momentarily cooling her down. Wait until Sparks heard this. He'd love it, since it involved food. She was sure he would insist on being a judge. Now, who had the contacts to get the word out big? Lifting up her hair to take advantage of the lake breeze, she laughed. She felt free and in the moment. It would drive her grandmother crazy and Emma was sure the news of it would skitter along the gossip line to Garden Terrace faster than the speed of light. Her steps quickened; where *was* Sparks?

As she approached Angel Way and Main, the unmistakably familiar sounds of Juggy's ancient car assaulted her ears. A blast of possibility hit her hard and fast. She stepped into the street to flag him down. Who had the only satellite internet connection in town? Juggy. Who spent time surfing the net? Juggy. Who never seemed to sleep and chatted online all night? Emma smiled.

He pulled over. She made her deal: advertising the Jamboree and the barbecue cook-off on the internet in exchange for Juggy getting the car parking assignment he'd always wanted. He appealed again for the Elvis look-alikes; she turned him down again. He finally agreed. Excitement propelling her, she broke into a trot. She'd call Sparks.

As she neared her grandmother's house, there he was, sitting on the steps of the bungalow, elbows propped on his knees, chin on his hands, surveying the street. The moment he saw her, he leaped up and jogged toward her, smile wide. They met, their eyes shining. Emma thought how right and natural it was for him to be there, sitting on that porch. Waiting for her? Here in Heaven? After she spilled out the terms of her deal with Vince and Juggy, he chuckled. "Tell Juggy maybe next year. He'll love it."

Emma simply stared at him. Next year he would be where? Next year she was going to be so far from Heaven, she'd have to buy a GPS to remember where it was. If it still existed. A shadow passed over her heart, even as the notion of spending next year with Sparks warmed her.

After Emma opened the door and Trouble shot out to properly greet his buddy Sparks, she and Sparks sat together on the top step of the porch. "With Juggy taking over the parking from Ed Groves, he can do what he wanted to do. What did he want to do?" Emma asked Sparks. She grinned and lightly tapped him on the head with a finger. "Stand still and let me wave over you with my magic wand. I am the granter of Jamboree dreams."

"Wood." Sparks smiled back at her, leaned into her for a second. All rational thought floated away. This time the dream involved a Hobie Cat on the lake and kissing. "He does something with wood."

"How are your ideas coming to ward off the flood over Heaven?" she asked, leaning forward to catch her breath. He *was* the most beautiful man she'd ever seen. Even a man moratorium couldn't eliminate that.

When Sparks didn't answer, she straightened and glanced over. His face was flaming.

Narrowing her eyes, she tipped up her chin, remembering her grandmother's lack of forthrightness. "I know what that flush means. You have a secret."

His tanned face instantly reddened. His grin was weak. "How can you know me so well?"

Then he leaped to his feet. "Gotta run. I need to hit the OD."

Did his urgency to get to the Organic District have to do with fruits and vegetables? Or was it a pretty bread baker who held the appeal?

The phone jangled inside. Sparks waved and dashed off. Emma frowned after him. Something was up and she didn't like it. As she opened the front screen door, she bent to pick up the colored envelopes of mail spilling from the drop in the door that the dog had trampled in his dash for freedom. Trouble darted in for a quick lick that landed on her mouth.

"Ew." *Dog kisses*. "Knock it off." On the heels of that thought came the forehead kiss. Fortunately, the very pleasant sidewalk embrace and Sparks's arm finding its way around her shoulders more frequently replaced that frustrating memory.

Then his comment about her knowing him. He had seemed surprised and—could it be—a little delighted? Emma had never met anyone like Sparks, who attracted her so strongly, plus she flat-out liked the guy. Neither of them were looking for long-term. Perhaps just for the summer? Could she rethink this man moratorium, or maybe ease off it for a while? It was only for a couple of months after all.

The mention of the OD niggled in her brain. Every time she got close to taking another chance, something always came up. Like in this case a petite bread baker in baggy clothes.

The phone jangled, and Emma caught it on the fourth ring. Sorting Nomi's medical statements into one pile and the rest of the envelopes into another, she said, "Hello," and placed the bundles on the mantel. Chet would pick them up and take them to her grandmother.

"Hey, Emma, I hear I'm out of a job with parking this year." It was Ed Groves.

She flopped down in Grumpa's old recliner, Nomi's present to him when he'd retired from the bank. The worn leather slid cool under her hot skin.

"Yes..." The glow of stair time with Sparks dissolved under the ever-present pressure of the Jamboree. "Are you okay with that?" she asked.

The cackle of laughter on the other end of the line reassured her. Her shoulders returned to their normal relaxed position. "I hated doing parking, but you know your grandmother, once you've done it and didn't screw up, the job's yours for life."

Emma knew that tune, had sung it until she was hoarse. He related that he liked to carve animal creatures out of wood and he would donate all his proceeds to the town. Though nothing spectacular, it was still generous of him to do so.

"How many souvenirs and such have you made?" she asked.

"About two dozen. Sorry it's not more. I've sold quite a few already."

Emma's heart sank. Two dozen little wooden statues that sold for what, five to seven dollars? Maybe, ten—tops. She smothered her disappointment and picked up the Black Binder lying on the floor. She added him under the tab for booths, then flipped to Schedule to pencil in when his carving demonstrations would be, how long and how often. She thanked him and he thanked her, delight evident in his voice.

After she disconnected, the thought ran through her head. If she was as ruthless as her grandmother, she would have told Ed it wasn't good enough to donate little wooden tchotchkes. Why hadn't she? That answer was a no-brainer. She knew it hurt to be told your ideas weren't good enough.

CHAPTER SEVENTEEN

IT COULDN'T BE.

A deep tremble wound its way through Naomi as a grimy white envelope fell from her hands. Chet, who faithfully delivered the mail, had brought the envelope yesterday. She'd not noticed it amongst the other ones. Today, it jumped out at her. She hadn't seen the handwriting in over two decades. It was Friday, June 20, and the opening day of the Jamboree was rushing closer. Meanwhile, her granddaughter still hadn't come.

She'd heard about Emma's decisions, like giving Juggy the parking concession, allowing Ed Groves to give up something he was good at for some hobby he tinkered with. Naomi shook her head. Fingering the envelope, malignant if-onlys swarmed at her. If only…she'd told Emma first about Sparks co-planning with her…told her about the lack of funds, the flooding. Naomi was angry with herself. Her own ways had sunk her ship. Her good hand fell to her lap and at the feel of the envelope, wetness appeared in the corners of Naomi's eyes. Now it was nearly too late.

A dry sob caught in an even drier throat. Reaching for the water cup and straw with her good hand, she gulped at the liquid. Once Emma knew about this letter, the past would tear away the last vestige of family from Naomi.

Family. The word tasted bitter in her mouth. She sucked at the water. She hadn't done well at family. At everything else...well, people said Naomi Chambers faced every challenge head-on. People said she was bullheaded but got results. People said she never quit. Each accolade accused her, slapped her and stripped her of all excuse. What would people say when the past was known all over town?

A sound at the door made her open her eyes and turn her head. Chet stood in the doorway, solid, comforting. To get here this early, he must have risen at dawn, dashed into the shower. Damp strands of hair slicked across his forehead, and he was wearing a different golf shirt but the same Bermuda shorts from yesterday.

"Beautiful day out, Naomi." His voice was soft, his eyebrows asking a question.

As she shifted toward him, pain surged out in a pathetic voice that couldn't be hers. "Oh,

Chet." Without the strength to say more, her right arm slipped onto her lap, the envelope rustling its evil.

He strode to her side, knelt and clasped her left hand in both of his. "I'm here, Naomi. I'm here."

Her eyes watered when they dared rise to meet his. Naomi choked back the emotion.

"Oh, Chet, oh, Chet…" She kept repeating his name, looking down at the envelope.

Chet glanced at the handwriting and the tension grew. He knew. He and Raymond…and one other.

Regardless of the outcome, she must get to Emma.

CHAPTER EIGHTEEN

SATURDAY, SPARKS WOKE up later than his usual time. He showered. He shaved. He dressed.

After a late-morning cardiac-arrest breakfast at the Dew Drop, he still had zip for a killer idea, but still, he felt bad for chickening out on a trip to the OD yesterday. In contrast, Emma had been glowing yesterday, generating idea after idea, coming into her own, stepping out of Naomi's shadow.

After Juggy's blast of the internet, the rush of phone calls on the BBQ contest indicated that Emma's notion would fly. Bull and Tilly—with Juggy's help—had pulled off getting them the midway. But what about the live musical act? Rockin' Sounds was good, he had to admit, but he could think of another act that would be even more popular for the Jamboree. A performance by former superstar Trinity would be huge and guarantee big numbers.

He speculated whether Trinity would insist, though, on him keeping his promise to her regarding her anonymity if her performance could contribute to the town's coffers and save everyone's homes and businesses. He headed toward the marina after a firm shake of the head. He couldn't ask her. It just wouldn't be right.

So deep was he in arguing with himself about what to do about Trinity that the shriek of the fire whistle made him jump. Every nerve responded. Old instincts thrilled in a way he couldn't discount yet. Then a stronger, sinister feeling slithered through his stomach, coiling up around his backbone. Things were different...now.

Seconds after the fire whistle blew, Chet burst out of the IGA with three men behind him. He headed for his red-and-white Ford pickup, saw Sparks and waved him on. "C'mon, son, we can use you!"

Before he could remind his body what his head had decided five years ago, he sped forward and hopped into the back of Chet's vehicle. He looked over at Pitch, who was muttering under his breath.

"Where's it at?" Sparks shouted.

Pitch ignored him, as did Pitch's brother, Oliver, who was scrunched next to Pitch, his glasses sliding down his nose.

"The OD—that bread woman, Jennifer," Vince volunteered, vaulting over the side of the truck, still wearing his butcher's apron. The solid guy flattened Juggy, who grunted.

Before they were all settled, Chet punched the accelerator while Sparks's stomach clenched. Her smile at Sparks on one occasion had elicited a searching glance from Emma. Did Emma think he and Jennifer had a connection? Well, they did, but not the one that she thought.

Father Jack's New Yorker, with Pastor Ned on the passenger side, peeled out of Cherubim behind them as they sped past the Feed-N-Seed, Juggy's father following behind them, coming from the Dairy Delite. From the volunteer fire department get-togethers and a couple of training sessions, Sparks was confident these men knew what they were doing…with the exception of Juggy, whose expression goggled between what looked like fear and determination. It being the guy's first year in the VFD, Sparks hoped the kid remembered his training.

He tried not to think of another rookie with a similar expression, but did anyway as Chet curved the county road, never touching the brakes as they hurtled past the various homes and ranches between town and the OD. The tinder-dry fields and grazing land increased Sparks's uneasiness both regarding this fire and the possibility of the fireworks not being reinstated. With a gray sky, no rain, yet parched ground, the whole area was a tinderbox waiting to go up in flames.

Another quick sideways glance at Juggy, and Sparks reflected on how he had seen too many rookies caught by surprise. The corresponding clutch in his gut reminded him that it wasn't just rookies; sometimes experienced smoke jumpers made deadly mistakes, as well.

Long before Chet spurted off the two-way and onto the gravel drive, billowing smoke signaled the site, flicks of orange-yellow leaping within it. The town's tanker and the four men within it, having arrived only prior, fought the flames on the east side, while two other men had commandeered the pump hose from the side of a larger building nearby. Assessing the situation out of old habit, while he donned the protective gear Chet thrust at him, Sparks noted the vulnerable wood-frame house burning like a torch. The heat reached out toward the men as they raced to take up their positions. Regrettable outcome: total loss.

Despite it being the smell of burning lumber, and old lumber at that, rather than a forest on fire, his pace slowed. *You know what to do.*

A volunteer dragged another hose to the well pump nearby. From the corner of his eye, Sparks saw a lone figure, arms wrapped around herself and a cat, watching. Worlds re-moved from the first time he'd laid eyes on her.

"The roof! Sparks, anchor the end!"

Jerking his head toward the sound of Chet's voice across the wide yard, Sparks saw Juggy near the older man, struggling to keep his balance with the hose pressure. He sprinted over, stepped next to Juggy and gripped the hose, a certain previous fire leaping unwanted to center stage in his mind.

It didn't take long for a yell to go up when the right forward portion of the roof sank simultaneously with a sudden shift of the flame—blasting back toward the firefighters. Awful memories of flames with the same sucker-turn, as it was called, blasted back just as fast. Sparks gagged, dropping the hose and hitting his knees. He saw Juggy stagger, then Juggy's panicked look over his shoulder to Sparks. *Get up, get up.* He'd been a fool to think he could overcome this, little town or not, yet the conflagration in his mind would not clear sufficiently for him to corral his limbs.

Fifteen minutes later, the women's auxiliary—headed by Tilly—had arrived, taken Jennifer and the cat into Bonnie and Ed Groveses' RV, and Chet had called the building under control and a total loss.

Sparks made tracks for the far side of Chet's

truck. Finally, when he'd gotten hold of himself and could finally think straight, he wiped his mouth, walked over to the RV and stepped inside. Jennifer and Tilly looked up. Although Jennifer had stopped crying, her puffy face was red. He expressed his sympathies for the house. She shrugged.

"It's a house." Jennifer stroked the tiger cat on her lap. Even from where he stood, Sparks could hear it purring. "I got Rewind out. That's all that matters."

Rewind had been Trinity's first pop chart topper. Standing there, the former superstar looked nothing like her extravagant stage persona. With her hair its natural color and no startling blue contacts, no one else would make the connection between the megastar and the introverted bread baker. Heaven had no idea they sheltered the biggest pop phenomenon in years. The large eyes in the thin face begged him not to give her away.

Sparks excused himself and went back to where the volunteers were packing up their gear. He helped them, hoping no one other than Juggy had noticed his misstep with dropping the hose. Whether Juggy would mention it was anybody's guess. Sometimes Juggy had a big mouth and sometimes he didn't.

"How's Jennifer?" Chet removed his helmet as he stepped away from the smoking remnants of the bread baker's personal residence, waving at the cars and trucks leaving the scene.

"More concerned about the cat than her house."

"Healthy sign," Chet responded, squinting up at the hazy sky. "That fire will smoke for a while. Wish we'd get a blue-sky day again."

"Yeah. If only those clouds would produce something other than promises." During this laconic conversation, after his check of the sky, Chet had begun eying him, but Sparks wasn't buying into it. The break during the fire had been enough emotional leakage. The past was the past; what good did talking about it do?

Chet clapped him on the shoulder. "What happened to you back there?"

Sparks stopped abruptly and stared at the ground. Never had he told a living soul, and he didn't intend to now. The only question was how to avoid it without being rude to a man who'd been nothing but kind to him. Chet remained silent.

"I was stupid to come—only did it by reflex," Sparks said finally. "Could have hurt the effort today."

Quiet hung between them. Then the older

man shifted from one foot to the other, one hand stroking his jaw. "No harm, no foul."

He and Chet continued toward the truck, climbing in, pulling out onto the road. The rest of the crew had found other rides back home or to the Dew Drop, where the fire would be recounted in detail, Sparks knew. He hoped Juggy would continue to keep quiet.

"You could...tell me about it. I'm not new to secrets. Stuff in your head usually digs a hole and it gets harder to leave it buried there," Chet said, eyes on his driving.

No, Sparks didn't want to talk about it, but before he could consider it any further, he heard his voice choking out the whole story, every stinking part of it.

It began to rain.

CHAPTER NINETEEN

A BOLD RAP on his door shocked Sparks awake. He'd been with a brown-haired beauty with deep hazel eyes in his dreams and his smile lingered. For a moment, he lay there. She looked a lot like Emma, this dream girl. They had kayaked to an island and kissed on a deserted beach.

Another heavy rap on the door.

Monday's bright morning light cracked through the gap in the drapes. Sitting up, he rubbed both hands across his bare chest and yawned, swinging his legs over the side of the bed, stumbling to the door. When he yanked it open, the yawn froze in place.

Tilly's thirtysomething daughter, clad in what had to be a child's T-shirt and a grape skintight pair of Wranglers, lounged against the doorway, a wicker basket dangling from her hand. In one fluid move—that seemed impossible in those jeans—she was in the door and offering the basket. A fruity scent wafted—banana muffins.

"Hi, I'm Little Red Riding Hood," she said. "Wanna be my big bad wolf?" Her eyes, darkly outlined in some shade of purple, roamed back and forth across his bare pecs.

Shirt, where was his shirt? He stumbled backward, and the cuff of his loose, slouchy pajama bottoms caught beneath his foot, prompting a throaty chuckle from Tilly's daughter. Turning in desperation, he grabbed the first article of clothing his fingers found, only to discover they were a pair of boxers.

"Uh, muffins. Thanks," he mumbled while his back was turned and he dug through a suitcase on the other bed. His frantic search finally yielded a shirt, and he yanked it over his head.

Tell Sparks, Emma repeated to herself, taking the corner into the motel's driveway at a dead run. Lynette waved from the office. Telling him wouldn't solve this new catastrophe, but at least Emma wouldn't be alone with the news. She ignored the friendly wave of the room cleaner, who had a family resemblance to someone she probably should know, and sailed through the open door of Sparks's unit before she could think of why it was already open.

The door banged against the wall. Sparks peered past Tilly's daughter and muttered a groan. On the threshold, her eyes took in his half-off shirt and Tilly's daughter. Sparks's blush deepened as a strange expression flitted across his face. Disappointed to see her? Embarrassed? Emma couldn't bear to look at him. Her gaze shifted to Tilly's daughter.

The two women eyed each other. And in that weird way that women seemed to have, Emma must have communicated to Tilly's daughter that an exit was in her best interest.

"We were just talking," Tilly's daughter sputtered. "Not doing anything." She looked regretful.

"I don't care what he does when he's not working at the Jamboree." What had she been thinking, losing her grip on the man moratorium? She was still a fool where men were concerned. Sparks was indeed no different than the others she'd dated.

Sparks pulled down the shirt like he wished it would cover him all the way to his feet. "Emma, it's not what you—"

"I don't care what it's not. I don't care what you do, man of the world, committed to none. You're merely the hired help." Each word ended with her jaw snapping shut. "I care that I just got a phone call—Rockin' Sounds cancelled—and so we have no musical headliner that Heaven has been advertising for six months."

Tilly's daughter paused at the door. "Catch you later, Sparks."

Emma knew the news would speed from her lips to the town's ears, compliments of Tilly's daughter. All of Heaven would know they'd lost their headliner before the fourth order of biscuits and gravy had landed on a table at the Dew Drop, and way before Starla slid open the window at the Dairy Delite.

Sparks sat with a thump on the sagging bed; it groaned.

With Tilly's daughter's truck outside laying rubber, Emma remained at attention near the open door, ready for flight. Her co-planner's face morphed into a deer-in-headlights look. Through folks in town, though, of course, that did not include her grandmother, Emma had learned that local bus-tour companies had committed to include the Jamboree on their itineraries after hearing the top tribute band, Rockin' Sounds, would appear. The booking had been Naomi's doing, convincing the popular group to appear after contacting the agent through the mayoral conference she'd attended.

As the words left her, she heard them, heavy, tired, defeated. "What are we going to do?"

She wanted to…wanted him to take her in his arms and tell her he'd fix it. Man of the world, committed to no one, though.

She knew Tilly's daughter by reputation and had difficulty placing blame at Sparks's door. Had seeing Tilly's daughter with him upset her? Yes. Was she angry? She had no right to be. Maybe she was jealous? That she would not think about.

Things had been looking up, too. She and Sparks were getting along. Yesterday's rain had reinstated the fireworks. The now-steady misting would vindicate Tilly's insistence on a grandstand cover. The problem was no musical act to play under the cover.

"There really is nothing between Tilly's daughter and me. Really." Sparks looked surprised at his words. A thin sheen of sweat appeared on his forehead. Emma's gaze remained locked on his. In a summer of nonstop surprises, that he was more concerned about her knowing that he wasn't having a fling with Tilly's daughter, instead of offering suggestions about the latest Jamboree crisis should have distracted her, but it didn't. She gritted her teeth.

"I'm sure you're holding something back. You must know a celebrity and yet don't want to ask." The words were accusing and she knew it. "Could you just *do* something? We both want to leave after the Jamboree." Suddenly, it hurt to say that. She pressed on. "We've got less than two weeks before the Jamboree starts. That and we need it to net three hundred and seventy-five thousand dollars."

CHAPTER TWENTY

IN THE EARLY afternoon during a sun shower, Sparks, hands shoved in the pockets of his khaki shorts, watched the crane place the second half of the premanufactured log cabin in the Organic District. He had less than a week with Emma.

Sure, from the outset he'd known he was leaving the town, knew her trip had fallen through, as well as her rescheduled plans, but for some reason, her still being here for now comforted him. The next six days marched in front of him. What was he going to do about Emma? For Emma. He was going to ask Jennifer to come out of retirement and sing at the Jamboree. After all, it was her town, too, that she'd be saving.

In another few moments, the house settled on its foundations. He pondered how to start the will-you-sing conversation while he marveled at the speed of Jennifer's "instant" replacement of a house. In the three days since the fire, she'd made arrangements to get a new place to live. She stood beside him, arms wrapped around herself as usual, neither happy nor unhappy. Hard to read, really. How would she react to his request to give up her privacy and sing the town right off the flood list?

Remembering Emma's forlorn demeanor at the motel this morning had prompted him to act. It was hero time. He'd been unreliable for Emma. One day there, the next he was leaving her to handle the Jamboree alone. His seesaw attraction to her and wanting to avoid contact had caused her problems.

Out of the corner of his eye, he watched the former entertainer. She rubbed her throat with long, bony fingers that could coax awesome sounds from a guitar. He wondered if she sang around her place or while she baked. Her voice had been a low, throaty, melodic sound that could soar to soprano sweetness and leave you breathless. In fact, "Breathless" was one of her songs he especially liked. He hoped she missed singing it in front of crowds.

She placed an arm around his waist, her head not even to his shoulder. She would disappear under his arm, whereas Emma fit perfectly.

They strolled toward the bakery, where an air-conditioner compressor worked mightily. "Gotta ask you a question," he managed to say.

"Hmm" was her response.

In her previous life, Trinity had been surrounded with people who wanted something from her. He didn't want to be considered one of them, yet there he stood. He ran his hand through his hair. If the stakes weren't so high… The sooner he spit it out, the better. He was willing to brave a cold, empty look like "how dare you" or worse. He watched her check a couple of commercial-size mixers kneading dough with huge hooks. You could hang a side of beef with those things. Sweet-smelling whole-wheat dough—looked like raisins in it—rolled and twined around the steel hook.

"About that question—" he began.

"Your life make you happy, Sparks?" Jennifer's intense gaze speared him before she shut off one mixer and plopped the dough onto a large marble slab. A sharp knife in hand, she sliced the mound into twelve smaller lumps. Her hands moved swiftly and with assurance.

About to blow off a glib answer, like he did when faced with most personal questions because he didn't want to answer, he parted his lips and blurted, "It does with Emma." *What's up with this?* In the air-conditioned bakery, Sparks shivered. Had he really said that out loud?

Jennifer's small grin dissolved her somber expression. She gestured to a stack of metal bread pans to her left. "Hand me a dozen of those, will you?"

He counted out the pans, handed them to her and leaned against the counter. He wanted to run, hop into his rental car and drive to— he hunched his shoulders—anywhere. With all his talk of man of the world, committed to none, he'd gone and done it. Found *home* with Emma. Except she didn't know about it and was leaving in a few days.

Swiping wax paper through shortening and then rubbing the paper briskly around the inside of each pan, Jennifer worked quickly as she talked. "Three years ago, an interviewer asked me that question." The faster her hands put the dough into the waiting pans, the more words tumbled out. "And I realized I had to get out of the business. Or die. The pressure. The unhappiness. And it never seemed to be enough, no matter how many new songs I wrote, or how much money I made. Reading crystals, hiring my own personal spiritual leader—I tried it all. Sure, I looked deep inside myself." She paused, her hands stilled. "All I found was *me*. And I was a mess. So I came here for a new start as Jennifer, not Trinity. Her, I left behind."

"Well, you had a lot of responsibility. A lot of people counted on you." In an instant, he realized, that Emma was the one who had it made. Emma, despite her growling about her grandmother and everybody knowing her her whole life. Emma *belonged* somewhere.

He swallowed hard and stared up at the ceiling. Jennifer had had to ask the question. His reply had hit him hard. Blast.

Moving over to the deep, double porcelain sink, Jennifer turned on the water and ran her hands under it. Looking back over her shoulder at Sparks, she lifted one eyebrow. "What did you want to ask me?"

EMMA WAS DONE. Tilly's daughter with Sparks. More bad Jamboree news. Should anyone really be surprised?

She didn't want to think anymore. She wanted something to wear her out so she'd fall into an exhausted sleep and not think.

But how? Then she remembered the old shed.

It took only minutes to run to her grandmother's house, drag her old bike from the shed, pump up the tires and wobble her way onto Main Street and toward the OD. There were stands with every known kind of comfort food out there, and she intended to spend big bucks on them and then she'd crawl behind one of the stands and hide. For how long? How about until after the July Fourth weekend?

It had sounded like the perfect escape if she couldn't take a plane to England. What she hadn't recalled was the leg-burning grade of the county road. The continued mist didn't help conditions, either; the humidity was like having a heavy blanket on a hot night. Soon, however, the rhythm of pedaling eventually brought some ease to her emotions, despite the moist warm air radiating from the blacktop.

She could work through these problems if she just kept organized. Okay, problem one: no major musical act. Solution: run off and never return. She kind of liked that one.

She puffed up another short rise. Tilly's daughter's tight rear end that morning reminded her of the pressure on her own waistband. Too many slices of cinnamon toast soaked with butter, eaten with Sparks.

Stay on track, please. Problem two: How susceptible *had* Sparks been to Tilly's daughter's enhanced assets? Was it her first time to the motel? Sparks's expression would have been funny if Emma's heart hadn't wrenched. Was he uncomfortable because Tilly's daughter was there, or because he'd been seen by Emma? Now the neck rub and the friendly arm around her shoulder seemed tainted.

Sweat ran down Emma's back and front, slipped off her nose. The lake breeze did not reach this far with the road curving away from the water for several miles before swinging back toward it. No helmet, no sunglasses to break the glare. She was a poster child for how not to ride a bike. She squinted at the fields around her. How far left to go?

Focusing her wandering imagination, she acknowledged that the solution for problem one was a no-go. She had recently come to realize that just because she didn't want to live in Heaven it didn't mean she didn't care about it. That revelation had smacked her upside the head when she heard about the town's spot on a potential flood list.

Problem two needed more thought. Why had she been so disappointed in Sparks a few hours ago? Did she want, A, Sparks to solve the Rockin' Sounds problem, or, B, take care of her forever? Or C, both A and B. Right about now she'd take a gallon of water over any guy, no matter what size diamond ring he offered.

Somebody help me... She snorted a dusty giggle. She had to get to the OD and water now.

Emma considered getting off the bike and walking the rest of the way. She considered turning around and coasting back to town. She considered that due to some perverse Naomi Chambers's gene of perseverance that had latently, and regrettably surfaced, she could not quit. *Finish what you start, Emma. If it's worth doing, it's worth doing well. Go, go, go!*

Her tired legs spun the wheels until they hummed against the road. She would finish big. She would gulp mass quantities of water. She would eat a sweet roll and one baked good from each stand. She would ride back, triumphant, and then she and Sparks would think of someone brilliant to replace Rockin' Sounds. They would celebrate. He would smile at her. He would never know the trouble he caused her heart. She was brave, independent, for Pete's sake.

She flew past the line of wooden stands with various fruits, vegetables and baked goods for sale. More dust floated up Emma's nose and she coughed; she gripped both brake calipers. How fortunate, she acknowledged, that her hands had cramped in the pressed position so she didn't ram into the tall windowless building with the scorched sides. The bike shrieked to a stop. A good thing. But her fingers didn't release. Not such a good thing.

In addition to the cramped hands, her nauseous stomach now released a horrifying belch.

She and the bike tipped over as the door to the bakery opened. Right before she hit the ground and vomited, Sparks and Jennifer appeared, squinting, into the midday sun, Sparks leaning in toward Jennifer's face.

CHAPTER TWENTY-ONE

"THAT WAS A pretty stupid thing to do," Sparks said an hour later, breaking a silence colder than the air blowing from the new rental car's AC. His expression had *stern father* written all over it. Great.

Paternal interest. Just what she'd always wanted from someone so beautiful, fun and *alive* as Sparks.

"Yeah, well." Sitting in the front seat of Sparks's rental car, smelling like vomit, was not how she had visualized her triumphant end to the bike ride. Worse was the sinking feeling she might need the heavy pottery bowl on her lap.

His right hand came off the steering wheel and patted her knee, like he would Trouble. Did he want to ruffle her ears, too, and say, "Who's the best dog?"

"How're you doing? Good thing Jennifer thought to send along the bowl, in case." He kept his hand on her knee. It warmed the chill until she moved away. From the corner of her eye, she saw his look of concern. A few hours ago, she would have thrilled that the concern was for her. Now her mood matched her sour stomach—he wasn't concerned, he just didn't want stuff on his seat.

"Yeah, she's great." Good ol' Jennifer. In a more gracious mood—which Emma hoped would surface soon—she'd thank Jennifer for dealing well with someone being sick in her driveway. Jennifer hadn't said much. She and Sparks had pried Emma's fingers from her handlebars, walked her into the bakery's bathroom, where Jennifer had shut out Sparks, took off Emma's tank top and disappeared with it. Emma sat on the toilet, shivering in the stifling space, still muddleheaded and wondering where she'd missed noticing the obvious coupling of the two.

Sparks paid attention to all women, for Pete's sake. However, the times he came with her to buy bread, he and Jennifer had never moved beyond a polite nod and greeting. Dehydration, though mitigated by almost three quarts of water enhanced with some type of herb tea, was nothing compared to her humiliation. Stupid, stupid Emma. Invisible once more. He had flirted with her, she realized now—way too late—like he flirted with the rest of the female population.

She grimaced as a lingering stomach cramp

gripped. If she continued to think about this for any length of time—which, she apparently was—it occurred to her that he grinned at her the same way he grinned at Violet and Mae Cunningham. And Chet and Father Jack. Sparks was…well, friendly.

On to self-abasement. Why did she get sucked in every time? Let some guy smile at her, even be nice to her, and her brains fell out, thinking it meant something.

At the intersection of Main and Angel Way, Sparks took the corner slowly, and finally broke the silence. He even smiled at her. "You can relax, Emma—everything's going to be fine. You wait and see." He imitated an old-time preacher. "I can see the light!"

For me, the light at the end of the tunnel is usually from an oncoming train. He could tell Mother Egan that one. She forced a smile that felt more like she was baring her teeth. Once on Seraphim, while the trees provided some shade from the sun, the contrast hurt her eyes.

Sparks parked the car in front of Naomi's place and ran around to open the door for Emma. She handed him the bowl and stood up, willing her legs to get her into the house.

"Thank you." She had manners, even if no luck with men. "I appreciate the ride."

"I'll put your bike in the shed and…see you later?"

Emma shrugged and stumbled into the house, ignoring Trouble's inquisitive fascination with her fragrance. She stripped off the damp clothes Jennifer had rinsed. They smelled like her day had been.

All in all, she had better stick to short-term relationships, she concluded as she stepped into the shower, since she couldn't sustain a man moratorium. When a quick romance blew up in her face, she would moan an allotted two days and then go back to her so-called life. She lifted her head to the stream of warm water. One difficulty with that, however, her heart informed her as an involuntary sob escaped. *Yeah, I know the what the difficulty is*, she thought to herself as she squirted shower gel into her palm. *I know, I know.*

SPARKS CLIMBED INTO the car and backed out of Naomi's driveway, then spotted Chet and his car, probably returning from Garden Terrace, pull into his driveway across the street.

Relationships were tough. Emma's earlier snap at him at the motel—*I don't care what he does when he's not working*—burned, as did her frigid silence in the car. He had explained there was nothing going on with him and Jennifer. Did she really think he preferred Jennifer over her?

His previous epiphany at the OD about Emma being "home" was clearly one-sided. She obviously didn't see him as long-term material. Back to man of the world, committed to none.

On top of all that, Jennifer hadn't said yes to his request when he'd finally asked her. "I'll think about it," she'd replied, stressing *think*. He couldn't even be a hero to Emma on his way out of town.

At the corner, he looked both ways before pulling out onto Main.

The loss of Rockin' Sounds had devastated Emma. His great plan to get Jennifer to sing seemed to fizzle like his past couple fireworks shows. How could he have thought that a small-town summer would improve things, get him back in the game? It had only served to remind him that old habits didn't die with new scenery. What had happened years ago had set his rambling ways in place.

As he neared the Safari Motel, his mood turned dark. Why should he have to figure out what Emma was feeling? Or solve the problems of the Jamboree? This was a simple summer gig, nothing more. He was on the outside looking in, the way he had been his whole life.

Well, he didn't need to moan about it. It was time to get out.

After inserting the key and opening the door to his room, he viewed his suitcases on the sagging bed. He had done his work, faxed the schematics. Now that the fireworks were re-instated, the techs from Evanston could finish the job. He would collect his paycheck. It wasn't the town's fault he and Emma had a falling out. She probably didn't think about him enough to know they'd had one.

While he traced the pattern of the bedspread with his eyes, the familiar ache crept in and among his deepest thoughts. This rant-and-run scenario, although a different town, a different girl, was not new. *Man of the world, committed to none.* His fists clenched.

The memories of Willard, Duff and Ray's first-day friendliness and the warning about the vegetable medley returned. His lips curved in a smile; his hands, holding a polo shirt, hovered over an open suitcase. With the lack of funds, Heaven would rise like the dust in the fields to the top of the flood list. The grocery store gone—no more Nick's BBQ, Dairy Delite's Dream Burger. Washed Ashore under gallons of water. Dew Drop demolished. His smile faded.

After a quick squint at his watch, he slapped

the shirt into the suitcase. It wasn't his problem; it wasn't his battle. He had one parasailing lesson left at Washed Ashore with Ben. He'd take that and then hit the road. It was what he did.

The light sprinkle under putty-colored skies and the lingering heat dampened his bare arms as he walked down the access road to Ben's marina. Washed Ashore had tickled his funny bone when he first saw the sign. Today, it hit too close to home. Jennifer's question had prompted a review that quickly revealed his life was not freewheeling, but drifting. He'd washed up in Heaven and been surrounded with the sense of community he'd always wanted. Blurting Emma's name in response to the pointed question had been a mistake.

Community brought heartache. The romantic kind and otherwise. *Don't forget that in your view of Mayberry, dude. And don't forget who you are.* Right now, he was a parasailing student. Right after that, he was history.

Leaning back on his heels, he made it down the steep half gravel, half paved street where stubborn grass insisted on growing. It was, according to the regulars at the Dew Drop, one of the streets on the town's To Be Fixed When We Get Money list, which the Jamboree was meant to pay for. Sniffing deeply of the lake air, he reminded himself that he'd had a great time and that was all that mattered. He looked at the parasail on the beach and anticipated the upcoming wind, the drop feeling that twisted his stomach when he lifted off the water, a feeling preferable to the others that kept plaguing him.

Ben was scanning the lake with binoculars with one arm, the other close to his side in a sling, when Sparks came alongside.

Gesturing to the sling, Sparks asked, "What happened to you?"

Ben patted his arm. "Wretched my shoulder. Being stupid—reaching for something I couldn't get."

I know what you mean. He'd wrenched his heart on this town—and Emma.

"Hold on," Ben said. "I'm just checking the lake for our boats, or rather the tourists in the boats."

"I'm leaving town."

Ben laughed. "I said that once about this place." He slapped the other man's shoulder. "About ten years ago."

"I'm serious. Right after the lesson."

With the binoculars in front of his eyes, Ben's response lacked interest. "Huh."

"Yup. Faxed my schematics as soon as the

BLM reinstated the fireworks. The techs can carry on now."

A startled exclamation burst from Ben's lips. "Gonna have to postpone that lesson, dude. Some tourists out there just swamped the boat." He grabbed a life vest and tossed it at Sparks. "It hasn't sunk yet, but it's on its way. Don't see the lake patrol out there. I hope those folks were smart enough to put on the life vests in the boat." Gesturing to the sling, he said, "There are kids on that boat with their parents."

Sparks broke into a run for the dock.

It seemed as though it took hours to tow the boat to shore. Each time he attempted to increase his speed, the two children, huddled with their parents, screamed. It was only after he unloaded his cargo to Ben, the dock boy, and the volunteer fire department that he found it had been less than an hour.

The couple thanked him with hugs and pats on the arm. The girl, appearing about four years old to Sparks's inexperienced eye, regarded him from her father's arms, large brown eyes wide. "I hate Heaven," she said, her small body jerking with posthysteria hiccups. Her father kissed her dark hair while his brown eyes twinkled at Sparks. "*Miha*, you don't hate Heaven. You hate this part."

As Sparks watched them go, the mist and humidity shot shivers through his wet clothes.

Ben said he'd make time for the last lesson in the early evening. "That is, if you can stand Heaven a few hours more. Thanks for the rescue... You're a handy guy to keep around." Then he asked him who was replacing Rockin' Sounds, which reminded Sparks of Emma and why he was leaving. Maybe staying even for the last lesson wasn't a good idea.

Ben strolled behind the counter of his shop. "See ya later this afternoon." He chuckled again. "Leaving, huh?"

Once he was at the Safari, Sparks had a shower and then lay on the bed, ignoring partially packed suitcases. Three empty hours spread out before him until his return to Washed Ashore. He wasn't sleepy, not hungry—amazingly—and if he saw Emma, he'd blurt out he was going and he didn't want to deal with that. Heaven was too small to sneak around. The pittering of rain on the roof increased. The family in the boat had been in serious trouble, worse now if they'd still been on the lake. He recalled the little girl's pronouncement and her father's, "You just hate this part."

Sparks had resented Emma coming to him, expecting him to help solve the town's problem. Just see what happened when he couldn't deliver. He laced his fingers behind his head and stared at the bumpy cottage-cheese ceiling. Was he, perhaps, fond of throwing the baby out with the bathwater, as he'd been told growing up? That he ran whenever things became difficult? His scheduling coordinator had said the same thing. Sometimes it wasn't fun when fireworks didn't explode like his schematics dictated. He hadn't quit that yet...but he'd thought about it. There did seem to be a pattern.

If he left now, he'd spend more time wondering what had happened and what he could have done to help. "It's not all bad. Just get through this part." Puffing out his cheeks, he blew himself a raspberry, sat up and started taking clothes out of the suitcases. "You're in for the whole deal, dude. Who were you kidding?"

CHAPTER TWENTY-TWO

TWO WEEKS BEFORE the Jamboree, Emma sat across from Jennifer at the small table Vince had near the deli case. Why had the woman called her that morning and asked to meet her at the IGA? Whatever the reason, Emma wanted details about Jennifer and Sparks. Last night she'd talked herself out of this meeting, since it wouldn't change anything between her and Sparks, but some perverted sense of closure changed her mind while she brushed her teeth.

The air outside hung stuffy and thick, yet Jennifer wore a hoodie and long pants about two sizes too big. Emma had on her last clean pair of shorts and a T-shirt. The humidity had torqued her hair. She noted how smoothly the other woman's hair slid into a shell clip, her face exquisite, though devoid of makeup. She looked about sixteen. After getting drinks from the self-serve soda fountain, they settled at the table.

Jennifer began the conversation. "Sparks said he didn't know you rode a bike."

Sparks doesn't know a lot of things about me, Emma thought. Primarily that she had fallen in love with him, slowly, as she'd absorbed his humor, his interest in people and, most recently, his growing interest in saving the day.

Now the story of his lake rescue was all over town.

Sitting next to the one he preferred hurt, but it wasn't the first time she'd seen her competition and knew she wasn't even in the game. Petite Jennifer had that air of fragility about her that guys loved. Emma had tried fragility and been told she was too needy. Which boyfriend had that been? They were starting to blur together.

"You and Sparks seem as if you've become good friends." Emma hoped she didn't whine.

Jennifer lifted her gaze from turning her iced tea cup around and around. "Sorry, been kind of distracted." She paused, then spoke. "Believe it or not, I called you for a reason. And yes, Sparks and I are good friends. He recognized me when you two came out to the bread stand the first time." She swallowed and released another tiny smile. "He kept the secret."

Why would they need a secret? They were both adults. Jennifer was speaking again, so Emma crunched on her ice. She found herself liking Jennifer. Drat. Could see why Sparks would be attracted to her. Double drat.

"I used to be a recording artist called Trinity."

Emma's eyes widened. The number of people on the planet who didn't know Trinity would fit into a very small cab. In the next breath, and in light of revelation, she took in the mousy brown hair and the hazel eyes. In all the magazines, Trinity had been a streaked blonde with vivid blue eyes.

Jennifer, aka Trinity, seemed to interpret her scrutiny. "Weekly hair weaves and contacts. This is the natural me. Finally." Her next statement left Emma gaping. "I heard Rockin' Sounds canceled. If you can use me, I'd like to sing."

As if they could afford Trinity, although it was sweet that she offered. She could see the commonality between Sparks's life and the superstar's. Jennifer—er, Trinity—would fit into Sparks's jet-setting lifestyle, unlike Emma, who couldn't seem to get more than two hours from where she was born. "You're great, but we can't afford you." Emma mentally watched the crowds depart and kissed away the ka-ching of profits. Crowds that would pay anything to attend a comeback of Trinity's.

"Yes, you can. And you can call me Jennifer. It's my real name."

She must be distracted again, thought Emma. They could never afford her. "Uh, Trin—Jennifer. You're great for offering…"

"I'm free."

The crowds in Emma's imagination swarmed back through the park, waving money.

"I had heard you'd retired." Or quit. Or disappeared. It depended on what supermarket tabloid you read.

"A few years ago, things became too much, and to survive I had to get out of the business… I've been hiding." She looked almost apologetic. "After the fire… Chet and Tilly and Sparks… People have been so kind, so concerned. They all…"

Emma was sitting next to *Trinity*, listening to her talk about her superstar life being awful.

"That day you arrived on the bike," the singer began, though graciously didn't add any descriptive qualifiers, "I asked Sparks what made his life happy. I'd been thinking it was time for me to get back into life… I feel like I'm resurrected, so to speak." Hunching her shoulders, she smoothed out the napkin she'd been folding and unfolding. "Sounds corny—it being Heaven. But true."

"The Jamboree will be very glad to have you sing," Emma finally acknowledged, then couldn't resist asking, "Just how did you and Sparks meet anyway?" She was talking to *Trinity*.

"At a gig, a long time ago." Jennifer pulled the wooden clip from her hair and it cascaded below her shoulders. "I ran past him, upset, headed for the bathroom. No one saw me break down but Sparks. He followed me right into the washroom."

It sounded like something Sparks would do—act first and think later—maybe.

"My people were suspicious of Sparks's motives, of course."

"Of course," Emma said.

"They thanked him, but ushered him out quickly. We saw each other at a few events—Sparks is in demand for concerts a lot—and then I noticed him with you at my bread stand." Jennifer said *my bread stand* with a sense of pride that wasn't attached to "my people."

Jennifer clasped her hands together on the table. "Well, I'm glad the Jamboree has a replacement."

Considering Jennifer as a replacement for Rockin' Sounds was like considering the hydroelectric power of the Hoover Dam akin to a toilet flushing.

"Thank you," Emma managed to say, feeling part of the weight of the world lift off her shoulders. The fireworks were a go again, and now a lightning bolt had resuscitated their center-stage act. "But you won't be anonymous here anymore once you perform," Emma said as an afterthought, a *very* late afterthought. "You know this town. Gossip at the speed of light."

"Yeah." Jennifer nodded. "I'd heard a few bits and pieces about the town having financial trouble and figured it didn't concern me. But then—" A small silence ensued between them against the hum of store activity. "My house was on fire and the volunteer fire department showed up. Normal people dropping everything to help me. After the fire chief's wife came to make sure I was okay, well, it just broke the need for isolation. They were there for *me*, Jennifer, not Trinity, and not because I was famous." She looked apologetic. "Bottom line. I can't be part of the town and hold myself back. It's a two-way street."

Try as she might, Emma had no words.

"I hope the Jamboree is a success," Jennifer added, lifting her gaze from the napkin to Emma. "I'm kind of nervous about singing again, but I'm glad I get to do it in my hometown."

Emma, still digesting the two-way street comment, grimaced. "All the places you've lived and this is home." She shook her head.

Jennifer shrugged and smiled her tiny smile. "Kind of funny. My first hit was bashing small-town life. I thought I was so superior, so destined for bigger things."

"But you were." Emma didn't like the direction this conversation was going. "You had to be yourself. Small towns are suffocating."

Pulling herself up from her slouch, Jennifer drew in a deep breath. "I used to think that, too, before, but it's a funny thing. You take yourself with you wherever you go. Think about it. There's you, your troubles, doubts and even inspiration. You still have to deal with things, no matter where you end up." She stretched like a small cat and rose. "Thanks again for giving me the chance to sing. Now, I've got some bread dough waiting for me." As she turned the corner by the canned corned-beef hash, she looked over her shoulder. "Oh, Sparks is the friend to me that he is to everyone. Nothing more. In case someone wants to know."

"Right." Emma winced. "I'll—I'll let... someone...know."

IT WAS TIME for both of them to fish or cut bait, put up or shut up and any other sayings Mother Egan might come up with, Emma theorized after a quick shower, pulling a clean top over her head. She finished getting dressed, turned off the blow dryer and surveyed her mane with satisfaction. Frizz under control.

Earlier, as Emma had left the IGA, she'd encountered Sparks on the street. Still in the glow of Jennifer's assertion that she was not involved with Sparks, Emma had asked Sparks for a date. The same perversity that had kept her pedaling in blistering heat had now induced her to invite Sparks out for a cruise on the party barge at dusk, where, in a masterful deviation from a life pattern, she would ask him what he thought about her. It was surprising that Sparks's reaction was a burst of laughter, but then he explained that he'd been hunting *her* down for a lake date.

No, she corrected herself as she carefully applied eye shadow for the first time this summer and several coats of mascara, not what he *thought* about her…how he *felt* about her. That sounded more direct. No… What was the *nature of their relationship*? Even better. Now that she had Trinity-Jennifer's perspective, it was time to find out Sparks's.

A rustle deep inside hinted at an impending emotional upheaval, but she ignored it. She would let Sparks know how she felt instead of waiting around to be asked. Seize the day. Spit into the wind.

Then, in a second stab at personal authority and self-determination, she'd told him not to pick her up, but to meet her at Washed Ashore as she'd taken care of all the arrangements. Ben had looked amused earlier this afternoon but had supplied the boat keys. Gracefully gliding down the hill toward Sparks at the marina would be as close to a slo-mo romantic scene as she could think of on short notice. Plus, she even had a plan: come-hither eyes and Renaissance eau de toilette, purchased at the Rexall. When the selection of scents on offer overwhelmed her, she had gone with the historical connection of a new birth, a reawakening. She added one more squirt to the several for a little extra reassurance.

There. She stepped back to view the end result. Not bad and with time to spare. All she had to do now was bring Trouble in and head at a sedate pace for the marina so she would arrive calm and collected, as arriving cool didn't seem possible in this heat.

Emma opened the back door to call Trouble in, whereupon he took one look at her, backed up and began running in large circles. Emma sighed. He knew she was going somewhere he wasn't. Twenty minutes later, she was across the street and in the Petersons' front yard, no longer calm and collected. Trouble had leaped over the gate and had begun an attack on every oscillating sprinkler head the Petersons' had in their front yard. Then he sped to the back and began digging in their flowerbeds. While it was truly fortunate they weren't at home, she thought, finally capturing the dog and chastising him all the way over to Nomi's, it had sucked all the grace time from her sedate glide, and, she noticed halfway to the marina, water and dirt had combined to add an interesting texture to her light blouse, summer skirt and strappy sandals.

By the time she had stepped carefully down the grassy hill toward the marina—now more than fashionably late—Sparks was sitting on the dock with his back to her, swinging his feet over the side. If she had made a grand entrance, he wouldn't have seen it anyway.

"Sparks! Sorry I'm la—" the sentence was not fully formed or out of her mouth when her right foot twisted sideways and she stopped, dropped and rolled the rest of the way down the hill. She, who had pined for drama and adventure, had made her grand entrance after all.

"Emma!" Sparks leaped up and acted the

hero, helping her on her unsteady feet. The shirt and skirt had taken another hit of texture, she found, looking down, as well as now having a lot more leg showing. She hastily pulled down the skirt that she knew now was too short. By the way Sparks was looking at her, the mascara also had not survived either the heat of the walk to the marina or the rock and roll down the hill. Putting a finger underneath one eye, she drew it away heavily smeared in black. "How bad?"

He offered a corner of his shirt. "Here, let me." As he examined her, his blue eyes deepened; she closed her eyes so he wouldn't see her emotion. He was close enough she could smell his sweat and the citrus-sage fragrance that clung to him. It reminded her all over again of how much she liked him.

Finishing with a final swipe, he took a step away from her; she clenched her back teeth and pushed away the desire to throw her arms around him. *Not yet.* When she asked about the state of their relationship, she'd be throwing her heart on the ground. This one might hurt too much if he stepped on her offering, or worse, ignored it.

"There. Back to normal." The edge of his shirt looked as if he'd been tarring a driveway. *C'mon Renaissance.*

"Thanks."

He sneezed. "You don't need that stuff anyway. You've got beautiful eyes."

"Oh. Um. Thanks. You do, too." A familiar tickle swept up Emma's backbone. He was so easy to be around.

They managed to get onto the boat and out on to the water without any further problems, Emma graciously suggesting Sparks captain their craft. The captain's chair and wheel stood in the middle, a half circle of plush benches ringed around it. She balanced next to Sparks as he eased the barge into deeper water. The lake breeze kissed her damp skin, cooling the heat of embarrassment. Twilight on the shore of Heaven Lake was one of Emma's favorite combinations. She could tell when it was nearly eight fifteen in summer—the slanting rays morphed golden over the lake, flowed up through the cottonwoods in the park and bathed the town.

When Sparks slung his arm over her shoulder, pulling her closer, she relaxed. Time for a do over; she could start this evening again. She could do this. Allowing herself to snuggle a bit into his shoulder, she opened her mouth to ask the question.

Sparks sneezed. Violently. "Sorry," he apologized.

She smiled sweetly. No prickly Emma tonight. In about an hour, the sky would be
loaded with stars. It would be spectacular, providing all the makings of a romantic evening, a
perfect time to ask Sparks a few leading questions. The island ahead lay as a dark smudge
against the diminishing light. A few boat lights
twinkled white and red at wide intervals. The
Wave Runner types were in, and other than a
few fisherman closer to shore, Emma didn't
see anyone else. The lake, with all its enchant-
ing possibilities, was theirs.

"Were you going to say something?" he
asked, wiping his eyes. "I thought we'd go to
the island."

Better and better. Promise Island was famous for romantic assignations. Would she
wait until then to ask her question? No, she
might lose her nerve.

"Yes, actually. I wanted to ask you…" she
said, turning and taking a half step away so
she could look up into the face that showed
up regularly in her dreams. "Rather, I'd like
to know—"

Another shoulder-shuddering sneeze. "I am
so sorry," he said, suddenly rooting around in
the boat's compartment and coming up with a
wrinkled tissue. His back to her, he blew his
nose heartily.

They were halfway across the lake.

"I better concentrate on getting us to the island before I start sneezing again," he croaked.

"Sure," Emma said, moving to the railing, disappointed yet determined. She didn't think she'd heard him sneeze much at all during their summer thus far. Odd.

A few more minutes and Sparks cut the motor. As he did, the night noises of frogs and lapping waves rushed in, in concert with the pungent mix of mud, lake water and soggy vegetation. The boat drifted toward a natural sand beach fringing the island with the cottonwoods and undergrowth about twenty feet from the water's edge. Shadows backed deep into it. Mysterious. Romantic.

Sparks joined Emma at the railing, where his arm rested against hers. She considered herself and Sparks together. Sometimes one of them had an answer for a problem; sometimes the other did. Sometimes neither of them did, but no matter what, these past weeks had shown her she had an ally in him. What had started as an uneasy alliance had moved into friendship and come out the other side as love. Emma shivered.

"Cold?" He moved closer.

"No." Not cold.

"I—I want to tell you, Emma."

Could this be the moment? Had her risk taking shifted the universe and Sparks would speak first? "Uh, yes?"

"I went back out to Jennifer's place to ask her to sing…after you came to my motel room," he blurted. "She used to—she is—well, famous."

So that was how Jennifer had learned of their plight. Conflicting feelings tumbled around Emma's head. First, it was great he'd gone there to solve their problem. But telling her tonight? Three's company, even though she now knew the singer wasn't competition.

"Oh?" Emma managed. The breeze shifted to her left, toward his face, and he turned away from her, removing his arm from the railing and sneezing three times. Her skin chilled at his absence.

"I wanted you to know I was thinking of ways to help the Jamboree." Rather than the low, silky-smooth tones of the romantic hero, his voice sounded thick and congested in the night air. Another three sneezes in a row. And again. As the boat bumped against the island's shore, he staggered and pulled her to him, murmuring against her hair, "Ebba, dis summer has been da best of by life."

The short-circuited kiss in Nomi's kitchen rose in her mind as he leaned closer. Part of her—the eager, needy woman who had become whatever previous boyfriends expected— told her to spill her heart. Yet after the summer she'd lived through so far, she held back. Sparks meant too much; rejection from him would hurt worse than anything in this moment.

He whispered again, still so close his breath tickled her ear. "I've nebber stayed anybhere for long. And you…"

He was going to kiss her. If he aimed for her forehead again, she was going straight up on her toes so he hit her lips.

"You don't gib up. You work so hard." The nasal tones continued.

This was sounding more like a 4-H Achievement Night than an intimate confession of his feelings for her.

"I want to spend the rest of my…"

Emma slid into a daydream that had something to do with Hobie Cats, waving bon voyage, Sparks at her side, her new green suitcases at their feet. His next words slapped her awake.

"…time left enjoying the town with you before I go."

CHAPTER TWENTY-THREE

Zoo bit into her Big D burger as she and Emma sat at a Dairy Delite picnic table under the green-and-white-striped umbrella. The shade cut the heat a bit, and only a bit. Emma hitched her sun-exposed left shoulder more under the umbrella. It was six days until Jamboree liftoff.

The burger stand was dealing with a hungry luncheon crowd; the smell of fried onion rings hung in the air. Zoo had insisted on an early lunch to catch up on news she'd missed while attending a vet conference in Fort Collins. So Emma filled her in on her grandmother's swift improvement—information gained through the faithful Chet—as well as the Jennifer triumph.

She was midway through an emotional recitation of the party barge debacle Saturday when Zoo interrupted.

"You're doing it again." Zoo's voice was matter-of-fact.

"I am not." Avoiding Zoo's gimlet gaze, Emma swabbed a square-ended fry through a pool of ketchup, thinking she simply ought to smear it on her thighs to save her body the effort. She didn't want to talk about Sparks anymore, thank you very much.

"I would think you'd be ecstatic. Jennifer and Sparks aren't an item. He told you last night he wants to spend time with you."

"That was a consolation prize, not a romantic proposal. Zoo, for Pete's sake, he sneezed the whole time. The man is obviously allergic to getting close to me!"

Her heart ached. She didn't remember it aching like this with the other guys. Mad, sure. Betrayed, yeah, a couple of times. Used… Oh, yes, definitely. But this…this feeling… She couldn't put her finger on it.

Zoo licked the secret sauce dripping from her burger. "You're avoiding how you feel about Sparks."

"Am not." Emma bit the fry in half. "What I'm *really* thinking about is it is Tuesday and we haven't had a town crisis since Friday." A personal crisis more recently, but not a town one.

"Same old Emma."

"Remind me to invite my *other* sympathetic friend Zoo to lunch next time."

Her friend's violet eyes held her gaze and Emma had the uncomfortable feeling she'd periodically had over the years. Zoo could be all clinical, you'd feel safe, and then out of no-where, she'd zap you with deep emotional in-sight. Hopefully Zoo was in vet mode today. That she, Emma, cared about Sparks after his apparent short attention span was more than she wanted to admit, for the rest of the sum-mer and beyond.

Setting down her burger carefully on the wax paper, Zoo wiped her hand on the thin napkin. "But I'm not helping you if I say, 'poor Emma.' You didn't like it when we were kids and people called you 'poor little Emma Chambers.'"

"'Poor Emma' fits."

"Denial is a warm lover on a cold—"

"—night of reality. What's your point?"

"My point is that, until Sparks, you picked guys—or let guys pick you—who didn't de-serve you. And as a result you start expecting them to dump you."

Zoo's kennel-cleaner fumes were eating her brain.

"That's crazy. Why would I want to set my-self up for heartbreak? Besides, your theory has a flaw. Sparks isn't like the others." Emma jammed another fry into her mouth. "So there."

"Exactly my point. He scares you. He could actually be the one."

Emma's stomach gurgled. If he was the one

and she missed it, would she ever get another chance? What if he didn't know he was the one? Who decided who was the one for the other one anyway? She sipped her iced tea. "So what if he *is* the one? What can I do about it?"

"You can stop holding him at arm's length like you do everyone else."

"Have you forgotten the disastrous lake date already? I tried." It was going to take another order of fries and possibly onion rings to get through this conversation.

"Are we revisiting that again? Yes, you do. Arm's length. You always have. You always blamed it on your grandmother and her ideas on who was worthy to play with and so forth. Well, she's not here now." Zoo leaned forward on her elbows. Uh-oh, she was getting into this.

"You grew up here. How many people in town do you know well?"

"You, for starters. To my current dismay."

"Thank you. I love you, too. Who else?"

"And Chet…and… Are you going to finish your fries?"

Zoo pushed the cardboard tray toward her. "Can I assume that your attempt to deflect the question indicates you know I'm right?"

Her old friend had done it again. Emma heaved a deep sigh and folded her hands in her lap while Zoo regarded her with compassion and, Emma suspected, more than a wee bit of triumph.

"So what now, Freud?" Emma said. She couldn't argue with truth when it permeated a French fry frenzy, even when she didn't want to feel the hurt slide out of the deep place where it had hidden silently for years. "Are you planning on telling me why I do it in…um—" Emma glanced at her watch "—less than fifteen minutes? I have to accept a load of Porta-Potties at the park."

"PORTA-POTTIES."

"Check," the postmistress said. "In place, and I made up extra gallons of my organic deodorizer."

At the table set up just inside the auditorium, Sparks bolted awake to see Emma look up from her list to smile at the woman. He must have dozed off after the report on grease traps. He tried to catch Emma's eye, but she ignored him, like she had since she'd dashed off the barge last Saturday. Chet, sitting next to him, was doodling Naomi's name inside a lopsided heart. Aw.

Sparks had told Emma that everything would be fine. Jennifer's performance alone would probably do it, even though there were no guarantees. But as for his relationship with his codirector...not so fine. On the boat, he'd tried to let her know how he felt and yammered instead about her work habits. He tapped his finger on the table until Emma swung an ultrapatient, would-you-stop-that-please gaze at him.

It wasn't an accident that he had a job that kept him moving. He'd assumed long ago that if he stayed in one place, people might find out what he was really like—scattered, undependable—and therefore conclude that he was a jerk. On the barge, he had wanted to be open, to let Emma know he wanted to learn to stick around, but he didn't know how. Of course, none of that had come out. Just the jerk, with senseless babbling about her civic pride.

Then he'd started sneezing and couldn't stop. He hadn't had trouble before being around her. Why had it bothered him so? Perhaps that heavy perfume she'd been wearing. Emma normally smelled like sweet air and lavender. He liked that.

"Parking concession," Emma called out.

Juggy jumped in as if he was presenting the solution to global warming. Sparks hid another yawn by sweeping his chin with his hand as though checking for five-o'clock shadow. This was the final meeting. Tomorrow all the volunteers would eat a donated breakfast early in the morning and then head to their stations.

"First-aid booth."

Emma had to be almost through that blasted binder.

Chet stopped scribbling and reported.

By the time Sparks had docked the party barge last night, Emma had barely muttered, "Thanks," before practically bounding up the hill. He, who could talk to anyone about anything, had blown it. It had been a big strike one in telling Emma how he felt—or wanted to feel.

The meeting agony ended forty-five minutes later, with Emma pronouncing, "We're done." He caught up with her as she hurried out the door.

"Hey, lady, let me walk you home. No telling what danger lurks on these streets." With the barge fiasco behind him, he would clearly express himself on the way to Naomi's. Tell her she'd made an impression on him. That wasn't right either. Impression? There had to be a better word. *Explosion? Illumination?* What were some of those big words she used?

Her laughter in reply lit up her face; the smile she turned on him made her eyes squint the way he lov—admired. Maybe he'd imagined her coolness postbarge.

"Sure. As if that'll happen in Heaven." Her pace didn't slow.

"Gives me a chance to escort a beautiful woman home."

"You tell that to all your girlfriends in town."

Now, how was he supposed to take that remark? As he pondered its connotation, they waited to cross Main Street and then headed over to Cherubim. Lights glowed in the windows and the sounds of air conditioners and swamp coolers hummed in the warm night air. The palms of his hands began to sweat.

"Emma…"

"It's all come together. Tomorrow, whether we've done it right or wrong, we've done it."

He slipped his arm around her, marveling at his new protective reflex, then groaned inwardly at her barely perceptible step away from him. "About Saturday night, Ems."

Her stride never faltered. "I'm thinking about the future from now on. Let's not talk about the past. Let's talk about your—your next job assignment and my getting out of town."

Her walls were up and he couldn't see over them. That she would make it out of Heaven and do well was a given. Emma was changing before his eyes.

He remembered the first night he'd met her in the canyon.

As they went past the darkened school, he recalled how they'd gotten reacquainted by his driving her nose into the end zone.

He'd seen her face fear, make choices to do something she didn't feel comfortable doing. She'd rescued him and been amazing and now was more amazing. She was stronger now. She deserved to know how he felt about her.

"Remember when I…" He trailed off, looking toward the school.

"I remember."

"Listen, Saturday I tried to say something and it didn't come out right."

"It sure didn't."

Once he left town—and she left—he'd probably never see her again. Panic coiled up his spine. Connecting with a woman had never been so crucial…or so difficult.

A gray sedan with tinted windows rolled past them, parking lights only, and turned onto Seraphim as they did.

"That car doesn't look familiar," Emma said with a frown.

"Probably relatives coming in for the Jamboree. Everyone I've talked to said they had invited every person they knew, including family they didn't like." He cupped his hand around her elbow and turned her toward him. She pulled away. The car kept going straight on Seraphim, past the corner for Angel Way.

She stopped in front of Naomi's and shrugged. "You're right. Tomorrow there will be all sorts of cars, I hope. Good night."

For a moment, she looked into his eyes with an expression he couldn't interpret. He thought she took a step toward him, but then, protective mask snapped firmly in place, she turned, strode up the walk and into the house.

Strike two.

CHAPTER TWENTY-FOUR

OPENING DAY OF THE jamboree and she, Mayor Naomi Chambers, wasn't part of it. A deep loneliness had settled on her the moment first light had poked her as she'd lain in the dratted hospital bed. She would miss seeing the crowds emerging from their motels and campgrounds as they gathered in the park for the day's events.

Her eyes darted to the envelope on the nearby table. It had taunted her for two days.

Several more minutes passed until she muttered, "Never put off till tomorrow what you can do today," and dragged the envelope toward her with her good hand. She couldn't quite get a deep breath before she held down the end of the envelope with the weight of her infernal bad arm, tore it open and pulled out the contents.

After reading the slanted, racing writing, she dropped the paper as though it'd scorched her fingertips.

Emma was in danger.

WE'VE DONE IT, Emma thought. As least, to start with. As she jogged to the double doors of the church/community center, she noted the parking lot was full and bicycles lined the fence. Red, white and blue bunting decorated just about everything in sight.

Folks had arrived for the inaugural volunteer breakfast prior to the opening of the Jamboree. It was one of Emma's suggestions that had been enthusiastically received. In spite of her grandmother's interference, the weather, a fire and an old musician having a heart attack, they had made it to opening day. She burst through the auditorium doors, wet hair flopping.

The two churches had provided all of their folding banquet tables, which were angled around the large room. The volume spiked as people moved off the buffet line and found seats. Emma's mouth watered as the smell of Vince's regionally famous ham sizzling and Jennifer's egg bread toasting blessed her nose. Emma marveled, as she had ever since her talk with the world-famous singer, that their humble Jamboree now touted *the* Trinity as its headline act. But where was Sparks? She headed toward the long food table, shooting side glances left and right so it didn't look as though she was looking for him.

Underneath the fragrance of food, the auditorium smelled of floor varnish, just as it had since her grandparents had paid for its refinishing years ago as a gift to the church. Someone had hung a pair of angel wings from one of the basketball hoops. Just as long as it wasn't an Elvis impersonator hanging up there.

In addition to the town stepping up with ideas such as the midway and small wooden creations, Beryl had pretty much stopped her protesting this summer. With Naomi out of the way, the fun must have gone out of it. She noted the usually feisty woman sat with Tilly and her crowd. Amazing. Although it wouldn't stop Heaven from being flooded if the Jamboree didn't net sufficient money, that they had given it their best shot remained amazing. Emma suspected Sparks had something to do with Beryl's softening. He had that effect on people. *Do not go there*, she admonished herself, stabbing a pancake from the warming tray.

Emma flopped the sunflower-size flapjack onto her plate, smearing real butter and maple syrup over it. Who cared about calories? It was a day to celebrate. She would make it through the next five days, and then it was her turn. She could leave with a job well done. The man moratorium, though tested by Sparks, would remain intact. Now, if only the image of Sparks and his crooked smile would stay out of her head. She shook that head until she felt dizzy. Eat, then Jamboree. Nothing else.

She spotted Sparks sitting with Chet and her resolve wobbled. Not everything would be tied up neatly. Emma took her plate and turned, surveying the room for a place to sit. Those wings had been another project she had given up fighting, deciding as long as it made money for the Jamboree, wasn't immoral or illegal and no one made *her* wear them, she could live with it. Did she dare sit by Sparks?

Chet, wearing another of his golf shirts, waved her over to his table. With a stifled sigh, she pulled her lips into a smile and headed over there. She could do this. It was only five more days.

"Great job, Emma!" somebody shouted, and someone else began to clap. The sound swelled, echoing through the high-ceilinged room. Heat surged to her face, and she collapsed in a chair next to Sparks who stood, fingers to his mouth, emitting an ear-splitting whistle.

"Sit down," she hissed, bumping his thigh with her elbow. He bent and drew a finger along her cheek.

"You're red."

"I know, you idiot." Her heart rose up to ask

for reconsideration of the man moratorium, but Emma stomped it down. Pleasant times with Sparks were allowed until the Jamboree was finished. She could do that. Then it was over.

"Mornin' to you, E," Chet greeted her. One mammoth slice of ham draped over his plate. He gestured to it, leaning back in his chair, and patting a flat stomach. "I've gone and made a fool of myself on this ham." He picked up his fork and knife again, a smile stretched across his mouth. "And I intend to go on doing it. Worth being a volunteer this year for the breakfast alone. Thanks for the idea, Emma. That Starla can cook, as long as you don't watch her do it."

Remembering Starla's healing cut, Emma inspected her plate, the enticing scent of ham, eggs and buttered toast wafting to her nose. She shook her head, firmly told her imagination to take a break and began to eat. A glance at Sparks's half-empty plate told her he had begun eating his way through the Jamboree as planned.

"Your grandmother loves opening day," Chet said with a lost look as he swirled his coffee.

Emma savored the bite of ham with pancake and didn't answer. Nomi did love it. For as long as Emma could remember, her grandmother had donned her Jamboree "uniform" of blue walking shorts, a white blouse and socks and navy sneakers, instead of her standard blue pantsuit. All she lacked was the whistle around her neck and a whip.

"Every year Grumpa used to make breakfast the morning of the opening," Emma told Sparks, to try to move the subject off her grandmother. "It was only him and me." Grumpa's breakfast had made opening day bearable.

"Your grandmother is not perfect, E." Chet's thoughts remained with her grandmother. "Never has been, never will be. You not talking to your grandmother is the first trickle from the crack in a dam. It can only get worse." Although Chet's tone was firm, his gaze on her was affectionate.

The man was nothing if not persistent. "Maybe the dam needs to break, Chet." After Emma swallowed her mouthful and reached for her glass of diet soda, she shrugged. "I don't want to argue about it. Anyway, today is our day. We did it. Whether we make it or break it, whatever's done or not done."

Chet opened his mouth.

She gestured with her fork. "I don't want to hear what didn't get done. I want to be dumb and happy today."

"Just goin' to say you've done a fine job of marshaling everyone together."

"Oh." She made a face. "Sorry. And thank you." Funny thing, this summer. While she had stood on her own and been more resilient than she'd known she could be, the elation she had expected remained elusive. For weeks, she'd been anticipating this victory; now it seemed a flicker, as though waiting…for *sparks*. She glanced at Sparks, met his blue-eyed gaze head-on and then looked away.

Feeling full yet not feeling compelled to stuff her face—a true moment of joy—Emma set her fork and napkin down. "I'm going to get Trouble for my first shift. It'll be cool enough for him to walk around the park with me and will give him some exercise. Unfortunately, he's going to feel ignored this weekend."

She thanked as many people as she could for their work as she made her way out the double doors, and then, in that moment, the revelation hit her. Despite the frustration and resentment, she knew why she wasn't celebrating yet. It wasn't Sparks. No matter the state of their relationship, she desperately wanted to share this morning with her grandmother.

CHAPTER TWENTY-FIVE

HOT GREASE AND frying bread dough from the Navajo Taco stand covered the park like a heavy blanket. Emma sniffed, sidestepping hoards of people as she made her way toward the first booth. The amount of people already here was incredible. More than any year she could remember. *Here's hoping it will be enough.*

She sniffed again. Sparks and his appetite for fried food had given her own guilty pleasure an avenue. At least, she thought, until he left town, or she did. Swallowing a lump in her throat, she checked the clipboard that said Starla was supposed to be ready to open the Dairy Delite–sponsored booth at eleven.

"Emma!"

Her stomach did the combo twist and flip as it reacted to Sparks's voice. He bounded up. "Hi, Starla. Smells good already." The morning sun shone on his bleached hair and he was, for Pete's sake, wearing a pair of angel wings attached over a T-shirt that said, Made in Heaven.

"You're wearing wings." A smirk slid over her face, after a not-very-strong attempt to stall it.

Trouble charged over to greet Sparks—one of most favorite people. Like a pro, Sparks sidestepped him, then bent to tease the tipped-over black ears. Lucky dog.

"Hey, when in Rome—"

That lazy lift to his lips made her want to dart forward and press her own mouth to his.

He straightened, and she caught the intense look in his deep blue eyes. "Can we—talk?"

Hooo... She needed one of Starla's chilled bandannas.

Starla greeted them, "Hey, you two."

"Hi, Starla." Starla wore a strappy tank straining to contain her bosom over a pair of capris, her permed curls bulging out from under a Central High baseball cap. She flashed a knowing look between the tall fireworks designer and Emma.

Emma made a check on her list and began to edge away. She had overheard rumors that Starla had made comments about Emma and Sparks.

"So you'll be gone come Tuesday," Starla remarked to Sparks, handing him a hand-dipped fried corn dog. "The way you eat, I'll lose money." A step closer to the long table separating them and she dropped her volume to half stadium roar. "You two gonna get going and get on with being an official couple any time soon? Might as well. Anyone can see you're—"

Face as red as the plastic ketchup bottle, Emma kept her eyes on the clipboard, yearning to punch the grin off her own lips. Waving a quick goodbye to the two who had begun discussing Trinity's upcoming performance, Emma checked the roasted-turkey-leg station, the ice cream booth and all the rest. Everyone had what they needed. Tucking the clipboard under her arm, Emma tipped her head from side to side, feeling the stretch. Done.

Now to call Nomi. It was time to make peace. Her grandmother couldn't cause her any more trouble now.

She and Trouble were hiking back up the hill when she heard Sparks call after her. Her heartbeat ramped up its pace. *Stop that.* She turned and met the full force of Sparks's singular smile.

He gestured toward the park. "Things look great. You done good, girl." He looked as if he was about to say more, but didn't. Given that he'd heard Starla's question, she was just as glad. They only had five days left. Why spend time talking about a future together they would never have?

"Where you headed now?" He squatted and rubbed the spots just over the dog's eyes that made Trouble close his eyes in bliss. Emma's hand stole to the back of her neck. "I just need you—"

The man had more charms than a bracelet. The sound of a chain saw being fired up reached Emma's ears. Her brows slammed together. The Black Binder had no plans for a chain saw. "What? Sorry, I—there's no chain saw demo in any of Nomi's instructions." She flashed him an apologetic glance.

They jogged back to the park.

The crowd surrounding the noise stood about seven or eight deep while others were swiftly migrating closer carrying corn dogs, hamburgers and soda cans. The air smelled of lake, barbecue, popcorn…and fresh wood chips. Once Emma and Sparks reached the edge of the crowd, she rued her short height. Even when she stood on tiptoe, she could only see pieces of wood flying.

"What's going on?" she asked Sparks. She could barely hear her own voice above the chain saw's whine.

"Ed Groves," he said. "Wow." And before

she could protest, Sparks had placed his hands around her waist and heaved her upward.

The warmth and power of his hands rendered her speechless and during those moments, she spied Ed and Bonnie Groveses' table, draped in patriotic bunting and decorated with silk greenery, providing the backdrop for detailed *life-size* wooden bear cubs.

Sparks's hands were slipping upward. Emma panicked. Wriggling, she pushed at his hands until he dumped her with a yelp.

"Don't." She shot him a look.

"I was just trying to—" Confusion clouded his face. "I knew you couldn't see—"

"Never mind." She could still feel his touch and traitorously wanted his hands around her again. *Stay focused.* "Local wood," she said, after navigating through the crowd to the Groveses' table. She turned a tag over. As she peered at the price, surely more than the ten bucks she'd figured tiny items would go for, Bonnie, a large straw hat on top of her short gray hair, spotted her, waved and turned back to her customers. "With tax, that's four hundred and fifty dollars, dear," Bonnie said to the visiting couple. They looked like money, as Lynette would say.

Emma watched, conscious that her mouth

was hanging open, but unable to shut it. Sparks leaned in.

"Little more expensive than you were expecting?" he said.

Wanting to lean into that arm and telling herself firmly that was not an option, Emma stood straight and nodded. "So much better."

Sparks removed his arm with a sideways look she chose to ignore. *Keep pleasant, keep the Jamboree moving and then it will be over.* That was her goal. Falling further in love with Sparks was not.

The woman smiled at Ed's wife, handing over a platinum card. "It's a bargain at four-fifty. We're saving a bundle on shipping, and besides, it's easier to see the detail here than on the website."

Emma pulled Trouble with her to a folding chair where she collapsed. Four hundred and fifty dollars a pop for a carved wooden bear. A *small* bear. Some larger ones stood as tall as she. She could only speculate as to their price.

Bonnie finished with her customer, moved over to Emma and flopped down in a wooden rocking chair behind the booth. Picking up a large fan, she waved it under her chin. Sparks roamed up and down the row of stalls after inspecting the intricately carved statues.

Finally, Emma found her voice. "Bonnie,

when Ed mentioned donating the proceeds from here, I thought—" She shaped the air with her hands. "Little…"

"We've sold all twenty-four that Ed had ready."

Standing halfway down the table, Sparks applauded awkwardly, one hand gripping a turkey leg in a paper cone. *Where does he get his never-ending supply of food?*

Emma performed a rapid mental totting up of Ed's bear sales. *Take* that, *flood project,* Emma thought, triumphantly.

"That couple bought the last. We have to keep a few now on display for orders." Bonnie reached down and brought up a small jug with a drink spout. Tipping back her head, she drank deep, reminding Emma how long it'd been since her diet cola at breakfast.

When she'd finished, Bonnie said, her voice breaking a bit, "We're happy to do it, Emma. The town's been good to us. We've raised our sons here and they're fine boys—" She paused. "Except that little Ed is stalling about marrying that sweet gal he's been seeing for five years." She shrugged with a what-can-you-do attitude. "My Ed's been wanting to show his wares, so to speak, in his hometown for years. It never came up."

After a little more chitchat with Bonnie and

Sparks, Emma said goodbye. She'd taken two steps to head toward the Omni, and Garden Terrance, to put her reconciliation plan into action when one of her former students, dashed over to her, followed by several others.

"Miss Chambers! Sparks! Come quick!" they shouted.

The look on their faces sucked the breath from her lungs.

CHAPTER TWENTY-SIX

AT GARDEN TERRACE, Naomi licked dry lips. My, she was cold. If only Chet would hurry. *Emma, it was for your own good.* How unnatural a mother could Naomi be that a letter from her only child sliced fear through her? She didn't want him to visit. She wanted him where she was safe from him. Where Emma was safe from him. His coming would only mean bad things.

The decades-old unanswered question of how two responsible parents like her and Raymond could have ended up with a son like Kent rumbled through her mind like an empty eighteen-wheeler coming through town. No matter how hard she had worked since and made things happen in Heaven, she couldn't escape that she'd failed as a mother. She'd finally given Kent up for dead after he ran off at eighteen. Based on this, his letter, so casual, with no mention of where he'd been or what he'd been doing, resurrected him and broke her heart anew. Thankfully Raymond had not lived to see this.

"Naomi?" Chet appeared in the open doorway, his hair awry. "You all right?" The concern made Naomi wish she was a clinging woman.

"Where have you been?" As soon as the petulant words were out of her mouth, Naomi wanted to take them back. Chet wasn't the enemy.

He came over and squeezed her right hand briefly. "Don't try your charm on me, Naomi Chambers, I'm immune." His faded gray eyes twinkled. "Now, what's the deal?"

"Kent's back," she quavered, and braced herself to convince Chet that she needed to leave. Now. To her surprise, he merely began putting her belongings into her bag. She would never understand that man. He'd argue till he was blue about whether they should plant a peace rose or a Mr. Lincoln in the front yard, but when she announced the sky was falling, he simply nodded.

She had to get home to Heaven before Kent did, get there before Emma could meet him. Before he started telling the lies that were logical, easy to believe. She understood, since she'd believed enough of them herself.

WHEN EMMA REACHED the parking lot on the south side of the park, dripping with sweat and gasping for breath, her Omni looked only half its size.

The local sheriff was writing something down. Juggy stood beside the vehicle, arms hanging loosely by his sides, his face crumpling further when he saw her. The accident involving her car was already one of the most talked-about events of the Jamboree so far. People standing on their toes, trying to get a good look. Dizzying waves washed over Emma. She wasn't sure if it was from running in the heat, trying to catch up with girls who ran track at Heaven Central, or because her means of escaping the town was now yard art.

"Oh, boy," Sparks breathed.

Knowing she shouldn't, Emma reached out for his hand. He clasped it snugly. Her brain cleared. They would get through this.

The sheriff approached her. Hands on gun belt, he bestowed judgment. "That car's not gonna be running any time soon."

No, her exit from Heaven now would have to include a Greyhound bus.

"The car Juggy was parking. Were the owners from out of town?" She should have changed the insurance liability. She should never have let Juggy park cars. Nomi had been right. No one under thirty should park someone else's car. "Have you identified the owner yet?" she repeated. Let it be someone who had six cars and barely remembered this one. Or someone who felt nostalgic about the continued existence of small towns and wouldn't sue them drier than they already were.

The sheriff looked down at his pad of paper. "One of Heaven's own."

Emma lowered her shoulders from her ears. If not mercy on the town, maybe they would have mercy on Juggy. Maybe he could get the town plows to do their street first this winter. Maybe... "Where's the car Juggy was driving? Is it hurt badly?"

"Parked over there. Not hurt like the Omni."

Some good news at least. Emma's eyes followed his gesture, recognizing the dark green of a Toyota Camry. She groaned. *Heat stroke take me.* It would be preferable to dealing with the owner of this particular car...the car that was parked nightly along the Berlin Wall next door to Nomi.

"I'll talk to Beryl," Sparks offered.

It was tempting. Beryl did like him. Perhaps it was ultimately better to expect nothing good to happen in life, she mused. Then it wasn't a surprise. Hooray that Trinity would headline the Jamboree, hooray that volunteers appeared to be happy, hooray that Ed Groves was bringing in unexpected heaps of money. Bummer that Beryl would sue the present and future coffers of Heaven.

Here comes the flood.

As much as she didn't want to, she needed to tell Beryl about this. As she shook her head, she muttered, "Beryl is not going to let this slide. You don't know her like I do."

"Then, the least I can do is go with you." Sparks linked arms with Emma. "She's on duty at the first-aid station."

He's equally as nice to everyone else, Emma. Remember that. Good thing first aid would be nearby, for Beryl would surely vivisect her with that acid tongue.

With a sigh as deep as the lake, Emma let her arm remain in Sparks's and gathered up Trouble's leash. *Deep breath...another...three's the charm.* No, she still shook.

Approaching the awning and banquet table that served as the first-aid station, Beryl's unmistakable bulk overflowed the folding chair behind it. Pinching her palm hard, Emma swallowed. She skipped a greeting; it sounded more authoritative. "Beryl."

The woman turned toward her, expression somewhat muted in the heavy folds under her eyes. Her gaze warmed, though, as it swung over to Sparks and remained so with a glance back at Emma. Sparks greeted Beryl.

The words rushed out of Emma's mouth before she turned tail and ran. "We've had a slight accident in the parking lot and your car's fender and grill are damaged, for which I take full responsibility." The remaining breath blew out in a gasp.

The hooded eyes regarded her. Emma shifted back and forth, bumping into Trouble. Then Beryl patted the empty folding chair beside her. "Have a seat you two. How's your grandmother? I haven't heard lately."

She'd expected such vitriol to spew from Beryl's mouth that she'd assumed the conversation wouldn't require any further input from her. As Emma sank onto the chair, Trouble disappeared under the table. Sparks turned a chair around so he straddled it and laid his arms across the back.

Beryl's chins quivered. "My car's insured. Don't worry about it."

Emma sat stiffly, back arched away from the chair. *Don't worry about it?* While Sparks began to chat with Beryl, Emma scanned the park in a daze. People milled around talking, eating and laughing. She heard the sounds of a few shrieks, and booth operators hawking their wares. She smelled the ubiquitous popcorn with an undertone of barbecue. But this could *not* be earth, not with the Camry crunched and Beryl acting *civil*...no, downright friendly. Hearing her name, she turned, bemused, back to the others.

While Sparks listened and grinned, Beryl commended her on her organizing the Jamboree. She rubbed Trouble's head while Emma watched closely for the canine's reaction, surprised by the hitch-and-snuggle move of the beast. He liked her. Beryl chuckled at something Sparks said. Minutes passed and Emma's spine relaxed enough for her to lean against the chair. A few times people interrupted them and Emma saw the gruffness she expected from Beryl.

The older woman was impatient with folks who needed bandages or water, cutting them off to sit back down with Emma, where she seemed to have all the time in the world.

Emma said goodbye about half an hour later, and, when she was far enough away from the first-aid booth so Beryl couldn't see her, she rested against the gate to the park's entrance. Only one likely reason existed for Beryl's thaw—a certain tall blond man with a good heart and a beautiful crooked smile.

"You must be magic," she remarked to Sparks, who seemed puzzled. Since Emma already knew he was magic, she figured surely he must know his own power. "What did you do to Beryl?"

Sparks winked. "I promise, all I did was yard work for her."

When a passing tourist mentioned the time, Emma remembered her grandmother and the phone call she'd committed to. Sparks said he needed to meet Ben and took off down the hill.

While walking out of the park the second time, she gave in to pleas of "Try this, Emma" and "New Jamboree tradition, you gotta eat at least a bite" until she'd consumed most of a roasted turkey leg, frozen cheesecake on a stick, a fresh corn dog and half a cup of fresh-squeezed lemonade.

Sucking on the sliver of penuche fudge she'd protested she absolutely had no room for, Emma and Trouble reached Main Street, which resembled a parking lot. She touched her stomach while waiting for her turn to cross. Despite the overeating, the tightness in her stomach that had dogged her for days was gone.

She lifted damp hair off her neck. The Thursday sun was straight overhead when a few raindrops splattered on the sidewalk near her. Then a few more. A *sun* shower? Soon big fat drops sent some more people under her tree while others stood out in the rain and lifted their arms. It had been a strange summer for weather, but she couldn't badmouth water of any type—except the flooding that might destroy Heaven. Intermittent rain guaranteed the rescheduled fireworks. And Sparks would be around a little longer.

You're going to have to deal with that, you know. Yeah, she knew. Emma checked her watch. A jaunt home to leave Trouble in the afternoon cool of the house, then she'd call her grandmother. To be followed by a quick wash, maybe even a quick nap, before going back at it. Tonight was the square dance. Did Sparks dance? A silly question. It wouldn't matter if he did or could. He'd be right in the middle of things regardless. Coiling Trouble's leash around her hand, she decided to make a run for it between the drops.

She glanced up at the still-sunny sky. The awning on the bandstand would come in handy—thanks to Tilly—should the clouds dump precipitation periodically. Leaving the noise of the Jamboree behind, she and Trouble walked down Seraphim. Cool—hot—cool—hot as they passed underneath ancient elm trees shading the sidewalk.

She halted. *I'm loving this.* The loss of her trip softened momentarily. Whether the Jamboree would make the money it needed or if Heaven would slide off the flood list loomed ahead. Sparks and she remained unresolved. But this moment—she resumed her way to Naomi's house with Trouble, savoring a deep breath of summer—*this* moment was good.

At Naomi's, Emma took the steps two at a time before pushing open the front door, unclipping the leash. Time to call her grandmother, break the ice. She let a smile curve her lips. Okay, and to brag a little about how well everything was going.

The jangle of the phone as she shut the door made her jump. How weird would that be if it was Nomi calling? Grabbing the receiver off the charger, she tucked it against her shoulder and chin as she leaned down to take off her sandals. The cool of the time-smoothed hardwood floors on her over-warm feet evoked a sigh.

"Hello?" Moving toward the back door, she opened it for Trouble, but the dog stayed next to her.

"Hello?" a male voice inquired.

Grumpa? Emma's heart seized as she heard what sounded like her grandfather's twang over the phone. She began to rub her forehead while Trouble began to bark, his body crouching low, tail on the ground.

"Trouble! Quiet!" Emma poked her finger

at the dog while she spoke into the receiver. "I'm sorry. I couldn't hear you."

The voice spoke again while Trouble continued his urgent bark.

"I'm sorry. Can you speak louder? The dog's barking... I can't hear you."

Since Trouble refused to quit, she edged around his crouched frame and stepped outside, onto the back steps, and shut the door closed, dampening the noise. What was up with that dog? She'd only heard that danger bark once before, for raccoons in the garbage. Even when Sparks had walked up on the porch for the first time, Trouble hadn't made a peep.

"I said, I'm looking for Naomi Chambers."

Trouble commenced an assault on the other side of the door.

"Who's calling?" she asked, stretching out her legs.

"Oh, a blast from her past, blown back into town."

Emma explained where her grandmother was. There was a short silence, then the voice uttered, "She must have finally blown a gasket!"

Even though whoever this was knew Naomi, Emma didn't like the man's tone. It was one thing for her to think that about her grandmother and quite another for some stranger to say it, no matter how much he sounded like Grumpa.

"Who *is* this?" she asked again, her voice sharpening.

"Sorry. I should have introduced myself." The man chuckled, nevertheless, the hairs on the back of Emma's neck continued to prickle. "To whom do I have the pleasure of speaking?"

"This is her granddaughter, Emma Chambers. Who is this?" As soon as she said her name, Emma bit her lip. She could hear her grandmother's scolding across the years. *Never, never tell someone on the phone who you are before you know who they are.* "Hello?" Emma frowned. The voice had gone silent again. "Are you still there?"

"Yes, I'm here. Her granddaughter, huh? How old are you?"

I don't like this one bit.

"Listen, why are you calling my grandmother? I've now asked you several times, who are you?" In about one second she was hanging up on this guy.

Another sound, rather like a snort.

"I said, who is this?"

"I'm a little late in the info loop, but if you're her granddaughter, I guess that makes me your father."

CHAPTER TWENTY-SEVEN

EMMA MADE HER way back to the Jamboree, bumping into people and muttering apologies. The clipboard's metal clasp was cutting into her chest, the only sensation piercing the numbness, so she knew she was alive. With his voice holding the ghost of Grumpa's drawl, there had been no doubt about what he'd said.

Her father was *alive*. All the dreams, all the fantasies about him were now manifested in a still-faceless voice that held a note of amusement, and what... What had been the other undercurrent?

I have a father. My father is here. In Heaven. On the heels of that thought steamrolled a darker one. Nomi had lied to Emma her whole life. Not only had her grandmother lied and was still lying, but she had punished Emma for lying as a child. *If you tell the truth, you don't have to remember what you said.* It was one of Nomi's mantras.

Emma's knees wobbled and she reached for something to support her. Nothing.

Then Zoo's voice, strong and close, "Are you all right, Emma?" A tanned arm braced her jerking shoulders.

Emma opened her eyes.

"Emma?"

The waft of kennel disinfectant soured Emma's mouth and she put her hand to it. *I will not throw up.* Her stomach begged to differ. She staggered to a cottonwood tree and slid down the rough bark.

"Breathe through your nose. Deep breath in, Emma. In and then slowly out," Zoo instructed from far away.

Right by a cottonwood tree in the town park, landing on her knees, Emma retched.

Curious onlookers slowed. Rolling back on weak legs and pushing against the tree to an upright stance, Emma turned Zoo. "Get me out of here."

Zoo helped her just yards away to her No More Hot Dogs: Hydrate Your Pet booth; Emma sank into a folding chair at the back, semiconcealed behind a couple of easels holding full-color posters on the dangers of leaving your pet in a car during the summer. Zoo handed her a bottle of cold water. Emma rolled it over her superheated face before she uncapped it and drank greedily. She moved just in time to throw up again on the grass.

Gasping, she hung on to the back of the chair while Zoo soaked her bandanna in the water and handed it to her.

"You have to tell me. What did you eat, what did you drink?"

Emma shook her head. "Not that. Ph-phone call. I—I—I got a phone call."

"Are you going to be okay? Is it Naomi?"

Nothing would ever be okay again. Why hadn't her grandmother told her? Emma had been walking around this town for thirty-some years and hadn't figured it out. She'd been told all those whispers were from ignorant people. How stupid did that make her?

"Emma."

"My father is alive."

Zoo's expression slid from concern to confusion.

"Your father is dead."

"Apparently not."

"Smoke jumping a fire in Montana."

"So you've heard the same lie."

Dropping into her own chair, Zoo regarded Emma, skeptically. "You're going to have to explain. Maybe I should get Sparks. He's had emergency training."

"No!" That much she could say. What would he think of her once he knew the family secret?

After Emma finished her story, she took

a tentative sip of water from the bottle. How many people know—knew—every time they looked at her, sat across from her at parent-teacher conferences, stood behind her in line at the post office? The haze filtered back.

"Okay, Emma. Stay with me. Keep talking."

"I don't think he knew I existed." Grumpa had known, too. The shards of betrayal cut cold, deep, and then the blood cooled and numbed. She sipped more water to moisten a desperately dry throat.

Zoo slid to her knees in front of Emma. "I'm so sorry, Ems. I can't find anything to say, except I'm so sorry."

With Zoo watching her as a dog watches a bone, Emma straightened up and stood, swigging the rest of the water. "I had wondered how Sparks felt, knowing his parents didn't want him. At least he understood from the outset and nobody lied to him about it."

"I'm going to find Chet." Zoo leaped to her feet.

"No! I'm sure he's in on it, too." She could not stop crying, gulping, hiccupping.

At that moment, someone came up to the booth, and, after casting a last glance at Emma, Zoo moved away to answer a question.

The Jamboree had faded from Emma's attention until now, when, like a rushing wave, the sounds and smells crashed in—kettle corn, peppers and onions, laughter, the midway. She leaned over and picked up the clipboard she'd dropped. Her first thought was she wanted—*needed*—Sparks. The second thought was she couldn't continue with the Jamboree until she submerged the raw pain, until…until whenever.

Wiping her eyes, she checked the event list and then her watch. Five to three. Had three hours passed since she'd learned her father was alive? Seemed like only a second ago. What she really wanted was to feel Sparks's hands on her neck, making all the pain go away. She drew in a shaky breath. She had to run the Jamboree for four more days, leave on the fifth.

According to the clipboard, it was time to head to the beach. The Silly Sail Race would be starting. Another new idea this year: Jamboree goers bought a chance on so-called "boats." The winner would be the first to sail out to the buoy, circle it, head to the next buoy, do the same and sail back to the finish line. Race requirements mandated a sail made out of material other than sailcloth, and the body of the boat—however uniquely constructed—crewed by two. The prize for winning was a place of honor in the parade.

Staggering down the hill, the babble of excited voices increased. Crowds of people stood around with most of the excitement centered on one entry. A familiar blond head rose above many others. *Help me.*

The sun seared her bare shoulders and stung her head. She'd forgotten her hat. Exhaustion seeped through every pore, softening her bones so that she felt she might totter to the ground. To sleep. To oblivion.

Zoo was eyeing the boats. "I see Sparks is entering a boat. He has quite a crowd around him."

Emma wanted the crowd to go away so she could be alone with Sparks. Maybe then she would cry. If she started crying now, without his arms around her, she wouldn't be able to stop. *I'll sound like some choking, wounded animal.*

"What is it anyway?" Zoo inspected the crazy flotilla cast about on the beach.

Emma shook her head. "I don't know. Ben has all the paperwork for the entries. But I hope whoever is crewing with Sparks has a good life preserver. He's not so good on details."

Below them, she saw Ben push through the crowd and say something to Sparks, gesturing to his clipboard. Sparks puffed his cheeks and started looking around. Apparently not finding who he was searching for, he raised his eyes and spotted Emma and Zoo. He began waving at them, smile wide.

Emma waved back. The tiny zip of pleasure from him looking for her momentarily cauterized her shock of the past three hours. He had a way about him, for sure. Whoever had his attention at the moment must be feeling special.

Sparks broke through the crowd, making his way toward her and Zoo. The midafternoon sun was reddening his tanned forearms. His eyes crinkled under the dingy white cap he wore, and he still sported those ridiculous angel wings and the Made in Heaven T-shirt. "Emma! You'll never guess what…" He paused, his eyes on hers. "What's the matter? What's wrong?"

Not now.

"Nothing. A little too much sun and no hat." And not enough truth. She turned the corners of her mouth up into what she hoped was a grin. "What will I never guess?"

"My crew member broke his ankle in the sack race he was running with his son."

"Ouch," Emma and Zoo exclaimed together.

"I'm sorry, Sparks. I know you were looking forward to this race." Emma raised on tiptoe, trying to get a glimpse of his entry. "What did you end up making as a boat?"

He gestured behind him. "It's down there."

"Ask Ben for a few minutes to find some idiot who will sail with you."

His grin grew wider and more lopsided. "Yeah, he already told me he'd give me ten minutes before he blows the starting whistle."

She pitied the poor fool who crewed with wild-man Sparks Turner. She also knew, as sure as she was standing in the sun and her grandmother was a liar, that despite his less-than-detail-oriented ways, any number of females would jump at the chance. "I'll be cheering you on." Fascinating how the human mind could numb trauma and compartmentalize. Sparks shoved his hands into the pockets of his khaki shorts, making her wonder if he only owned one pair of khaki shorts, or if all his shorts were khaki. Another oddity: the human mind could fixate on one superior pair of male legs when another part of the mind was calculating how far she could run away from her emotional pain. "You'll have to choose from all those clamoring."

"I've already chosen."

Apprehension assailed her when he kept those blue, blue eyes on her. This time the question in them was clear. "I want you to crew with me."

"Sure, Sparks. I'm going to crew with you." When her grandmother stopped lying to her.

His face lit up. As he headed back to the beach at a dead run, he threw the last words over his shoulders. "Better take off your shoes and socks. You're gonna get wet."

"Wait!" she called after him over the sounds of Zoo's chuckles. The man did not understand broad sarcasm. "I am *not* going to crew with you!"

But he was out of earshot and, judging from the clapping and happy nods, he'd already spread the word that his problem was solved.

Emma clenched her back teeth. This day continued its horrific descent. How much worse could it get? "Lightning," she said aloud, making her way down to the beach. That would be worse. Struck by lightning, sitting in a pseudosailboat with a wild man, they would pull her lifeless body from the lake. They'd call her "poor little Emma" again.

Her feet reluctantly started toward Sparks. On her approach, Emma noticed his craft. "I'm not getting into that." She was no boat architect, but a large plastic pool with an add-on bow and a makeshift tarp for a sail harnessed to the floor with paint cans was a blueprint for disaster. Taking a step nearer to confirm her suspicions of unreliability, a swell of cheering and applause rose from the crowd. Just what she needed, an audience for her refusal to get in.

The starting gun popped. She jumped.

"There's the shot! Push, Emma, push!" Sparks dragged the front of the boat into the waves, leaving her on the beach. She hesitated, sighed and ran in, pushing with him. Due to the drought and the resulting recession of the lake, it seemed like forever until the crazy craft floated. Sparks tossed Emma inside it as if she hadn't been eating fries all summer, and then with a final shove, hopped into the back.

"Yee-haw! Duck, Ems! I'm unfurling the sail and the boom!"

She bent over, her forehead splashing in about an inch of water. Oh, yes, this was fun. At Sparks's next command, she raised her head, only to duck again as the boom swung toward her. "We're sailing with my head in the water?"

His reply to these muffled words was a pat on her back. Emma could feel water soaking through the socks and sneakers she'd neglected to take off.

As they headed toward the first buoy, the craft's sail flapped less and less, so Emma did not have to kiss the plastic bottom as frequently. She lifted her head to turn toward Sparks to express an opinion on this whole disaster when he shouted, "Boom! Down!" And he tacked to the right, circling around the buoy.

Slamming her face into the water, her hips arguing on the continued wisdom of sitting cross-legged, Emma fumed. This day... Shifting to the right, she tried to unfold her legs. The movement caused the right side of the boat to wobble and dip and more water poured in.

"Don't move! Don't move!" Sparks yelled, yanking her to the left by her belt loops to balance that crummy excuse for a boat. "Bail, bail!"

"My hips are cramping!" she shrieked. Did nobody care how she felt about anything?

She scrabbled frantically for something with which to bail, but came up empty. "With what?" she asked, turning around, only to be smacked with a full-fledged deer-in-headlights look from Sparks. Muttering unkind things, she ineffectually began to scoop the water out with her hands, but more water continued to pour in. Kind of like her grandmother's lies and omissions. No matter how many were uncovered, there just seemed to be more of them.

The injustice of the summer, linked with her shorts now soaked in the ever-deepening

water—as well as, she noted, no life jackets—
flamed into a gut-deep rage. With the wind
and the boom out of her way, she emitted the
howl of heart pain that had been festering for
longer than she wanted to admit.

"What?" Sparks tapped her on the shoulder.
"I can't hear you in the wind!"

At that, she began to wail as they neared the
second buoy. Other sailors, in crafts equally
as bizarre as theirs, didn't seem to notice her.
Big surprise. The midafternoon sun seared her
face. She would never forgive them. Any of
them.

CHAPTER TWENTY-EIGHT

"No, I don't want you to see me to the door." Emma's sneakers squished against the floorboards in Sparks's car as she gritted her teeth and locked her knees. *Ugh.* "I want to get into the shower." She looked at her watch and then at the rain splatting on the windshield. She had to report soon to Inez at the main entertainment stage. "And lie down for a minute." Anything but think.

"You shouldn't be by yourself." Sparks swung the car along the grass in front of Nomi's house. He put it in Park and hitched around to look at her.

If Emma had not expended the last bit of physical and emotional effort on the boat, she would have laughed at his appearance. Sparks's blond hair was spiked all over, his face reflecting the forgotten detail of applying sunblock. A bruise from the boom, right before they landed in the lake, already darkened his right cheekbone.

"From what I, uh, heard, you…need a friend," he said.

Before they went in the drink and someone had to haul them out, the wind had changed direction, and Sparks had gotten quite an earful of her hollering. Every word shot crystal clear across the water. Then, as she had risen to her knees, the boom had struck between her shoulder blades, Sparks's warning a second too late. She had pitched off the side, Sparks lunging for her. The boat, already unstable with too much water, had capsized.

Wild Man Sparks, it turned out, in addition to forgetting the life vests and a bailer, couldn't swim. She'd had to apply her WSI training to keep them afloat until they were rescued.

"Sometimes if you don't talk about it, it circles around in your head and digs a deeper hole."

"This can't get any worse." She remained in the car, regarding the front of Naomi's house. Home, supposedly. Where she'd grown up, at least. She had to get dry clothes and feed Trouble. The house would be empty. Dry clothes and sleeping seemed the best solution for the aftermath of her screaming rage at just about everybody. She was beyond exhausted.

"If you don't want a…guy around…I'll call Zoo after I walk you to the door. She'll come over and be with you," Sparks urged, sliding out of the car. "I think you're more...drained than you realize... You know, after..." He stood and shut the door, leaving a moist patch on his seat, Emma noticed.

After saving Sparks's life, which he had said nothing about, the least he could do was comply with her wish to be left alone, despite her holding back hot tears as a result of his concern.

She really did want to be by herself. She'd done enough sharing with the world to last her the rest of her life. Unless she was lucky and the world ended tonight, she would meet her father here. Although she would have rather met him anywhere, but the prospect of the town watching the whole scene had made her insist on Naomi's for when they would eventually meet.

Walking up the front steps with a finally silent Sparks, Emma wondered, What does one say to one's father when one has never met him?

Shrugging her shoulders and grateful she had several hours to plan her response, she put it out of her mind. She could already feel the warm deluge of water from the shower and the smell of clean cotton sheets. As she reached for the screen door, she frowned.

"Trouble usually gets all excited and barks when you hit the porch." Sparks halted behind her, so close the summer heat of his body rushed to warm her deep chill.

Would it be so terrible if she collapsed against him? Her eyelids fluttered down. She rocked on her feet. He was so close. Blinking, as though awakening from a dream, she straightened and nodded. "You're right. He's always right by the door so he can escape." Trouble's frenzied barking burst from the backyard. "Hey, I know I left him in the house. It's cooler."

The lead glass in the wooden door behind the screen glinted, then opened slowly from the inside. Her gaze flew to Sparks.

Who was in her grandmother's house? They'd seen Chet at the park.

A man about her height, with the same hazel eyes, pushed open the screen door and stepped through the doorway. Ironically, still soaking wet, her mouth went dry. His smile was wide and also like hers. His straight white teeth showed through thin, pale lips in an even paler face fringed with brown hair flecked with gray. Compared to Sparks's robust and sunburned self, the man resembled unbaked cookie dough without the benefit of color from the chips or raisins. Emma managed to mirror his smile and put out her hand slowly.

"So I have a daughter." His pulling her into an awkward hug made her stumble.

"Uh, hello. You're early." A day early. A lifetime late.

Again their smile was identical. "Yeah, I couldn't wait."

She couldn't stop staring at him, but felt awkward being this close to him, so she disentangled herself. Sparks nodded at the man, excused himself and went past them into the house. An uncharacteristically serious expression had frozen his face. Emma had the feeling that Sparks had no intention of leaving her alone with her father.

"You died smoke jumping." She could hear Trouble barking in the backyard.

Her father's gaze slid away from hers and a moment's silence closed in. "I put that dog in the backyard. Not too friendly, is he?" His expression remained still. "She told you I died?"

"He's friendly to those who deserve it. She told me you died a hero in a Montana fire."

"Oh, a hero. That makes all the difference." He muttered something Emma didn't catch.

"How did you get in?"

He patted his pocket. "This town never changes. Key under the mat."

She could barely identify one emotion before another shot up from her toes: anger, shock, excitement, disbelief and now embarrassment from embracing him in soggy clothes, hair plastered to her head, smelling like lake water. "I'm really wet. I…need to take a shower and…change clothes." She gestured toward the hallway. "If you want to wait, there's the living room."

An enigmatic smile from her father. "I know."

Emma flushed. "Oh, right."

"Think you might offer me a drink?" He pushed his hands into jeans' pockets. "I'm sorry. I couldn't wait, now that I know you…"

"Exist?" So he'd really wanted to meet her. All those years Naomi kept them apart. Emma's rage at her grandmother fanned itself back to white hot.

Sparks had come into the hallway with a now quiet, though still obviously hostile, Trouble. "I'll get you something." He glanced at Emma. "You go. I'll raid the fridge." He grinned and gave her a little push. "It's not as though I haven't before." Without Trouble, who refused to leave Emma, Sparks moved toward the kitchen.

"No wedding ring. Must be the boyfriend?" her father asked, with Sparks still within earshot.

Emma flushed. "Coworker," she replied, looking down at Trouble, who had not taken his eyes off Kent.

How to explain Sparks?

DOWN THE HALL, in her room... Her father's old room... Emma closed the door, Trouble shooting in at the last minute. She held the doorknob tightly, trying to find the center in a life spinning out of sync again. When her hand began to cramp, she released the knob. Shoulders sagging, she pulled off the T-shirt and jiggled out of her shorts.

The first day of the Jamboree already felt a hundred years long. Running her tongue around her teeth, she threw on her robe and walked to the bathroom. She could hear her father's voice farther down the hall—*her father's voice*—and Sparks's one-word responses. Sparks, ever friendly and full of conversation, was cool toward her father. What was up with that?

Moments later, she sighed with pleasure after brushing her teeth. She then turned on the shower, stripped off her underwear and stepped under the water. As the warm drops hit her bent head, she dissolved into tears.

She wasn't ready for this, but how would someone get ready for a family secret that negated everything she'd been told? It would take months to sort the lies out. A lifetime to get over it, if she ever did.

"If I'd read a novel like this, I wouldn't believe it could have a happy ending." The more she massaged her head with tired fingers, the more the citrus fragrance clarified her thoughts.

That was all she wanted, a happy ending. Though only a master novelist could make a happy ending from a mess that looked as if it could still get worse.

She had not only broken her promise to her grandfather, who had kept this secret from her, but she'd lost her dream trip. What else? "Find a father, one who isn't dead, but one the friendliest dog in town doesn't like. Oh, and the guy I never should have fallen in love with but did leaves after the Jamboree." She continued ticking off the crises as she stepped out of the shower, the open window under the pulled shade chilling her body despite the high temperature outside. "And no job."

Yanking a puffy terry bath sheet off the towel rack, she rubbed her shoulders and legs and then wrapped the towel around her, catching a quick look in the mirror. She looked like someone the Red Cross had plucked off the roof of a house. Pulling on her robe, she scuttled back to her room where she dressed quickly, stepping over a snuffling Trouble.

Her father—her father—sat in the kitchen. She had to help Inez with the talent show an hour before its seven o'clock start…but her father wanted to get to know her so badly he had come a day early. He'd *come*. Another sigh. She wanted to skip to the end of this book and see how it all turned out.

Emma took another fast glance in the mirror and shook her head to loosen up her wet hair. "So what do I do?"

Trouble turned at the sound of her voice, then back to the door.

Grabbing her shoes in one hand, she pulled the door open a crack. The dog barked, squeezed through the opening and sprinted down the hall. Right now, she'd find out more about who her teen mother was, hopefully where she was and why she had abandoned her baby and vanished. So many secrets would be solved this day. What else hadn't her grandmother told her?

As she entered the kitchen, Trouble moved from Sparks's side to Emma's. Sparks was leaning against the counter under the cabinets, bulky arms crossed against his chest, a rare frown between his dark eyebrows.

Emma's eyes darted to Kent, who sat at the

table finishing up a sandwich. He looked up, smiling.

"So—Emma, is it?"

Absolutely surreal.

"Yes. Kent, is it?" Her pique slipped out. *For Pete's sake, remember my name,* Dad.

"My mother actually said I was dead?"

Sparks spoke up. "Kent and I have been talking about what he remembers from growing up in Heaven and stuff like the Jamboree." A line remained carved in Sparks's tanned, smooth forehead.

She noted the protective stiff-legged stance that Sparks and the dog were currently sharing.

Her father took a deep swig of coffee, grimaced and set the mug down. Sparks must have made the coffee. Leaning away from the table to balance on the back legs of the chair, her father laced his fingers behind his head. Emma used to get in trouble for the chair thing. "There's a reason chairs have four legs, Emma," Nomi would say.

"Yeah, growing up in Heaven was hell." He chuckled. "Everyone knowing your business and having an opinion on it. Narrow thinking, if you ask me." He winked at Emma, who had finally moved in from the doorway and sat opposite him. "I'm more of a free thinker."

Sparks waved the coffeepot at her. She shook her head.

Her father laughed. "You must have had this guy's coffee before. It's worse than in the joint."

Emma stopped breathing. *The joint?* Her face must have telegraphed her reaction, for Kent lost the smile and brought the chair back to rest on all four legs.

"Guess I should have said that a little better." He chewed on his bottom lip and stared at the tablecloth. "I was in prison for a while."

"Twenty-nine years," Sparks supplied, his arms still crossed. Her father flushed.

Emma looked over at Sparks.

"We've been talking."

"Yeah, it was an unfortunate incarceration," her father said, playing with his mug. "It wasn't my fault."

The phrase sounded familiar. She stretched her ankles under the table. Oh, yes, a standard excuse from junior high students. Perhaps, she reflected, chastising herself for the sarcasm, if she hadn't swallowed half the lake within the past hour, she might be in a friendlier mood. Rising hostility wouldn't make a good first impression.

"What about my moth—"

"I got some bad drugs and the stuff made me crazy."

"Crazy enough to do what?" She shook her head. "Never mind. I don't want to know."

Trouble growled and moved closer to her. Her father stopped twiddling the mug and regarded her like a cat watching a mouse. His easy smile returned. "You're like me. Like father, like daughter. I say, why dwell on the past when the future's where it's at?"

Emma jumped up and yanked open the fridge, the cool air decreasing the flush she felt in her cheeks. Grabbing a container of yogurt, she pulled a spoon from the drawer and leaned against the counter next to the fridge. She opened the lid and stirred its contents. While her stomach was rumbling, she wasn't sure she could keep anything down. She took a tentative spoonful, swallowed and waited.

So her father wanted to forget the past. *Not so fast, buddy.* She'd lived it, was still hearing whispers about it. *You don't appear in my life and get to erase what doesn't suit you.*

She stuck out her jaw. "I have some questions about the past."

Sparks turned and filled his coffee cup from the coffeemaker. Looking at her over the rim of his cup, he nodded. "I think you should ask all the questions you want." He turned to Kent. "Don't you? After all these years?"

Her father laughed.

She glared at him. Was everything a joke?

Her look didn't seem to faze him, but then, in *the joint*, he must have encountered worse glares.

He looked amused. "It must be weird for you to have me show up."

That's an understatement.

"It's weird for me too. Trust my mother not to tell me."

"You've been in touch with Nomi all these years?" she blurted.

A slight flush tinged his pale skin. "Is that what you call her? Yeah, *Grandma* doesn't really fit her, does it?" The color faded from his cheeks. "No, I haven't, but she should have found me and told me. I would have come right home. I'd have been a fun dad." The easy smile returned. "First I'd have taken you away from this place. We would have had a great time, you and me."

"You've been in prison about as long as I've been alive," she pointed out, poking the spoon in his direction. "How could you have come and gotten me?" Emma checked her watch. Less than twenty minutes until the talent show. She was losing her window of opportunity to find out who her mother was.

"I meant that it would have changed my life and things that happened wouldn't have happened. A kid changes things."

Child, please. She wasn't a goat. Petty comebacks. What was the matter with her? A dream come true sat in front of her, yet so many questions still lingered. She couldn't handle much more. She traded the yogurt for a glass of water.

Sparks banged his coffee cup down; both Kent and Emma jumped. He ran his fingers through his hair. "Isn't it about time for the talent show, Emma? We better be going." He turned and put his cup under the faucet, swirling water around in it, and then opened the dishwasher and put it in. *How housebroken he is* flittered across her mind, again reminding her of mental compartments that continued as though life were normal.

She stood up. "Just one question. At least for right now."

Her father's eyes narrowed so slightly she thought she'd imagined it. She concluded she must have imagined it, for his smile was in place with the next blink.

"Sure. Shoot." He laughed.

Emma swallowed the bile, shoved her hands into her pockets where she clenched her fists. "Who's my—"

The screen door squeaked and then slammed.

Emma raised her eyebrows at Sparks and he shrugged, his expression telling her he was as puzzled as she was. Considering the kind of day it had been, Emma wouldn't have been surprised if her mother walked in. She heard shuffling steps accompanied by Chet's soothing voice.

Emma froze by the counter, clutching the glass. *It's her.*

She slid a peek at her father to gauge his reaction at seeing his mother after all these years. A couple of expressions flickered across his face, but since Emma didn't know him, she couldn't tell what they were. Some kind of hurt, maybe, erased and followed by something that chilled his doughy features. She gulped her water.

Trouble barreled out of the kitchen with a happy yip. The shuffling halted for a few breaths, then the click, slide, click, slide resumed on the hardwood floor. It took agonizing seconds for the pattern to near the kitchen door. *Go. Run. Do something.*

The shuffling stopped. The trio in the kitchen jerked their heads simultaneously toward the silence.

Three generations of Chamberses locked eyes.

CHAPTER TWENTY-NINE

EMMA NOTICED A new look had slipped over her father's face. Solicitous. Bland. He rose from his chair and offered it to his mother. "You don't look too steady there."

"She's steady as can be expected, Kent."

Emma heard the edge in Chet's voice. Exasperation directed at her grandmother, she had heard from Chet. Indignation, yes, but never a thin edge of steel that belied his sparse white hair and age-spotted hands.

Kent nodded, helping Naomi into the chair. She peered at him, drawing her arm away with great effort.

"You're so p-pale."

Her dragging speech ripped at Emma. Nomi's words were always crisp, blunt, perfectly articulated. Part of her wanted to shriek at her grandmother; the other part wept for her. How could she hate and love this woman at the same time? She couldn't. She must put some distance between her and Nomi.

Chet tenderly mopped her grandmother's brow with his red bandanna, then he looked up at her.

"Hi, E. How's the Jamboree going?" He stood protectively next to Naomi, who was also looking at her. Meanwhile, Sparks had remained by Emma's side. Two knights guarding their women? *I wish.* The desire flashed fresh and clean out of the chaos tumbling in her mind.

The Jamboree. The talent show. Her escape. She checked her watch. She had exactly ten minutes to hightail it over to the park to help direct budding divas and comedians on stage. Inez would panic if she didn't get there pronto.

"I've got to go!" Relief poured through her words. *To do that,* she reminded herself, *you have to move your legs. Now.* She avoided everyone's gaze: Chet's pleading, Sparks's wide eyes, Naomi's fixed look and, finally, her father's considering assessment. She grabbed the clipboard from the table, said goodbye to no one and everyone and left the room.

"I'll go with you," Sparks called out.

She noticed Trouble didn't leave Naomi's side to escort Emma out.

With the screen door slammed behind her—*take that, Nomi*—Emma hit the sidewalk running. One big happy family they were not.

NAOMI TURNED HER head to get a good look at her son after Emma and Sparks blew out the front door. He looked so old.

He was a middle-aged man now, not the handsome boy of eighteen who'd stolen what money he could find in the house and hurled obscenities about how he was getting the hell out of this town. He'd roared off in that noisy truck of his and she'd never heard from him again.

Until that letter.

She'd made up the hero lie on a weak day when Emma had asked for the hundredth time where her daddy was.

"Been a while, huh, Mother?" The smile still curved like Emma's.

"You look..." What could she say? He looked puffy, older than his forty-seven years. He looked tense. But then he'd always looked like he was waiting to go somewhere other than where he was. She noticed his jiggling knee.

"Old?" He clucked. "Yeah, prison tends to age people. But you should see the other guys. I look great compared to them." The grin.

Surely, he hadn't said *prison*. Her heart seized and she struggled to breathe. Chet moved away from Naomi's side to sit across the table from them.

She needed him near. If only it was just she and Chet in this kitchen with its yellow and white, so cozy in winter and cool in summer. She had turned down many of his marriage proposals. Would he ask again? If he asked right now, she might say yes.

Kent leaned on his elbows. He appeared at ease, betrayed only by a jumping knee. "I sent you that letter from Seattle. Things weren't working out for me there, so I thought I'd come home to see you and Dad." His smile briefly slipped, revealing the despondency she remembered and despaired of; it was quickly gone. "I found out about Dad when I stopped at the bank on the way into town. I didn't recognize the teller."

Was that how he had learned about Emma? If only she had gotten home before him.

Years ago, the girl had said the same thing that night Emma arrived. Things weren't working out for her to be a mother. That, combined with the mention of Raymond just now, tightened Naomi's throat. She was glad her husband wasn't here for this.

"I'd have called or sent flowers if I'd known," her son said.

Uncertainty pulled at Naomi's heart. Maybe he would have.

Back then, that night, the stocky woman she

so disliked, wearing a wrinkled white uniform, had come up the walk behind the girl. The girl had half twisted to see who it was, then sullenly turned her back on the newcomer. Given their physical resemblance, it had solved the mystery of the girl's identity, but didn't improve matters.

Now, at the kitchen, across from the baby's father, she thought about how hard she had worked to accomplish her vow to do better by her granddaughter, no matter what the cost. But then there was Emma's surly mouth and stormy departure moments ago. Had she done enough to negate the selfishness of Emma's parents?

Kent peered at Naomi, the smile drooping. "You look a million miles away. Thinking of Dad? I would have been here for him. For you."

As he spoke, the words cooled her warming heart. They were Kent words, easy words. Words never acted on, never followed through on, though still, always the right words, the right expressions.

"How l-long are you s-staying?" Darn her tongue, tripping her now. It happened when she was tired. Showing herself strong was her only defense against his lies. She needed to know why he'd come…come now.

As Naomi had entered through the doorway, seen the bleakness in her granddaughter's eyes, a deep trembling had commenced. What had Kent said to her before Naomi had gotten there? Would he sense Sparks and Emma's growing attraction and strive to drive a wedge between them? She trusted nothing about the man.

"Now that I know I have a kid, I want to be a father, since I was never given the chance." He drained the last of the coffee from his cup, stood and placed it in the dishwasher.

"Glad to hear that, Kent. Emma's an amazing young woman. Her grandmother and grandfather did a fine job." Chet's voice lingered on *grandmother* and *grandfather*. He had never been taken in by Kent.

Trouble growled whenever Kent raised his hands.

Household things he'd never done in his life, Naomi thought, watching him wipe the table. Maybe she was looking at him the wrong way. She wanted a second chance with Emma. Why couldn't she give him one? *Don't you want a second chance with your son?* the exasperated little voice that often chattered in her ear piped in. She hesitated. She was so tired.

Kent moved toward the doorway. "I'll get my suitcase from the car and put it in my old room." He walked over to Naomi and put a hand softly on her shoulder. "I would have helped you settle Dad's estate if I'd known."

Stay here? He didn't even ask. He'd always been like that. But then again, this was his home. Or was it, considering how he left all those years ago? She was having trouble thinking clearly.

"N-no." Was that weak voice *hers*?

"C'mon, Mom. I'm finally home again, doesn't that count for something?"

Maybe this time…their relationship would change. They needed each other, could help each other.

"Emma's in your room. You'll have to take the couch." Chet's voice chipped out the words.

Naomi spoke up. "Kent, it will b-be busy here. The therapists will be here. Chet and Sparks will be c-coming in and out…and Emma." Silly, but she wanted Kent to know she wouldn't be completely alone.

CHAPTER THIRTY

"Emma?" Sparks didn't recognize her in the darkness at first. It had been difficult to locate her, as so many people had shown up to participate in family field games and to eat their way through the various food booths until the talent show started.

She sat on the hill above the beach, looking as if someone had sucker punched her. His protective desire rose again. And this time he wasn't going to get hung up on Emma as civil servant. His time with her was running out, and the appearance of the sleaze who claimed to be her father had ramped up his sense of urgency to declare himself to Emma. To support her.

With an overflowing hard-roll sandwich in his hand, he hunkered down beside her. Her eyes flicked over the sausage, peppers and onions and then turned away. "I am so sorry you had to be in on all that—" she paused, searching for the word "—drama. It must have been even more embarrassing for you than me screaming on the lake earlier."

He was close enough to see the hazel eyes radiating raw hurt, which made his heart ache. If only he could have gotten everyone to relax and mellow out. Instead, he'd been fighting the intense urge to throw her dad out the door.

Somehow, being with her during that… trouble, he knew it was where he was supposed to be. It had been a revelation. He'd spent his life avoiding conflict and issues, even more since his last day as a smoke jumper. No more. Tonight, if he died trying to get the words out, he was going to tell her they needed each other. He swallowed hard. "Man, the tension sucked the oxygen out of the air in that kitchen," he said.

A bubble of laughter popped up out of her. Good.

"Probably not what you'd expect from a family reunion," she answered, turning back to the lake.

"No," he said, relieved she didn't think he was a jerk for his comment. "More like some awful reality show. You really didn't know your father was alive?"

In her next breath, a dam must have broken inside. "No, and that makes me feel stupid. As if I should have figured it out. How could she lie to me like that for years? So if he's alive, is my mother? How many people in town knew and thought I was an idiot? Why didn't some-one, anyone, during all these years, tell me? Or maybe I did hear and discounted it because of what *she* told me."

While she talked, the sounds of the midway filled the park. Someone had burned a batch of kettle corn. He kept eating, with nothing pro-found to say. If he chewed long enough, some-thing tender and heartfelt would come to him.

"Sorry to dump on you. End of ranting." Emma lifted her hair off her neck.

Sparks swallowed the last bite of his roll too fast and choked. He wanted to hold her, kiss her even. Tell her she would be all right.

The temperature had cooled off some with the rain, yet it was still hot. But when Emma actually shivered, he did move closer and put his arm around her, holding his breath that she wouldn't freeze up and bolt away. With what she'd been through at the house, how could she trust anyone? With more intensity than he'd ever wanted anything, he wanted her to trust him. Forever. "You're cold?"

"Not really. Just feels good to have the breeze on my skin. And—have you close." The last words limped out of her mouth, and she snuggled into his shoulder. She fit right into the spot. Turning to look at the lights of the Jamboree, she sighed. "It feels good to sit and stare."

So they did, until the urgency to get on with it pushed him to speak.

"Wanna go for a swim?" He winced. There he was, backing away again from what he really wanted to say. If he lost Emma, he lost it all. The job wouldn't matter, the travel wouldn't matter and he'd be stuck watching reruns at 3:00 a.m. for the rest of his life.

Bless her, she laughed at his offer. The woman was a saint.

"No, thanks. I've had enough water for a while."

"I'm sorry about the boat." *Still rambling, Sparks.* "Sorry I forgot the life preservers... and a bailer. Thanks for saving my life." *In so many ways.*

"No problem." She faced him, the hazel eyes widening.

Say it, say it. "I've been thinking." His eyes never left hers. His voice rasped, roughened by swallowing lake water. "I've learned a lot from you."

Her body stiffened. "Like...that your life's better off than mine?"

He tightened his hold. "No, that you *stay.* Family, or community, stays. When people heard about the town being on the flood list, they stayed to fight for Heaven. They still don't know if they'll win. You didn't want to give up your trip, but you came and stayed because Naomi's family." Sparks released Emma and leaned back in the grass, regarding her. "After Mother Egan's, I've never stayed anywhere long—no longer than to prep a show."

"I think I've made a mistake by staying here." Her tone was bitter.

"Now, *that* is drama."

Her tone iced. "You know, I have too much going on in my life right now to try to be what you want. This is me right now. I'm hurt and I'm mad. I'm sure Tilly's daughter is in a better mood. Go find her."

Placing his hands on her shoulders, he leaned close, blue eyes on hazel. "I'm not doing this right. Give me another chance?"

Those hazel eyes regarded him frostily. "What?"

"I want—I want to try staying, like you. Get a home base. *Here*." There, it was out.

"I want to leave and sort things out," she replied.

Not the response he was looking for, but once he said this right, she would change her mind. "What—what I mean is, I want to be with *you*."

The hazel eyes softened so dramatically his breath hitched.

"What do I have that you could possibly want?" Her eyes remained on his.

"Loyalty, faithfulness, tenacity."

The corners of her mouth turned down. "You sound as though you're talking about Trouble. Your approach needs a little work. Like my smoldering eyes, my unbelievable beauty or my sparkling wit."

"You're *home*."

"Okay, that was a *lot* better." The lips curved into a full smile. Emma swallowed and her voice croaked. "I don't want you to commit to me. I may not be worthy of anyone committing. I haven't remotely reached the fun-in-dysfunctional stage, I'm unemployed, homeless and I'm leaving Tuesday."

Tuesday. A flash of life without her chilled the summer air. He'd learned enough about Emma to know she now meant what she said. Before she left, he had to make her realize he was worth taking a chance on, even with—everything.

CHAPTER THIRTY-ONE

WHEN A ROOSTER somewhere crowed for the third time, Emma opened her eyes. Where the heck was a rooster? Oh, right. She'd spent the night at Zoo's. Chet and Sparks had suggested she needed a twenty-four-hour break after Thursday's events. Chet would remain by Nomi's side and—Emma was sure—keep an eye on Kent.

With relief, she'd handed over all her duties for the day to Tilly, who'd only nodded and given her a quick hug, asking no questions.

She swung her feet over the side of the bed, blearily remembering it was the Fourth of July. Although she wasn't feeling particularly festive.

As she stood, the sheets scratched her new sunburn from spending the previous day on Promise Island with Sparks. An oasis in this conflict. Still, she was glad she'd be confronting her father alone later, because really, how much could Sparks hear before he rethought his wanting to spend time with her?

Last night rushed back. Sparks had said everything she'd ever wanted to hear from a man. Tears stung. Too many other crises short-circuited her permanently wrapping her heart around his words. She'd tried to show him she wanted to be in a relationship with him... though maybe it would have to be another time, another place.

Their day had been glorious, and she resolutely placed interrogating her father back far enough in her mind that it disappeared entirely thanks to the pleasure of the island and Sparks's company. If she never saw him again—a tear slid down her cheek—she could treasure their final time together.

She stretched and rolled her shoulders forward and backward, then grabbed her clothes off the chair by the bed and dressed. *Saturday morning.*

Today, however, was the day she would tackle a discussion with her father.

Forty-five minutes later, Emma let herself into Naomi's. Early-morning quiet prevailed, yet the smell of toast and coffee tinged the air. Since she wasn't talking to Naomi yet— second on her list—Kent would have to supply her mother's name. He wasn't on the couch, so he must be the one with breakfast. She heard

Trouble's dog tags clink against the floor in her grandmother's room, but he didn't appear.

Her father did his best to avoid the past, but she couldn't blame him a bit. There didn't appear to be much in Heaven that was a happy memory for him. Although she, too, had suffered at whispers and still lived under Naomi's imposing influence, she had realized this summer spent in town was filled with a lot of good memories for her. Regardless, she would have to get him talking about the ol' days. Unless she came right out and asked him about the identity of her mother, and all the other questions that were rattling around in her brain?

Bluntness wasn't—or hadn't been—her strong suit, although, over the past weeks, and especially the previous few days, she'd blurted out more than she ever had before. She'd just have to ask.

As she entered the kitchen, Kent was spreading peanut butter on buttered toast.

"Hey, beautiful," he greeted her, their common smile lighting his face. "You get up to be with me?"

It was straight out of her dreams: breakfast with Dad. She smiled back and put more bread in the toaster, folding the wrapper back around the bread with the twist tie. Why should a dad matter now, after all these years? She thought about Sparks, how he hung around Chet, thought every word that fell from his lips was a diamond. Maybe people never lost wanting their parents around.

"Why don't we eat out in the backyard? It's nice in the morning," she said, eyebrows raised in a question.

"Anything you say." Kent stood up and filled his cup again from the coffeemaker. "I talked with that boyfriend of yours last night at the Jamboree. Couldn't find you in the crowd. More people than I've ever seen at one of those things, and I saw a lot of them growing up."

Delight shot through her. *He looked for me.*

"Yeah, he sure asks a lot of questions. Must make a ton of money doing those fireworks."

Kent had set off quite a buzz at his return. Some people had come up to her to express their shock and dig for more information. Others, when she stopped at the IGA or wherever, avoided her, zooming off in another direction. She hazarded all of Heaven knew Naomi had lied. From what Chet had said, Kent still looked enough like he had when he lived here for people to figure out who he was.

"He—he's a great guy, but we're—we're not a couple." She filled her mug. Those words didn't sit right.

Kent laughed his nasal snort. "You're like me. Lots of fish in the sea."

Not really.

The toast popped up. Emma spread butter and then peanut butter on the two slices. Prior to seeing her father do the same, she thought she was the only person who did both butter and peanut butter on toast. How did her mother prepare her toast? Emma added it to the list of questions she would ask.

She balanced her plate and cup and walked to the back door and pulled it open. After the steps, they headed toward the cottonwood tree where two plastic lawn chairs sat. Together, she and her father ate in silence; she tried to watch him when he wasn't looking and knew he was doing the same. A couple of mourning doves cooed on the Berlin Wall, with Beryl's garden sending over fragrance from unseen flowers. As she crunched her cooling toast, Emma heard Beryl moving near the fence. What did the woman do in her backyard for hours? She must have quite the garden.

These questions with no answers danced with the others in her head, and after trying to sort them into categories, Emma tabled them. Might there be another woman walking around Heaven with a heavy secret?

Her father smacked his lips on the last sip

of coffee and set the mug down on the lawn. "I overheard someone at the IGA say before Dad died, you and him had a big trip planned."

Emma nodded. It seemed like decades ago.

"You must have saved a long time for that trip."

Emma took another swallow of coffee to wash down the now-cooled toast. "I did."

"If I'd been around, I could have helped you invest that and make a mint."

"That might have shortened the time it took. I liked the people I worked with, though. Teaching's more interesting, being with the kids and all, but the money was better with curriculum development." Time to turn this conversation around. "What do you want to do now that you're…"

"Free?" Something dropped behind Beryl's side of the fence. They turned toward the sound, then back to each other.

"Yeah."

"I've got some ideas that will net me some serious cash. The money's out there if you're smart enough to find it."

"That's great. Tell me who you dated, growing up stories, you know, that kind of stuff."

He laughed and shook his head. "Don't dwell on the past, that's what I say."

Emma frowned, sliding an edge into her

voice. "I need the past to put you in my present to see if maybe we have a future."

"Well, since you put it like that—" Heaving a sigh, he began, "I've never had a problem with the ladies. Mother tried to get me into all the stupid clubs at school. She even tried to get me to play sports. Not my thing. I'm better at the head stuff than the muscle stuff. I was ready for the real world and taking risks. Considering that trip you and Dad planned, you're like me. How much does a trip like that set you back?"

"Yeah. Enough." Indeed, in the face of direct questions, this allergy to talking about the past was worse than she'd imagined.

"Which of the ladies was my mother?" Putting the mug to her lips, she watched him over the rim.

Kent glanced at her sharply, then as realization dawned, wagged his head. "You don't know?" His jaw tightened, twitching a muscle in his cheek.

A hot flush suffused Emma's face, and for a moment she couldn't speak, couldn't think.

"Sorry." He looked around the yard. "Leave it to my mother to let someone clean up after her. How did you get to my parents' in the first place? When's your birthday?"

She choked out her birth date with a halting

summary of what she knew. That her mother had asked Nomi and Grumpa to take care of her, and that she'd never come back. "When I was little, I'd ask Nomi about what happened, but all she ever said was that it would make me sad. So eventually I gave up asking."

Pursing his lips, her father stared past her at the Berlin Wall. The moments ticked by. Emma envisioned a parade of women walking through his mind. He looked again at the Berlin Wall. A low whistle issued from his lips. "It could be…huh. I bet it's Jeanine. Timing's about right." He looked at her as if he was seeing her for the first time. "I remember she had the same nose. Well, I'll be."

His laugh grated on her ears. "Jeanine Winsome's girl…"

The roar in Emma's ears blocked out any words that followed. Her mother was Beryl's daughter? Who even knew that Beryl had a daughter?

Her father burst into chuckles at her expression, even slapping his knee.

Emma's neck stiffened. "You *think* it was her, given the dates?"

His Adam's apple bobbed, his smile no longer assured in the face of her ire.

"I—I'm not sure. She was here and then gone." Kent opened his mouth to say more, closed it partway, appeared to reconsider his answer and then simply shrugged.

"I didn't know Beryl had a daughter."

"Neither did I, until Jeanine showed up that night. Dad was out of town on bank business and Mother, of course, was still at work. Jeanine came to the wrong house."

"What do you mean, the wrong house?"

"She was looking for her real mother."

Was nothing related to her life up front and easy to understand? "Beryl wasn't her real mother? But you said—"

"If you'd quit interrupting, you'd find out," her father snapped. "Beryl had Jeanine when she was a kid herself and gave her up for adoption."

"What was my moth—Jeanine like?"

"Jeanine? She was seventeen. She had a great body and hair like yours—kinky. When she knocked on the door, I'd had a few beers by then. Kept 'em stashed in the shed that used to be back here. Offered her one, and the rest, I guess…" He trailed off, not meeting Emma's eyes.

"Is me."

"So to speak. We partied the rest of the afternoon. Right before Mother came home, we drove in my truck to the top of a hill outside town. As soon it got dark, she ripped off her shirt, danced around and screamed at the moon." Reaching down to pick up his mug, he looked in it and snorted. "She left a few hours later… She said she was going to Beryl's." Now he watched her. "You asked."

"You never knew she was pregnant?"

He leaned back in his chair, front legs off the ground. "You're talking about a girl who screamed at the moon. I never saw her again." His voice dropped away. "She swore she was on the Pill. They all do."

Emma stood up so quickly his chair fell backward. It startled her father and he flailed to catch his balance.

She turned on her heel toward the garden gate.

He sputtered and called after her, "You can't blame me. She wanted it."

Emma didn't turn around.

He called after her again. "Where are you going?"

She whirled. His expression had changed into something ugly, but fear didn't pierce her rage.

"To introduce myself to my *grandmother*."

With that, she ran from the backyard, slamming the gate so loudly Trouble objected inside the house. It would wake her grandmother if the raised voices hadn't already. Tough.

Beryl Winsome. Naomi Chambers.

Sparks was the lucky one. He was the orphan.

CHAPTER THIRTY-TWO

ON EACH SIDE of Beryl's cracked walk, the grass was neatly trimmed, the result of Sparks's work, Emma knew. Blown along by a spreading maelstrom of abandonment, Emma raced up the walk, trying to slow down her heartbeat. *Breathe in, breathe out.*

Climbing the steps, she remembered this was the house that didn't like kids, that kept balls that went over the fence...that housed the witch who lived inside. Today, the Victorian gingerbread trim was freshly painted, again, thanks to Sparks, and nary a weed intruded in tidy pots of geraniums on the porch. Emma banged on the door. She would have her answers.

"Beryl!" She kept on pounding. She waited, then raised her fist to pound again, when the door slowly swung inward. Emma quickly lowered her hand when Beryl gasped and took an involuntary step backward.

The older woman stood still, backlit by the morning light. For a moment, granddaughter and grandmother surveyed each other, as though they hadn't met in the grocery store, the post office and in church for years, Emma seeing nothing in the stout lady's face that resembled her own.

"I guess you'd better come in," Beryl said at last, stepping aside.

"I guess I'd better." Emma darted over the threshold and then stopped, at a loss as to what to do next. As she scanned the main room, a familiar photo in a crystal frame caught her eyes. It sat on a coffee table placed in front of a worn love seat. It was Emma…in her cap and gown from high school. Taking a step closer, she noted smaller framed snapshots of herself at different ages: on her first two-wheeler, as a potato in a school play, with a tennis trophy in high school.

The most recent photo was one Grumpa had taken of her shortly before he died. When she looked to Beryl, a frown creasing her forehead, her arms prickled.

A knock sounded on the door. Beryl moved toward it and in bounced Sparks, concern wrinkling his face. "I was just over at Naomi's. Your— Kent told me you came here. Hi, Beryl." His grin at the older woman flashed full and real. Like him.

Beryl gestured to the love seat. "Sit down.

Do you, um, want something to drink?" She trailed off as though rusty with hospitality.

Emma's militancy fizzled out. "No…thank you," she said quietly. "What I want are answers." She fell onto the green love seat.

"You shall have them." Beryl sat down across from her on an equally shabby mustard-colored velour chair, nearly filling it with her bulk. She folded her hands. This took the rest of the wind out of Emma's sails. A tight silence filled the space between them.

Emma crossed her ankles, leaned forward and plunged in. "Is your daughter my mother?"

"Yes."

"Jeanine was your daughter." She needed to hear precise words. Sparks lowered himself to the love seat, requiring her to move away or their thighs would be touching. She didn't move.

"Yes. I had her when I was seventeen. My parents made me give her up. Later I figured she was better off, given how my life had gone." Beryl's eyes never shifted off Emma's.

So many questions. "When did you meet her?"

"She found me the day Kent met her. She went to the wrong house and asked Kent where I lived. After their—time together, she came to see me."

"How come she didn't stay?"

Beryl hesitated so long Emma feared she wouldn't tell her. "I think she was disappointed with what she found."

Sparks leaped up and began to pace.

It must have been a painful admission; Emma admired her for making it. "Did you see her again before she came back with me?"

"No."

Silence. Sparks's voice rang out from behind her, where he'd paused in his marching. She jumped.

"Ask it, Emma. You've got to ask."

He was reading her mind again. He surely had the same questions that he'd never had answered.

"Why did she give me away?" The hurt underneath that question rubbed like salt in an open cut.

"I assume Jeanine thought it would be fun to have a baby and do what she wanted because she was the mother." Beryl sighed and rubbed her knuckles through her short gray hair.

"She must have been surprised." Babies had feelings. *This baby's feelings were bursting all boundaries.* Emma wanted to scream, cry, pound her heels and throw things. But she made herself sit still, lean against the cushions, will her spine to relax.

"Eight hours after you were born, she realized she couldn't handle it. Discharge questions like where are you going to live, how will you support the baby, who will provide medical care. Things like that." A tiny smile lifted the corner of Beryl's mouth.

Emma looked toward the most recent photo, then swept through all of them again. No new pictures after her grandfather had died.

"Grumpa gave you all these photos."

Sparks leaned over and squeezed Emma's shoulder. "Why not tell her once she was older?" A second squeeze. "Sorry—"

"No, it's all right." *So very all right*, Emma thought. She wasn't alone. He *saw* her, knew what she was feeling.

"He was my operative, I guess you could say. He wouldn't cross Naomi openly, but he felt— I had rights." Beryl's voice trembled. "Even though I was the invisible grandmother."

Emma started at the word *invisible*. "Why didn't she bring me here? You're her mother."

"She did. At first." A lengthy pause filled every corner of the room. The older woman lifted her eyes from her lap. "We had words." The familiar bitterness flashed across Beryl's face. "She wrapped you up, said she'd take you to Kent's, where they had some class and money. I followed a few minutes later. Jeanine had already given you to them, screamed at me to stay away."

What a toxic couple her parents were, Emma thought miserably. How much of them was in her? This would be the death blow to Sparks wanting anything to do with her.

"Why didn't Nomi ever tell me you were my—" she pushed the word out tentatively "—grandmother?" Sparks's hand dropped to her shoulder and remained. "Why—didn't you fight for me?" The final sentence emerged as a croak.

"It was better for you to be with Naomi and Raymond." Beryl's voice was so low Emma had to lean farther in to catch the words. "Naomi made a-an arrangement with me. If I didn't tell anyone Jeanine was your mother or what my relationship was to you, neither would Naomi, and she would raise you as a Chambers." A deep sigh rose from her bosom. "We thought it best for you to grow up with the advantages Naomi and Raymond could provide for you, and it would mean a lot less gossip." Beryl looked at Emma.

Emma was sure the "we" was "I," as in Naomi. It would have killed Nomi to know her granddaughter was living next door with Beryl.

"But you've acted differently this summer," Emma said.

Beryl's color surged and receded. "Once you came home...and I heard you were planning the Jamboree, and Naomi wasn't around, I knew I had a chance to...to be a part of your life without anyone suspecting anything." After she shuffled her feet, adjusted her caftan, she continued. "Then I met Sparks." She raised her gaze to Sparks and the smile was big. "He treated me decent. If he heard stuff about me around town, he didn't let it bother him. He... Well, he's a fine young man."

Emma swallowed a lump in her throat. Yes, he was. She tipped her head back and smiled a watery smile at him. He stared down at her, blue eyes dark and full of questions she still didn't quite understand.

Emma's heart ached. What would it have been like if Beryl had had the chance to be a grandmother? If Emma had had a sanctuary next door? Grumpa did his best, but his refusal to challenge Naomi's stubbornness and her rules for raising Emma so sternly had left her confused and resentful toward Naomi, even though her intentions had been good. She wondered if on that night, when Jeanine had left her with Grumpa and Nomi, whether Nomi had written in her planner, "New life goal: make sure Emma doesn't grow up to be like her parents."

Anger began to simmer. How did Nomi live with herself forcing Beryl to watch life go by from over the Berlin Wall?

Beryl lurched to her feet. "I'll get iced tea. Your grandfather told me how you like it with no sugar and lots of ice." She disappeared from the room.

Sparks slipped back onto the love seat, joining Emma, taking her hand. "Wow, you have family coming out of your ears now."

Swallowing a sputter of laughter, Emma at last felt her backbone unbend enough to rest against the cushions. Trust Sparks to say the most perfect thing in the most unexpected way. "I'll miss you so much," she began.

Holding two plastic tumblers, Beryl came back into the room and handed one to Emma and the other to Sparks. "Sparks and me, we talked a few times." Beryl sipped her water, chuckling. "Boy, can that boy eat."

Sparks *knew*? The warm fuzzy feelings vanished. Of course. He must have, with all the photos. She leaped up. He'd said he wasn't good at keeping secrets. Well, this one was a whopper. "You *knew*?"

A low chuckle halted her intended exit. "Just wait, Emma." Sparks stared anxiously at her. "Cool off."

After a puzzled glance at him, Beryl shook

her head. "Can you believe it?" She sighed. "I always fed him on the porch, Emma. I never let anyone in the house. I couldn't risk people seeing my pictures, so everyone thought I was unfriendly and inhospitable. Which I guess I was." She took a deep drink. "Am... But trying not to be anymore. So where does this leave us, dear?" Her grandmother's voice wobbled. The tremble awakened the rest of Emma's slumbering compassion. She stepped toward her grandmother, hands extended. *Invisible grandmother, meet your invisible granddaughter.*

"NAOMI, YOU ASLEEP?"

Naomi jerked her head toward the sound, drawing the sheet up to her chin. Chet stood in the doorway where Emma had stood moments ago. Emma, Naomi's reason for living... had told her she didn't think she could forgive her unless Naomi admitted she'd been wrong to swear Beryl to silence. Emma's outrage clanged through Naomi's head.

"No." She sighed. "I'm very much awake."

Chet sat beside her in the chair by the bed. Taking one of her hands in his, he smoothed the weathered skin.

"I saw Emma just now. She looked pretty upset."

"She found out about Beryl today. From Kent. Went to see her."

"And?"

"And she wants me to admit I did everything wrong."

"Oh, a little request, huh?"

She was so grateful he didn't press the issue; her mind was already whirling. So many revelations, explanations... Naomi nodded. Clarity now. Even if Emma didn't believe her, she owed it to her to tell her the why of it all. Something no one, not even her beloved husband Raymond, knew.

"Naomi. I actually came here to tell you something about Kent."

A familiar fear from long ago dried her mouth. So often she'd heard that phrase as her son grew up. Briefly closing her eyes, she clenched her back teeth and raised her eyebrows at Chet.

"I found out why he went to prison."

CHAPTER THIRTY-THREE

DUSK SLID OVER the lake and up the hill, that green expanse filling with blankets, folding chairs and people, some loaded up with picnic baskets, others with food from the booths. Traffic on Main Street was again at a standstill.

Word about Trinity making her comeback had spread faster than the Heaven grapevine with more will-call ticket money than the Jamboree had made in its lifetime, if someone wanted to count it. Emma didn't. She would have to watch the counting of the proceeds soon enough, right after the fireworks.

It had been hours now since she and her grandmother had eyeballed each other and Nomi had uttered that unrepentant comment, "I did what I had to do. For you." Emma had turned and walked out of the bedroom.

Checking her watch, she dropped down to the ground by a big cottonwood tree. She and Sparks had planned to meet at dusk, so depending on Sparks's casual interpretation of when that was, she could be early. As she tried to stall negative thoughts, she reflected that at least the Jamboree was going well. Sales for angel wings were more than robust, and the BBQ Contest at the fairgrounds had been nearly at capacity. Francine had redeemed herself with the Navajo Tacos opportunity Emma had given her.

After weeks of despairing that her time in Heaven would never end, it now neared with frightening speed. Jennifer sang tonight. Tomorrow morning, there was the combined lakeside service with Pastor Ned and Father Jack and their free breakfast for anyone who wanted to eat. The fireworks would explode as scheduled that night. Monday was the parade, then they cleaned up and it was over. She would leave Tuesday on the Greyhound that stopped at the Rexall.

If she didn't talk with her father again soon, she wouldn't have a chance to know…know what? Nothing was left and everything was left to know about him. Then, too, there were the dwindling hours she would have with Sparks. For the first time, *she* was leaving a relationship…if what they had this summer qualified as one. She had yet to see him today.

The next second, the smell of sage, citrus

and popcorn hit her nose, and Sparks was beside her. Emma's mood instantly improved.

"I missed you," he said, bumping her shoulder. "Even a little while is too long. Yesterday was great."

She agreed and closed her eyes as his lips touched hers. He tasted like buttery popcorn. After a satisfactory length of time, they parted. They'd made a quick return to the island for a picnic and swim once they'd discovered neither was scheduled at the Jamboree.

"Jennifer okay to go on?" she asked, taking a deep breath to settle herself. She reached into his popcorn bag.

"She's pretty nervous, but she really wants to do it for Heaven." Sparks regarded Emma guardedly. "Speaking of Heaven, I had Juggy put out some donation canisters for the tourists to donate to the no-flood fund. That okay?"

Emma agreed, putting a kernel in her mouth and chewing. "More than okay. You're great." She hoped she hadn't been that persnickety about people doing their own thing. A canister wasn't an Elvis impersonator leaping out of a plane.

The sun sank behind the mountains and night descended. The crowd's volume rose. The lights on the stage flooded on.

Sparks's lips brushed her ear. "Here goes."

Despite the enjoyment of being near him, her responsibility lingered. "How do you think we're doing on holding off the flood committee?" She peered at her watch. "Two minutes to Jennifer."

Shrugging, he tossed a few kernels of popcorn in his mouth, then flashed a smile at her. "All clouds don't bring rain."

"Mother Egan."

"You got it."

Emma thought of the clouds this summer that had teased the town with their unfulfilled promises of rain to cool the scorching heat. All those years of Beryl's bitterness clouding everyone's view of who she really was, an invisible grandmother. Naomi's dark clouds of control blocking others from growing and contributing. The blue of Sparks's eyes drew her in as they always did. Clouds. "If she was wrong about Beryl, maybe my view of my father has also been clouded."

The blue deepened as Sparks's glance slid away to a kid passing with a candy apple. "Sometimes you need to go with a first feeling." He rubbed his knees; she'd noticed he often did this when his normal happy-go-lucky attitude faded.

As the introductory streams of a synthesizer filled the air, Sparks and Emma's fingers found each other in an easy lacing. Jennifer walked onstage, the audience left their seats and blankets and rose as one, applauding and shouting before the initial notes of Jennifer's melodious voice floated up the hill.

While Jennifer sang to a packed park, with media from local and national stations in attendance, Emma scanned the area for her father. With Sparks at her side, more than a little regret saturated Emma. What texture Sparks added to her life. She should think she was crazy to leave a guy like this, and yet she also felt contentment at not having to beg him to come with her—or to change her plans to fit his. The goodbye, nevertheless, would be painful. Growth didn't seem to come without pain.

CHAPTER THIRTY-FOUR

As Sunday dawned, people sat and stood on the beach and sang or meditated, the smell of potatoes, bacon and onions filtering across from the south. Sparks and Emma basked in the peace and warmth of the sunrise.

Time was running out, Emma thought. What a wild ride this summer had been.

An hour later, still feeling the tranquility, she sat between Zoo and Tilly, savoring her breakfast. Sparks sat across from her, next to the Groveses and Bull. He kept trying to speak quietly to her but was thwarted by constant interruptions from townsfolk congratulating her or him or both of them on the Jamboree's success.

A couple of times Zoo kicked her under the table and smirked. Emma kicked her back and pointed a fork at big Jem Silver seated on Zoo's left. Zoo kicked her again and whispered, "Be quiet."

The table's occupants shared their Jamboree stories. Every one of them ended with the same question: Had all the effort been enough to save the town?

Although Emma kept an eye out for her father afterward, she never saw him. By noon, she was hot, tired and more than a little miffed at his elusiveness. When Sparks found her coming out of the Wayside without any sighting, he insisted on taking her to the beach for fun and relaxation. It didn't call for much to convince her. She'd put aside the pain of losing her grinning fireworks man until later.

IT WAS FINALLY time for Sparks's fireworks. At the park that evening, Emma cupped her chin in her hands and leaned her elbows on her knees. With the help of lit spotlights loaded onto trailers, she spied a shadowy figure down at the display on the beach. The figure straightened, looked up the hill and waved. Sparks. How could he see her among all the others? Because he was good at seeing people. A different kind of special, she thought, the memories of their day spent together almost reduced her to tears.

He looked kind of blurry, and she worried if the same would happen to her memories of him, too. Today, laughing and talking by the lake, her heart had warmed more than the sunburn on her nose and shoulders. For a moment, her resolve to make her life her own adventure wavered. No, she told herself, wrapping her arms around her bare knees. She'd decided to try for the England trip again, and she'd succeed. *You have to do it on your own.* She needed to, to fulfill her promise to Grumpa, make the dream a reality. Her nose ran and her eyes stung. *I'm in love with you, Sparks.*

Even as the emotions began again, she knew that no man in his right mind would want to get involved with her. Especially after seeing her family's dirty laundry fall out of the hamper on a holiday weekend. Sparks headed up the hill toward her, and as he neared, she could see more of his lopsided grin. A sweet ache throbbed in her. He sported yet another Made in Heaven T-shirt, but the angel wings were gone.

He smiled. Her stomach knotted.

"Hi," he said, looking down at her, his smile seeping away. She wondered if what had caused the smile to dim was the same thought that made her want to bawl like a baby.

"Hi yourself," she replied.

A shower of light popped in the sky over their heads, illuminating the crowd's upturned faces. Emma gasped. The white scintillation reflected on the boats moored on the lake and on the lake itself. It was breathtaking.

"You like that, huh?" He flopped down beside her.

She heard the oohs and aahs from the other spectators. A ripple of applause trilled across the park. Sparks was good. His casual approach to details belied a technical exactitude in his work, Emma thought, leaning back on her hands, looking over at him. He was grinning at the display, as though someone else had created the show just for him.

The smell of old beer wandered into her nose. "Thought you might be here, looking at the boyfriend's show." Her father sat down to the right of her.

"Hi," she said, smiling and staring up at the mesmerizing fallout of color. When she turned toward her father, she saw more than a little facial flush, even in the glow of the fireworks. Sparks had not greeted him, she noted. "I've searched all over for you. Where have you been?"

"Jeez, you sound like my mother." He swiped at his face with his bare arm. "I just saw you yesterday."

The Jamboree didn't sell any alcohol because Sheriff Zimmer said he didn't have enough jail cells to deal with "all those fool people who can't hold their beer."

Time had indeed stood still for her father.

Looking at him without the filter, or as other people did, nonetheless revealed the same conclusion. When her father spoke, it was about him, or the pressure on him, or what he would have done if someone had or hadn't done something to him or for him.

Sparks's hand slid over her knee. She hadn't realized he'd been paying attention. A big boom drowned out her father's answer. The grand finale.

She admired the beach display of the American flag and then lifted her head with the rest of the crowd when a shooting spray of the whitest of white sparks exploded into chrysanthemums of more white light with a resplendent surge of dramatic sparks up the center. It shot higher than Emma had ever seen fireworks go. Even though her neck began to ache, she couldn't look away. Then it was gone.

"That part is called Emma's Smile," Sparks whispered in her ear, tickling her neck with his popcorn breath. "When you smile, there's the first smile and then the full effect."

A moment of silence held the crowd in awe and then hooting, hollering and cheering broke out. Emma leaped to her feet with the rest of the people on the hill and glanced down at her father. He was gone. Shrugging, she clapped till her hands were red. Sparks stood beside her. She wrapped her arm around his waist.

"You are good," she said. "You named that for me?"

His arms held her and she breathed in his scent.

"You're good for me," he whispered in her ear. "Emma—"

People streamed past Emma and Sparks; some who knew them congratulated Sparks, inquired about her grandmother, while others hurried by, avoiding her with their eyes. No one mentioned her father.

"This wraps up most of the moneymaking events. Tomorrow's the parade and whatever anyone else spends at the booths." Checking her watch, Emma decided she should make a move. "I'll walk over to the Jamboree office and see how the counting of the money total is going." Time to tell if they'd made it. A little coil of worry wound up inside her. If they had worked this hard, sacrificed this much, and still it wasn't enough…

"I'll walk with you," Sparks offered.

"Thanks." She looked up at him, taking in his look of concentration on her. "Great show. The crowd loved it."

Two more days with him.

His smile edged back. Shoving his hands

into his pockets, he placed one leg downhill and stretched, then stretched the other leg. "Let's wait till the crowd thins out," he said.

They stood together silently as the crowd dissipated. Emma's heart constricted, torn between the new her who needed to do what she needed to do and the old Emma who wanted to cling tighter to Sparks as time slipped away. He hadn't told her he loved her.

She was on her own when it came to her heart.

Even though the fireworks had been a big hit, she could sense his unusual agitation. She'd first noticed it actually, when he'd sat down beside her. But she attributed that to pre-event jitters. Now, with him standing close, she saw his Adam's apple bobbing. He was clenching and unclenching his hands.

"I don't want to say goodbye," she blurted, the words flying past all reason. She sat down hard. He crouched down in front of her. She could feel the heat from his knees near hers, the breath from his sigh.

"You're the girl I think I'm in love with," he said, looking into her eyes with an expression that told her there would be no forehead kisses tonight.

So she wasn't the only one blurting.

"You *think* you love me?"

"Yeah, I think I do. But I don't know if I'm worthy of you."

She matched him, truth for truth. "I don't know if I can trust anyone, much less you, after all the lies that have come about."

"I haven't lied to you."

"You left stuff out. Same thing."

"I won't do that again."

"Yes, you will. Everybody lies."

"If that's true, what are your lies?"

He had her there. "Um."

Did she dare? She did. "I think I love you."

"That's a lie?"

"Yeah."

His mouth drooped. "So what's the truth?"

Emma sighed, the defeat of the words sweet and heavy. "I know I love you."

The crooked smile had never been bigger. "I can work with that."

She poked him. "So what's your lie?"

"I'm not going to try staying."

"After I said I love you?"

"Yeah, even after, because—"

Pounding feet disturbed their calm. Two volunteers, whose names escaped Emma, raced up to her, breathless.

"What's the matter?" *Nomi. She's had another stroke. Beryl?* People running up to her this summer had yet to be a good sign.

The taller of the two paused to reclaim his breath. "The money, Emma. The Jamboree money is missing."

By the time Emma and Sparks raced across the park and arrived at the small office, rumors and panic were bouncing around like balls in a bingo hopper.

"It was here and then it wasn't!"

"I saw it on the desk by the phone."

"No, it was by the fax machine."

"Check the bag from the front gate."

"I did. It's only the front-gate money."

"Maybe it fell on the floor. Everybody look."

The group of them, all anxious, dropped to their knees and started crawling.

Zimmer stepped up to her.

"What happened?" she asked, getting to her feet.

"It's the cash from the concert tickets. Money had been collected from all the booths one by one as they closed. I had three people. One took the money and counted it in front of the booth operator and the other two. Then someone else recounted it and deposited it in the bag with the rest of the takings for that booth. On to the next booth and the same procedure took place." His complexion behind the wire frames was an unhealthy reddish-purple.

"And then the bag was brought directly to this office?"

The sheriff straightened. "Of course it was," he snapped. "We followed protocol."

That was the trouble. Everyone knew the protocol. Grumpa had created the process years ago when he'd started the job.

Emma chewed the inside of her cheek. The bag must have merely fallen somewhere out of sight. It wouldn't escape the barrage of people crawling around, searching, sifting through trash cans, the shredder and every drawer.

Twenty minutes later, Emma had changed her mind. Someone had stolen their money. Who knew where to find it, and who didn't care about it being the town's lifeblood?

Sparks appeared next to her. "It wasn't someone from Heaven."

She looked at him with a wisp of impatience at his ingenuousness. "Every town has rocks and people who live under them."

He frowned like a little kid who had been told there was no Santa Claus. "It couldn't be. That money is too important to everyone here."

"I called the state police. They should be arriving in a little while." Zimmer nipped the end of every word.

A deep sigh gushed forth from Emma's

chest. "Good. Sooner's better than later." There was no putting it off any longer.

She headed for Naomi's.

CHAPTER THIRTY-FIVE

Trees swayed as the growing night wind cooled Emma's skin; however, it brought no comfort. Her steps dragged south on Main and continued onto Seraphim. Sparks said he would stay at the Jamboree office so he could get her the news as it happened. She dreaded telling her grandmother, even though she felt the older woman deserved to know. The moon hung high at this hour and reminded her of her mother.

She wondered if Jeanine ever had regrets about abandoning her. It struck Emma that she and her mother were similar. They both wanted answers to big questions in their lives.

Licking dry lips, she sniffed the fragrant night air. Little more could go wrong this tragic summer. Better to think about the pleasant evening she'd had with Sparks at the fireworks. Yet that was tainted with an undercurrent of tension emanating from him. What had been bugging him?

She climbed the porch steps, noting Trouble's absence, and recalled Chet had decided to skip the fireworks and keep the dog with him at his house. That way Naomi wouldn't have to deal with the border collie's panic at loud noises once the fireworks started.

Emma opened the front door. Once inside, when no summons were issued from the bedroom, she let out the breath she'd been holding. Naomi must have taken one of her prescribed sleeping pills. Emma could wait until morning to share the bad news, she decided, yawning, then massaging her head with both hands. She would check on her grandmother, get a glass of water and return to the office to wait for the state police.

Who had taken the money? Anyone who lived in town knew how crucial that money was this year.

Emma stuck her head into her grandmother's room and heard the rising wind tease the screen door open and shut. It was blowing right through Naomi's open windows. Her grandmother's breathing was heavy. She was asleep.

Emma stepped to the kitchen, flipping on the light switch. A muffled curse hit the air. Emma heard it before she saw him, her eyes blinking in the change from dark to bright. Her father with his hand in the cupboard over the stove—she wished she was still in the dark.

For years, Naomi had kept their household money in that spot in a cracked creamer.

Her father blushed a deep red, then smiled. "You startled me."

"*What* are you doing?"

He pulled his arm out of the cupboard and, following its direction as he pulled it back, Emma saw the bank bag sitting larger than life on the kitchen table.

"I'm getting back a little of what's mine. It's not working out for me here. I've got no choice. I just need some help to get there."

She couldn't speak.

He leaned against the stove. "You know what it's like here, Emma. You're like me. I saw it right away when I met you."

"You stole the money." Deep sadness mingled with her shock.

His lips tightened. "Now you see? That's what I mean. A self-fulfilling prophecy. How can I be anything else in this town but the screwup? I need a fresh break."

"Then, go, but don't take the money."

"Why not? Heaven owes it to me." He used ugly words to describe how he viewed the town's supposed treatment of him.

"You haven't been here in decades. Aren't you dwelling on the past a little bit for someone who says he's all about the future?" Without looking at the phone, she thought about how close she was to it versus how fast her father could move.

Her father shrugged, then smiled, his tone now warm and beguiling. "I thought maybe you and I could take that trip to England." He nodded toward the bag. "With this, and what you've saved, we could go in style."

Emma shuddered. "I wouldn't go across the street with you. I'm calling the police."

Instantly, his smile became a menacing scowl. He took a step toward her and she was genuinely scared.

HALF AN HOUR LATER, Sparks accepted there was no point in hanging around the Jamboree office. The money was gone. Although he wasn't hungry—which let him know he was truly bummed about this whole thing, and about leaving—he would stop off at the Dairy Delite to give Emma time with her grandmother.

He wished Emma had let him accompany her. He couldn't get Kent Chambers off his mind. Hadn't liked Kent from the moment he'd shown up in Naomi's house. Always seemed to have an excuse for things not to be his fault.

Hands in his pockets, head down, Sparks

walked, watching the tops of his cross trainers—right, left, right, left—until Chet's voice brought his head up abruptly.

"Hey, Sparks!" The older man was waving at him from across Main. "Naomi—"

Sparks couldn't make out what followed, but judging from Chet's face, it wasn't good. Adrenaline surged. There had been something to his uneasiness.

After darting between cars, Chet made it to Sparks, panting. "Why aren't you with Emma?" He bent over to catch his breath, then turned and pointed toward Naomi's street. "He's got—to—have—the money. I'm praying he loses interest as fast as he used to and leaves town before he hurts her." He waved Sparks past him. "I'm too old to run this fast. You go. Get to Emma and Naomi. If he feels threatened, he'll hurt them."

Sparks halted so quickly he staggered and almost fell over. "Hurt them?"

A heavy sigh came from Chet. "I told Naomi today, so I might as well tell you. You've become like family this summer." He told Sparks that Kent had been in prison for armed robbery and assault.

Sparks's first reaction to Emma's father roared back to life. Chet was right. The money and Kent were in a little bungalow, right where Emma was headed. He took off. *Let me be on time.* "Chet, call the sheriff!"

CHAPTER THIRTY-SIX

IN THE SMALL KITCHEN, father and daughter squared off. Emma's muscles cried out for sleep, her eyes burning from the glare of the kitchen light and the strain of persuading her thought-lost, newly discovered, unstable father to turn himself in.

"I'm not going with you," she repeated.

"No, you're not, I guess, and you're not calling the cops," Kent said, the redness fading, his expression smoothed out. "You're a Chambers. Dad ignored it, Mother fixed it. You can ignore it or fix it for me." He jammed the money from the cupboard into his jeans' pocket. Since Emma had used some of it for groceries a few days ago, she knew there wasn't much in there. Short of clubbing him with the bank bag, nothing came to Emma's mind as to how to stop him, so she decided to keep him talking, at least. For what? How long? "She didn't know you were in prison," she said suddenly, urgently.

"She wished I was dead so I wouldn't mess up her life." His eyes narrowed. Moving toward the table, he picked up the bag and stepped up to Emma. "Don't know when we'll meet again. I don't think I'm cut out for the father thing."

"You've got to stop sometime."

His chin jerked up. "Everyone tries to ruin my breaks. I'm always on the verge of a big one." He gestured with the bank bag. "Nice knowing you, and have a nice life. Now get out of my way."

"No." Emma braced herself in the doorway. "I won't. You'll have to—"

Before she could finish her sentence, he'd elbowed her and, using a hip check, sent her flying across the hall. Her back hit the corner of her bedroom doorway and she was down. Pain sucked in her breath. On the floor, her mouth, her lungs wouldn't work without air, and her vertebrae screamed. He was walking away from her. He wasn't even running. As he disappeared down the hall, she heard something tip over and then cursing.

"Emma? Emma, are you there?" Her grandmother's sleepy voice quavered through the haze of hurt.

Emma had to stop him. It wasn't fair and it wasn't right that Heaven should disappear under a wall of water because of one selfish man. She heard more crashing, thuds and invectives in the living room. What was he doing in there?

Again her grandmother's voice, more imperious. "Emma! Emma, are you all right? Answer me!"

Grumpa's gun. In Emma's memory, it had always resided in the wood secretary in the living room. More bumps. That was, it had until the day of the funeral when Naomi had loaded it and put it back in the bedroom.

Pulling herself up from the floor, stifling a gasp of pain, Emma leaned against the doorjamb. Urgency gave her soreness speed and she burst into Nomi's room, making a beeline for the dresser.

"Emma! Wh-what on earth is going on? Wh-what's all that noise?"

Emma paused in her trajectory. She stared at her grandmother, who appeared small in the bed, and a weird peace—antacid to the bile—flowed through her, reducing the heat of injustice, cooling the magma of invisibility and humiliation. Another hit to Nomi's system would only weaken—possibly kill her. Being a protector of Nomi was a new feeling for Emma, but one that seemed right. Her grandmother had enough of a burden to carry right now. A booming thump and her grandmother's eyes widened.

Emma reached into the drawer with her right hand as she drew Nomi's sheet up to the neck with her left. "I'm so tired, I guess. I got klutzy and ran into the doorjamb. Everything's fine."

"I hear crashing."

A long pause. "Raccoons in the garbage. You know how they are."

Her grandmother's disbelieving gaze rested on her for several seconds. "If you say so," she said.

Emma raced from the bedroom as fast as she could with her back muscles clenching like a fist. The living room looked as though an oversize toddler had raged through it. A deep shaking began around her heart and spread through her body.

Her father, on the opposite side of the room, was throwing magazines out of the cluttered rack. He'd already pulled out the drawers of the secretary and had flung them to the floor; the desk itself was on its side.

"Stop," Emma said, trying to control the trembling. She raised the Colt, thinking of the irony of pulling a gun on the man she had once wanted more than life to *have* in her life.

He turned, his face shiny with sweat and rage. Defeat filled his eyes before scorn snarled across his expression.

"It's not loaded, babe." It was not a term of endearment; rather, "Hey, stupid, you're trying to be a hero and you're doing it wrong."

He grabbed the bank bag and moved toward the screen door. "Dad never kept it loaded. All that gun safety crap."

"It's loaded." The gun was warm and heavy in her moist hand. She looked at him; he looked at her. *Make a good choice. For you. For us. Please.*

Another flicker of doubt from him. Then the cocky look reappeared. "You're too soft, like my dad, to shoot me," he told her and pushed the screen door open.

The instant she pulled the trigger, Emma saw red and blue lights and heard the squeal of brakes. Her father screamed, falling through the half-open door, clutching his right calf. The bank bag spilled over the front porch bathed in moon glow. Surprise replacing the sneer, he stretched his neck to see her as the screen door banged against his feet.

For Pete's sake, I've shot my father.

Then she spoke crisply. "I'm a lot like my grandmother, too."

SITTING UPRIGHT IN BED, Naomi heard Zimmer's voice and the answering murmurs of Chet, the higher breathless tones of Emma's and Sparks's taut interjections in the living room.

"We were already on the way when Naomi phoned in."

A lower voice—one she couldn't make out—resonated intermittently.

Kent had crossed the line of no return by threatening Emma. She felt frantic in her need to see Emma, but as she tried to get out of bed and lean on the walker, her legs collapsed, and she fell back against the pillows.

Coming into the room, Chet pushed the walker out of the way, saying matter-of-factly, "Kent's not feeling so good."

As much as she wanted Kent out of their lives, Naomi didn't want him dead. "I heard him…yell."

"Emma shot him in the leg." After helping her on with her sweater, Chet helped stabilize her on the walker.

"Emma shot her father?" Naomi tried to imagine it and couldn't.

"Sparks and I had just made the porch when the screen door blew open and we heard Kent tell her she wouldn't shoot him because she was soft like her grandfather."

I must get to Emma. Naomi took a step, then another, with Chet behind, hand lightly on her back.

"Yup. Then we heard a shot. Kent fell at our feet. Emma said something at that point, but I couldn't make it out."

She'd made it to the door.

Chet continued, "Juggy and Bull are loading him into the ambulance now. Zimmer and Sparks are here. The troopers will follow the ambulance to Regional."

Chet's warm hands rested on her shoulders as she made the turn and headed toward the living room. Chet, so comforting. Would he marry her now that the whole town knew the Chamberses' secrets? *Oh, Emma.* Naomi had been so wrong to keep things from her granddaughter. Stopping to wipe a tear from her eye, Naomi blew out a breath.

"You'll be all right, Naomi. That Sparks is a keeper. He read my mind as soon as he saw me shouting on Main Street to get to you and Emma. He starting running for your house right away, shouted to call the police. He knew Emma had been headed here."

"I have to see him."

"Sparks? He's sitting and holding Emma's hand in the living room, and I don't think he's going to be letting go anytime soon."

"No, Kent." She swallowed. "I have to see Kent."

NEVER HAD SPARKS seen someone look so defeated. Naomi's shoulders sagged and her shuffle-slide with the walker added to the demoralized picture. Her glance shot to Beryl, who was squeezed with them on the couch.

What was that expression? Difficult to tell, since he didn't know Naomi all that well.

Emma was pressed up next to him. Her hand was tucked securely in his and for once, she showed no intention of moving away. When he'd come through that door and watched her drop the gun and look at him wide-eyed and openmouthed, he knew he would never be able to move on without her. He'd found home, and if it took the rest of his life, he'd work to show Emma they had been saving each other while they tried to save the town.

Moments after the gunshot and flashing lights, Beryl had come to help Emma. Just like family.

Naomi raised a hand now, clearly wanting to touch her granddaughter. "I'm so sorry. Are you all right?"

When Emma stared at her blankly Sparks knew she had been through too much to talk. Naomi turned the walker toward the front door and the troopers. "I want to see my son." The two, one skinny woman and a taller stocky man, traded looks. Naomi raised her chin and took another step. "Please."

The woman opened the door, and held it that way for Naomi. "He's not saying nice things right now, Mrs. Chambers. Are you sure you want to do this?"

Kent's obscenities tainted the front yard. They had him handcuffed to a gurney, immediate first aid applied to the flesh wound, and were ready to lift him into the ambulance. As much as Sparks didn't want to hear the mother-son summit, he wasn't letting go of Emma's hand. She heard the rant, too, and closed her eyes, leaning into his shoulder. They were a captive audience.

"Ma'am?" The thin woman tapped Naomi on the shoulder. Naomi gave her a weak smile and restarted her slow progress to the yard.

"Yes. I'm sure."

The front door was left ajar and Sparks watched Chet steady Naomi as she rested heavily on the walker, gazing down at her son. Kent regarded her through half-closed eyes, breathing quick, shallow breaths.

"Son." Naomi's voice was a near whisper, and yet every word was heard clearly as the group in the living room held their collective breath. "I'm—I'm sorry. Please forgive me."

Panting, he raised his head off the gurney. "This is all your fault, not mine." He fell back, licking his lips.

Even though he'd never had a family, Sparks knew that had been a heavy blow to Naomi.

Despite what she'd done, she'd loved her son in her own way.

Emma whispered, "Oh, Nomi." As Juggy and Bull lifted the gurney into the ambulance, Naomi crumpled backward into Chet's arms.

CHAPTER THIRTY-SEVEN

IN THE SOFT darkness of Naomi's front yard, Emma and Sparks sat together on the porch swing. His foot languidly tapped the floor to keep the swing moving. After all the chaos of the past forty-eight hours, sitting in silence felt good. Emma saw no reason to fill it with the sound of her voice. She rested her head on Sparks's shoulder just as Chet pulled into his driveway across the street.

Emma nudged Sparks. "Watch. He'll look over here, hoping to see Nomi."

The older gentleman did that very thing. They chuckled softly. Emma loved feeling the rumble of laughter from Sparks's chest. So little time left. So much had happened.

Sparks squeezed her shoulder. "He's a man in love. I think I know how he feels."

Chet waved to them and crossed the street.

"I'd like to be that predictable some day," Sparks muttered.

Emma's lips curved into a soft smile. This was a bit different than "man of the world, committed to no one," which seemed to be all he could say when he'd arrived in Heaven in May. While she loved it in him, it posed a problem with her wanting to be more unpredictable, albeit with more finesse than her outbursts of recent days. She squirmed. Sparks looked at her, his eyebrows raised.

"You two seen Beryl's car?" Chet asked, sporting a big grin as he stepped onto the porch.

"Uh-oh," Emma replied, with a jerk of worry. As far as she knew, the car was in Beryl's driveway. Surely the Juggy parking incident wasn't going to come back and haunt Emma.

"I heard at the Dew Drop that she hotfooted it to Evanston today with Tilly and bought a new license plate frame," the older man explained. The grin seemed stuck in place.

Emma knew he was up to something, but she wasn't sure what, so she waited.

"And?" Sparks queried. "What's so newsworthy about that?"

"It's what it says," Chet said, unruffled at their questioning looks.

Emma decided to help speed him up a bit. "And that would be?"

"'My granddaughter is cuter than yours.'"

Emma burst into tears. Sparks looked concerned until Chet reassured him they were happy tears. They *were* happy tears. It was nice to deal with happy tears.

"I can understand that," Sparks said. "I cry, too."

Choking on her sobs, Emma looked at him skeptically.

Chet asked the question. "Okay, Sparks, what do you cry at?"

Sparks's smile crinkled, suddenly erasing his somber look from the moment before. "I tear up at gift-card commercials, cute puppies at the pound and any time 'God Bless America' is sung." Despite the sobbing, Emma's smile was huge, and he slid an arm across the top of the swing and dropped it down on her shoulder. "I've even been known to cry at some of my grand finales."

Emma giggled while she wiped her eyes with a tissue provided by Chet. She'd been fine to cry, she told herself. If there was one thing she'd learned these past weeks, it was that you have to deal with what must be dealt with, or it will inevitably snap at you where you least expect it.

It was why she and Sparks were sitting on the porch swing. They needed to talk about the future, or as far into it as they could see. Now that everything was over, the parade had been paraded, the money counted, the cleanup complete, nothing was left to keep Sparks and Emma from focusing on each other.

Where were they with each other?

No doubts remained about her feelings for Sparks, and still she knew she wanted to explore and see new places.

Her father would return to recover in the prison hospital and face violation of parole, attempted robbery and grand theft auto charges, since that gray sedan had been stolen. A shadow of sadness passed over her, but she let it slide on through, instead of dragging her down. She could not make him the father she had longed for and, she reminded herself, despite that tragedy, she had acquired a new grandmother who wanted the world to know about her. Some good had come from all the secrets.

Once Emma ceased her sniffling, Chet nodded toward the house. "Your grandmother will never live it down, will she, what with her collapse being an anxiety attack?"

Anyone who knew Naomi knew she wouldn't think an anxiety attack was a noble collapse. Emma was pretty sure her grandmother classified only stroke and/or death as legitimate causes for a person to lose consciousness abruptly. She laughed, recalling Nomi's drill-sergeant ability to rally just about anyone in town, no matter how blue they might be feeling.

Emma gestured inside. "Nomi's been holed up in her room since we brought her home from the hospital this afternoon."

Her grandmother was blessed to have had two fine men who loved her.

"Why don't you toast a couple of slices of cinnamon bread and take them in to her? I think you're just what she needs," Emma suggested.

"Before I do, I should update you two on the proceeds. It's all been counted now, with everything pretty much in."

"And?" Sparks asked, his arm tightening around Emma.

"We're ten grand short."

Emma gasped.

"Were." Chet held up his finger to forestall any comments or noises. "An anonymous donor has made up the difference. We're off the flood list." A different flood flowed through Emma. One of relief. And elation.

She exchanged a look with Sparks; he flushed and then winked. She had a good idea who that benefactor was.

"And now," Chet continued, "about your grandmother."

Emma's earlier conversation with her had given Emma hope that Nomi just might ease up on life.

"I'm already seeing a difference in her. She even let Trouble on her bed. She's told me how proud she is of me. We're talking change." Her expression grew sober. "I also understand her now. She's been through a lot these past few weeks."

Crossing his arms over his chest, Chet nodded. "Doesn't seem a woman could endure much more and live."

"Emma did." Sparks's long fingers began working her neck muscles. She sighed, not only because he was so very satisfactory in his work, but also because having him speak up on her behalf soothed some of the grief inside her. Getting through everything that had happened this summer she knew was in some way connected to him. Finally she'd found a special man, a good man who respected her and who she was, just as much as she respected him. He was so unlike the others; it had been a hard lesson for her to learn. But a rewarding one.

Chet acknowledged Sparks's correction with a nod. "Yes, you're right."

"That night after the fireworks was like a movie," Sparks said, pointing to a chair for Chet to sit. The older man shook his head.

A movie Emma never wanted to see again.

"On our way home today," Sparks told Chet, "Naomi admitted she set some bad things in motion by lying to Emma...including how Beryl was treated. She thought she had to use everything within her power to make sure Emma turned out right. It was misguided, but no one can deny how much Naomi loves her granddaughter."

Chet looked at her knowingly and asked, "Will you be able to forgive her, E?"

Emma stretched her tight back muscles by leaning forward to pet Trouble. The pain of her father slamming her into the woodwork would linger for a while. "If you'd asked me a few days earlier, I would have said no. Absolutely not. But in the car last night, when we were following the ambulances to Regional, it struck me I had just lied to her for the same reason she lied to me. Talk about a family legacy."

"What do you mean?" Sparks frowned and leaned away to regard her.

"I lied to her when my fath—Kent was stealing the money from the creamer, having already stolen the Jamboree money. She called to me...wanted to know what was going on.

I made a choice. Told her it was raccoons. I didn't want her to try to get up and get hurt."

Chet's lips curved.

"She protected me with her lie for all those years, as I protected her with my lie." Emma could feel the flush creeping up on her cheeks, and buried her face in Spark's neck. Her voice was muffled. "Sick, huh?"

"No sicker than me giving in to Naomi to keep the secret from day one," Chet admitted in a ragged voice. "Emma, will you forgive an old man?"

"I'll add you to the list."

"I thank you. Then, what's the answer to stopping this Chambers legacy?" Chet asked.

"We certainly have established a pattern, haven't we?" Emma shook her head. "Our motivation for why we did it is always good, but the execution gets twisted."

"From now on, when you're deep in a hole, *stop digging*." Sparks smiled, and she smiled back. His hands had found a particularly nasty knot in her neck, and she reveled in his gentle touch.

Emma continued, "Think of my father. He lied to himself so much that he believes what he says. I think he actually thought the town owed him the money." She turned to ask Sparks,

"How did you know Kent would come to the house with the bag?"

Sparks pressed her closer to him. "The way he stared at the cupboard that day when you and he and Naomi met in the kitchen. As if it had reminded him of something. And he'd need a car to escape. Everyone in town knows Naomi keeps the keys under the floor mat in her old Buick. Stuff like that." With a regretful shrug of his shoulders, he carried on, "Wish I'd figured it out before Chet told me what he'd been jailed for. That really scared me. That he might hurt you or Naomi."

In the dark, she suppressed a smile. On one hand she so appreciated that Sparks would rush to her defense. But on the other hand, she felt badly that Sparks blamed himself unfairly for not having been at the house to play the knight in shining armor. She fidgeted. Her tense back muscles rebelled at her position.

Slipping a pillow behind her, Sparks tapped her knee. "If I had been ten minutes earlier…"

"But we're okay." She had to face Sparks. This was too important. She needed him to understand. "I didn't want to do what I did, though I am proud I had the courage to do it. I was frightened, but just letting him go, not stopping him seemed…unthinkable."

Sparks hugged her while Chet nodded.

"You've got a lot to sort through," Sparks said.

"Nomi and I both do. I told Nomi today that we needed a new Chambers way. We need to protect each other with the truth. We're strong enough to handle the truth. Now we have to figure out how to build the trust with the truth."

Sparks's arm fell away from Emma. He was eyeing his knees. Was he going to start rubbing them? What worried him?

The smile he gave her was weak at best. "What did she say after she recovered from the shock of you taking charge?"

It was what her grandmother hadn't said. She'd cried, and Emma had held her for comfort for the first time in both their lives. When Naomi had composed herself, she'd looked Emma straight in the eye and said she was proud of the woman Emma had become and that she could learn from her.

Emma wouldn't share what else she had learned from her grandmother. Naomi's mother had given birth on the wrong side of the blanket, even though she'd married the father. Naomi's grandmother, who could never forgive herself or her daughter for the lapse in judgment, had hammered at Naomi day and night to be responsible and never stray from the straight and narrow. This family secret had only been revealed as Naomi's mother had lain dying.

This confession had helped more pieces fall into place for Emma.

She shrugged. "Oh, you know, she said she had a brilliant granddaughter." Needing to change topics, she clapped her hands and said happily, "I, for one, am glad all the secrets are out. It's a good start."

Chet swung his gaze to Sparks, whose hands were now resting on his knees. In Emma, the familiar rush of stomach acid interrupted the tranquility.

Seriously, after this summer, what secret was left? Murder, dismemberment...?

"Glad to hear it. Well, I'm going to go in and propose to Naomi again. Sparks..." Chet hesitated. "Sparks, you're a fine young man, one I'd be proud to have as a son. No matter what." He excused himself and went into the house with Trouble following and bumping the back of his knee.

A moment passed after Chet's departure, although Emma thought it lasted for about a year.

Sparks turned to Emma. His eyes were bright with tears. "One last secret."

She shivered as a chill swept over her shoulders. She hadn't expected an immediate test in this new-truth thing. "I don't think I want to hear this. Do you have a wife and kids anywhere?"

"No."

"Been arrested for fraud and or extortion and or murder?"

"No. Emma. Let me get it out." Sparks clasped her hand as he looked beyond her into the night. "I—I let someone down when I was a smoke jumper."

"What? What happened?"

"I was responsible for a rookie, and I looked away for a minute to check my gear and the fire changed that quickly. I instinctively threw on my shield. As I did, I saw the guy out of the corner of my eye. He was frozen, staring at the fire coming toward us. He never used his shield..." Sparks clutched her hand so tightly it tingled.

"That wasn't your fault."

"I should have been watching out for him. He depended on me and I let him down." A guttural sound sprang from his lips, from a deep, dark place Emma recognized. She held him, stroking his head, kissing his cheeks, murmuring words of comfort.

Realization dawned for her on that porch with the big wounded man in her arms. She recalled his mantra: man of the world, committed to none. His avoidance when it came to making a decision. The times he'd moved close, but then retreated into his own moratorium. The gnawing feelings of unworthiness and undependability. How heavy his own secret must have been.

"I'm a great one to talk about forgiveness, but…" It was true; Naomi and she had a lot left to sort through.

He nodded and sagged back into the swing. She leaned her head on his shoulder.

"Yeah," he said. "Counselors told me I have to forgive myself. Easy to say."

"We're a fine pair," Emma whispered. "You were running away from what you had. I was running toward something I didn't understand."

Besides their soft voices, only the creak of the swing could be heard. "So what do we do now?" she asked.

Sparks gave her the crooked smile, reassuring and familiar. She liked it. No, she loved it. She loved him. "I think I'm moving along on that forgiveness road, after learning from Jennifer, and even your dad."

Emma waited. No twinge of jealousy at the mention of the pretty singer. *Nice growth, Emma.* "Now, that's a contrast—Kent and Jennifer?"

He nodded. "Jennifer ran away to get whole, and found wholeness. She told me that she had to forgive herself for getting lost from what she really wanted."

Emma smiled as Sparks began to nibble her ear.

"Your father ran, and ran toward something and is still running." Sparks switched to her other ear. "As long as he can only see his side of the story, he'll be stuck running." He paused to look at her. "I don't want to be the way I was, committed to none."

"And no more man moratorium for me," she declared, a warm feeling inside.

"I'm glad we ran into each other," he murmured against her skin. "That we take turns saving each other."

Sometimes he said exactly the right thing. She kissed him, starting at the corner of his forehead and moving across, then down, to settle on his lips. Several minutes passed, maybe hours, maybe days. Emma didn't know and didn't care.

When they broke the kiss and Sparks once again set the swing to swaying, he said softly, "Emms?"

"Hmm?" She felt so deliciously safe and happy.

"I think I love you."

"Think?"

"No. Not really. I know I love you. Thank you for saving me."

She turned toward him to bestow a you're-welcome kiss. "Thank you for saving me."

* * * * *

LARGER-PRINT BOOKS!

GET 2 FREE LARGER-PRINT NOVELS PLUS 2 FREE MYSTERY GIFTS

Love Inspired®

Larger-print novels are now available...

LARGER-PRINT BOOKS!

**GET 2 FREE
LARGER-PRINT NOVELS
PLUS 2 FREE
MYSTERY GIFTS**

Love Inspired®

SUSPENSE
RIVETING INSPIRATIONAL ROMANCE

Larger-print novels are now available...